Th...
So happy you could talk
to her, Chloe & Sandra
Friends for the next
40 years

David
Aug 18/2016

ESSENTIAL PROSE SERIES 123

Canada Council for the Arts
Conseil des Arts du Canada

ONTARIO ARTS COUNCIL
CONSEIL DES ARTS DE L'ONTARIO
an Ontario government agency
un organisme du gouvernement de l'Ontario

Guernica Editions Inc. acknowledges the support of the Canada Council for the Arts and the Ontario Arts Council. The Ontario Arts Council is an agency of the Government of Ontario.

We acknowledge the financial support of the Government of Canada.
Nous reconnaissons l'appui financier du gouvernement du Canada.

....

David MacKinnon

**GUERNICA
EDITIONS**
TORONTO • BUFFALO • LANCASTER (U.K.)
2016

Copyright © 2016, David MacKinnon and Guernica Editions Inc.
All rights reserved. The use of any part of this publication,
reproduced, transmitted in any form or by any means, electronic,
mechanical, photocopying, recording or otherwise stored in a
retrieval system, without the prior consent of the publisher is an
infringement of the copyright law.

Michael Mirolla, general editor
David Moratto, cover and interior design
Guernica Editions Inc.
1569 Heritage Way, Oakville, (ON), Canada L6M 2Z7
2250 Military Road, Tonawanda, N.Y. 14150-6000 U.S.A.
www.guernicaeditions.com

Distributors:
University of Toronto Press Distribution,
5201 Dufferin Street, Toronto (ON), Canada M3H 5T8
Gazelle Book Services, White Cross Mills, High Town, Lancaster LA1 4XS U.K.

First edition.
Printed in Canada.

Legal Deposit—First Quarter
Library of Congress Catalog Card Number: 2015952375
Library and Archives Canada Cataloguing in Publication
MacKinnon, David, 1953-, author
The eel / David MacKinnon. -- 1st edition.

(Essential prose series ; 123)
Issued in print and electronic formats.
ISBN 978-1-77183-059-1 (paperback).--ISBN 978-1-77183-060-7 (epub).--
ISBN 978-1-77183-061-4 (mobi)

I. Title. II. Series: Essential prose series ; 123

PS8625.K553E45 2016   C813'.6   C2015-906636-0   C2015-906637-9

I will be a man fulfilled if, when my time comes,
I can disappear anonymously and without regret,
At the originating point of our world, the Sargasso Sea,
Where life first burst from the depths of the ocean floor towards the sun.

Se Deus quiser, amanhã ...

Yes, Se Deus quiser, tomorrow, we shall arrive in the new world.
Already the waves have changed in hue.

—Blaise Cendrars

HIM

*H*e saved me. Cendrars, that is. Not for what he was—one-armed legionnaire, millionaire three times over, bankrupt, tracker of African and Brazilian tales, inventor of French modern poetry. Thief of Chagall's paintings, drinking pal of Modigliani. Vagabond.

Ah, wait ... vagabond. That word begins this story. Vagabond. That came like a message from afar. There was a way out of this shit. This impossible problem of being alive. If you were serious about breaking the shackles, you didn't plan. You went into a trance. You surrendered to voodoo, or you were just rattling your chains.

Cendrars the legend. A friend of gypsies and gangsters. A whaler. A warrior. Leave that for literature. When you're lying down, forced into the supine position, when illness has removed your very manhood—the ability to move, to fuck, the ability to fight and to fend for yourself—in other words what a man is meant to do ... when the world leaves you as a rotting carcass, and then finishes the job off with Christian pity, you don't need a legend, you need to go into a trance. You need *fugue*.

To be sure, Blaise Cendrars was a legend. He exuded the deep, unfathomable mystery of the Sargasso Sea and the Amazonian jungle. But that's not why I owed him my life, and now as I look back at the tumult of my own existence, a flash. 1989. The middle of the night in Macau, in the year that China prepared to swallow up Hong Kong—a spit in the South China Sea—the way that Stanley Ho's Dragon Mouth entrance at the Kingsway Casino, where I was headed that evening swallowed up its patrons and emptied their pockets of a lifetime's earnings. Where suicide and murder and whores and windowless VIP rooms and toothless millionaires and one-armed bandits mixed with the chack-a-chack staccato of the baccarat tables that was the governing drumbeat of those islands in those days. And, where the easy purchase of a stiletto-heeled hooker gave an unworthy sod a brief taste of the vices of the gods.

I had just finished a bottle of Vino Verde and half a dozen plates and bowls of seafood in an open door café with a dirt floor. Lee Fook Lam and I were moving along the rue de la felicidad. The air was thick with an acrid vapour that enveloped us and the baked dirt alley we turned onto littered with mini-skirted whores, the lights of Friday night junks and floating restaurants illuminating the South China Sea, and Kowloon marking the dark silhouette of the mountain passes leading into Guangdong province. And, I felt so alive, voluntarily abducted as I was from that cocoon of certainty that had nearly asphyxiated me with its policy of love and morality. And I felt that my lungs had been pre-designed to feed off the fumes and the stench of whores trampled upon by other men before I too would leave my imprint. And I felt that I couldn't get enough of this corruption, and lit up a cigar to stoke the cauldron within that was my soul, ready for every sin under god's hemisphere, if only I first got a taste of life, this accelerated life, where every minute contained an eon, and where the China night sky regularly exacted human sacrifices to appease the untamed passions of those in the ether watching the theatre being played out beneath.

Cendrars dead twenty-seven years, now safely in Orion, the realisation of his secret right there for the taking—within his name—and that knowledge blinding me with gratitude. But to burn the old self to the ground and rise as a phoenix, one first had to flee. Fugue. The inseparable trinity. Flight, death and rebirth. Simultaneous, not sequential. For a man to tear up his roots and to flee, you must burn your past to the ground, you must surrender to the trance, move into it, be swallowed up into the fly-trap as you were surely swallowed up by China, when you flew the precarious last descent into old Kai-Tek airport.

Escape! I was the one in a million. So what if one billion Chinese moved in the opposite direction. Danger was everywhere, and yet death's vice-hold had never been so weak. The man who walked the old Macau lanes with me that evening—a man operating under his fourth name, and from whom lies sprinkled the air like petals from a dying flower, was gesturing at the Friday night lights of the boats and the Friday night visible stench of the putrefying cloud of sin, and me realizing in a flash the acute scintillating beauty of the industrial smoke, and the sounds of gunshots and rolling dice and the cacophonic chatter of street whores, and the scythe like sharpness of the Vino Verde slicing into my own corruptible psyche.

Lee Fook Lam smiled, not knowing my thought, but understanding perfectly the emotion that lay beneath.

"You are now part of all of this. This can all be yours."

I laughed, and sucked deep on my cigar, and saw in the mind's eye an image from the past, eight decades old, Cendrars in Beijing, stuffing old copies of *Le Mercure* into an old stoking oven to keep warm.

"It is already mine, Lee Fook Lam. It is already mine."

Orion appeared out of nowhere, God too impatient to remain invisible in the firmament, but Cendrars' silhouette clear against the skies. I swore that if the opportunity ever arose, I would pay him back. It must seem a strange thing to make a vow to a dead man you've never met, but I knew for a fact that the gods would call upon me to make good on my promise. So, to me, none of this was stranger than the carnivorous, eight-gated path of life itself. Everything crumbled before that reality and until this moment I had been unable to crack the logarithm of the puzzle.

This moment came from nowhere and all at once, like a sword out of the sky. I was glad of the neon night and secure in my privileged position as *gweilo* barbarian in the dying days of the Empire and the ever-present dangers of 1989 China. Within that hair-fracture second that split celestial heaven and infernal earth, I made my sacrifice and felt instantly the trance of fugue take hold, and I willingly pissed my soul into the gutters of the Macau netherworld. Let anything be visited upon me, I recall thinking, give me the teat of the succubus, that I may suckle upon her myself.

I was drinking of the same fountain as Faust, in full knowledge that the debt would be called in with interest at a time least expected. I knew equally that the flames of hell would engulf me via a woman, and teach me that hubris is not a consummation devoutly to be wished, because the final payment exacted teaches you that your mistake in playing beyond the constraints of human boundaries brings upon the wrath of those whose power we can barely fathom, and by then it is too late.

you

The world doesn't have to see why I did this, but you do. Don't confuse this with any sentimental attachment either—sentiment comes only with physical proximity, and you and I have had none for two decades. My sensitivities have long since atrophied. Although I no longer enjoy the usual feelings of other human beings, the gateway to my inner soul is safely shut. I am long past the day now where others openly question my lack of orthodoxy. Since I have ceased to have any impact upon the world, I can be safely ignored, and since the result of awakening the beast that lies within is unpredictable, I am largely left to my own devices.

Naïve as I was, even when I undertook this folly at such a cost, I presumed only that one person would believe in its aims and purposes. Of course—and this has been the experience of my life—this person ultimately proved to have no distinguishing features from the great amoebic mass of humanity. Behind the mish-mash Vedantic credos, the eccentricities and the claim that she was the reincarnation of her father, lay a hard-boiled pragmatist who believed in nothing. Generally, it's not that people don't believe. They just don't want to believe. I have reflected on this and know it to be true. And because the world won't believe, cannot bear to believe, the world will soon enter into a deep slumber.

During the fleeting and rare moments when I pause to consider those who would judge me, I detect the question "Why?" writ large in their faces. Why—after you had taken such pains to do all the right things, after you had picked up all the pieces of your broken life, why would you embark on yet another shambolic escapade? Why would you torment this old woman and exhume ghosts that are best left in the uneasy slumber of death. Why reduce the tragic story of a poet who lost his arm and recreate the world in its place to a madcap escapade to the Sargasso Sea?

The answer to that question is contained in a single world—you. You are the part of me that was amputated. You are my right arm, removed by malign forces from the unknown, independently of my actions or my worth. You alone are the reason for all this. Why else would a man, otherwise rational, suddenly yield to the urge that perversely led me to do what I have now done?

If a man loses a limb, he cannot replace it. Yet if his imagination and his courage are sufficient to the task, he may yet make something of that loss. And, if a life is removed, can the past be recuperated? I once thought it couldn't, but the discovery that the line between the living and the dead is more fluid than we surmised changes this.

For a time—a number of years in fact—I believed that delivering Blaise Cendrars' ashes to the Sargasso Sea would deliver me from my own fathomless depths, my own Sargasso Sea of suffering. Of course, nothing of the sort ensued. My suffering remained, but, for reasons unknown, so did my faith.

There was a time not that long ago, when it was fashionable for certain experts of a sort to claim that men were no longer necessary, except as procreators. While we foolish men mulled over our existential posture, our partners in destiny reduced us to being nothing more than carriers of seed. Of passing physiological interest, and little more. None of this is important, but it brings me to a short anecdote that I wish to recount.

While walking to Chartres in 1990 on a pilgrimage, I came across a Portuguese immigrant out gathering mushrooms with his son. During my brief conversation with the man, I learned that he had no gainful employment. And, although this man would feel shame in my homeland, here at least, both he and his son's universes appeared to be complete by the mere presence of each other. There is no moral to this tale, other than to say that I had an immediate realization that my own life had been filled with such frescoes, except that no figures had been traced out within and there was no discernible narrative tale. And, so I picked up the easel and the paintbrush, and I began to fill in the empty spaces.

Still, not even that proved enough, as you will read in the following pages ...

PART I
Doldrums

Nares Abyssal Plain

Doldrums. The horse latitudes. Between parallels 20° north and 35° north and meridians 30° west and 70° west. The waters are entropic, at the nexus of a vast ocean system of eddies, currents and gyres spiralling clockwise and paralysing everything within the unknown, shoreless Mare Sargassum—the sea of algae. Under the bathyal zone, on the pressurized intensity of an ocean floor too dark for photosynthesis, 20,000 feet from the surface, lies the obscure eye of this maritime hurricane, known to oceanographers as the Nares Abyssal Plain.

Se Deus quiser, amanhã ...

A larval form feeding on plankton has multiplied its weight by five in less than two months. The larva drifts slowly from the entropic waters towards the periphery near the western ridge of the sea and, for fifty-five days, it moves through the horse latitudes over the long-dead corpses of the brave men of the schooners *Rosalie* or *Ellen Austin*, over the crew of the barque *James R. Chester* in repose five miles beneath, in a north-northwest direction, weaving as it were through the doldrums towards the great forest, the thick weeded mats of Mare Sargassum, until an eddy propels it from the entropic calm into the Gulf Stream flowing eastward. The quickly multiplying organism now moves north-northeast past the Bermuda Rise and into the wide Atlantic Ocean over the Continental Shelf. During the 300-day transatlantic voyage, the larva metamorphoses into an unpigmented, transparent swimmer known as the glass eel, finally arriving in the estuarine waters of Europe's shores to begin its life as an elver for the next decade. *Anguilla Anguilla*.

1

Nothing is true ... so everything is permitted.
—Hassan-i Sabbah

The road which led me to the mission which is the object of this tale was an indirect one. Despite an education and upbringing designed to prepare me for a destiny as a leader of the most promising country in the world, my life quickly proved to be governed by the laws of attraction and intuition. I have generally moved in the direction where the gravitational pull upon me was strongest. Whether that pull came from god, or the stars, or manifest destiny, or a general lassitude is impossible to say. When my life hit these crucial, intense vortexes, shooting me into unforeseen new trajectories which involved escape, rupture, flight, abandonment and utter censorship by my conventional, bourgeois entourage, I was ruled by a fatalistic passivity and moved as if in a trance. Unlike Cendrars, whose life I emulated and relied upon, everything that had conditioned me from birth onward acted as a curse and infused me with dark guilt that only the welcome relief of drink would assuage.

I am quite certain in retrospect that the attempt to create leaders of the world carries with it a commensurate risk of producing unintended results and causes attrition and collateral damage which has yet to be properly charted. The human soul contains a history stretching backwards across infinity. Chalking a few strokes across the fresco of the soul with recently conjured ideas is a random exercise, only allowing for a sort of delineation of character and qualities already determined well in advance. Whether one becomes Gilles de Rais or Thomas Merton is more a question of chromosomes than of cognition.

Given my sojourns at the Sorbonne and the Katholieke Universiteit Leuven and further tutelage under the sharpest minds of both French civil law and English common law, it was natural that a number of doors would open wide for me. Get your paperwork in order, the judge had advised, and the world shall be your oyster. And since the judge exercised the strongest gravitational force at the time when he uttered these words, I temporarily acceded to his worldview. But he was a man of destiny—soldier, barrister and statesman—whereas I was a shooting star, or imagined myself as one, bright, transient and ready to disappear into the firmament. Even a bad reputation isn't built overnight. But my credentials were acquired within a relatively short time frame, as I assumed successively my career postures of lawyer, English teacher, immigration consultant, hack copywriter and oil field worker on a progressively declining scale as the deeper contamination of my friends Dostoyevsky and Blaise Cendrars tightened their grip and sent me into a jagged, unending spiral of misadventures. But prior to recounting that, a brief word on how Cendrars helped me to break the shackles of the provincial Catholic family into which I was born.

II

I have no roots.
—Blaise Cendrars

My father and mother were both children of the depression and the dust bowl years in the badlands of Alberta. He was a soldier at 18, a hero at 23. His life philosophy was simple and similar to that of other Scots Canadians—bite the bullet. I resembled him to a tee, and that brought me nothing but the reproach of those who knew him, as our resemblance ended at the physical. By the time I was an adolescent, the family I was born into had expanded into a clan which reached just about everywhere through Canadian society. Just like families, clans are organic entities living in accordance with a set of immutable laws which survive long past individual interests. A man can revolutionise the world, but the same man is powerless to alter the most banal realities of the organic trap from which he emerges.

The logic of a clan is to push out tentacles, each of which is an extension of the original body. When the tentacle doesn't exercise its designated function properly—i.e., either to gather food or to defend the host body—the remedy is excision. Childhood is the temporary illusion that this genetic cage is actually meant to protect you. So it went with me for 12 years. Things changed in the course of 10 minutes one day when a band of feral youths savagely beat me to within an inch of my death while I walked home from school. There was no warning of this, no motive, no familiarity with the attackers, whom I never saw again.

Looking back, it seems to me that everything stems from that one day, and the arrival home, and the first understanding that no one intended to do anything about it. The man whom the world universally regarded as a hero had left me to my own devices. During the days which followed, while I lay in a hospital bed with my eyes tumefied and several broken bones, I only knew that whatever I'd been told up until that moment was of no use to me, and I vowed to find out where I had gone wrong and to change everything.

Time moved on, and the incident was forgotten, except by me. Probably the only outward sign of the event was that I started smoking, a habit which brought me great solace and allowed me to mark the passing of time in units measured between the contemplative pauses afforded by a good Marlboro. As I excelled in school and followed politics from an early age, the presumption was that I would eventually play a significant role in public life at a crucial point in Canadian history. That statement, which strikes me as absurd in the extreme today, served as my governing myth right through early adolescence.

As my illusions had yet to be utterly shattered, I still harboured the belief that things would right themselves. Then my father decided to ship me off to boarding school with the Christian Brothers of Ireland. At the time, a tribe of thugs ruled its corridors and dormitories with absolute *pater familias* powers. The punching and strapping was called discipline. The practice of dark sexual arts with orphans or disturbed children was later characterised by their overlords in the ecclesiastical authority as "looking for comfort in the wrong places." During the early stages of investigations, parish priests and archbishops glared down at us from the pulpit with righteous anger or with mournful sorrow. Who indeed had the right to cast the first stone? A man had to look honestly into his heart; forgiveness was partaking of the divine. We knew they were lying, but even we were too naïve to realise that the sermons were a ploy to buy time so that the Church could move assets out of reach of the jurisdiction of the courts. Later, when the Vatican itself had no choice but to stop the cover-up, it never wasted a chance to label it the "Irish problem."

Thus, my formative years were spent serving a five-year sentence under those Christian brothers from Ireland. During the day, it was a war zone. The brothers, in black, swirling skirts, rosaries hanging at the belt, gave full vent to their raging, unbridled tempers, swinging the strap, smashing heads against bulletin boards or against other heads. Where the early days were terrifying, a paradoxical reversal of psychology occurred as we sized up the measure of our enemies: the threat of violence creates a climate of fear, but the execution of it punctures the illusion and deflates authority. When a skirted brother crossed the Rubicon into the zone of turbulence and released the beast within, it acted like a curse. The perpetrator became vile and tainted and marked for revenge. My classmates—a motley crew of scavengers, vagabonds, orphans and delinquents—were seasoned veterans of revolt, and we marked the brothers early on as an enemy to be sabotaged at every turn. They were no match for us, because they still feared exposure, whereas we had lost everything.

When the school bell rang, we drifted down to the train yards on the docks of the Fraser River. There we awaited the first passing freight train and hitched a ride to the south side of the river, where we trespassed onto farmland to steal mushrooms rich in psilocybin. We had found our first bootlegger, an ill-shaven animal out of the Cariboo-Chilcotin district who had an eye for young boys.

The Caribooster, as we labelled him, was our go-between for beer and whisky. Then it was down to the river for more scouring or just watching the tugboats and river sturgeon, log booms and barges move past.

On occasion, we spotted the keys in the ignition of a half-decent outboard, a temptation too good to pass on. One afternoon, we managed to steal a Carolina skiff boat with an Evinrude outboard from the local marina and sped downriver towards the delta while gobbling down mushrooms. Strange, atavistic life forms seemed to spring out of the riverbanks—rebels, bums and outlaws inhabiting ramshackle bric-a-brac constructions, balancing on makeshift cedar pylons planted into the shifting silt of the riverbed. These men sat on their porches, indifferent to the relentless buzz of stevedores unloading ships, sawmill workers pouring into the mills and river dredgers fighting against the great river's currents. They reclined on makeshift scraps of furniture, passively observing, drinking beer or coffee and smoking.

It struck me that these supposedly worthless and shunned river dwellers didn't look all that unhappy. Within the haze of my beer- and mushroom-induced fantasies, they were guardians of another realm. The sight of them as the river took on shapes of the sidereal Eiffel Tower or a Gaudi cathedral untethered a dream within—of the day I would flee my drab existence.

Adversity is meant to build character, but in my case it simply confirmed a growing suspicion that the world did not correspond to the user's manual I'd been handed. On the home front, it looked like the judge had long since concluded that his son wasn't made of the same fibre as he. I saw things differently. I'd spent my formative years devising various strategies to keep myself and my handicapped brother from being slaughtered by local thugs or, when on school premises, from being set upon by a clique made up of psychotically violent tyrants, pederasts or both. The casualty of this paradoxical quandary was morality, an obsolescent credo better suited for other places and times.

One teacher, Barnett, seemed the only regular man of the lot. A former truck driver, he taught mathematics and Latin, and he taught them well. A long time later, while reading the case law, I fell upon an Ontario decision in Chambers, ruling on a plaintiff's motion to seize all the assets of my alma mater to pay off 36 million dollars in execution of judgements for complainants of sexual abuse. The motion was dismissed. Apparently, the entire share capital of my alma mater consisted of three shares, and one of them was held by Barnett. The bastard was sitting on 10 million dollars' worth of blood money. I filed that for future reference, and a long time later, from another country, I dealt with this treachery in my own way. But that is another story.

On my 16th birthday, Banahan, a close friend and fellow scavenger, dropped by for a visit to make the following announcement: "I'm leaving tomorrow. For Europe."

"Sounds good. Can I come?"

"Have you got a passport?"

"No."

For the next year, I climbed the walls, living for the arrival of Banahan's sporadic but lengthy air-mail letters, which recounted the bohemian life. He lived with a Chelsea stripper and made regular side trips to the cathouses of Hamburg or the coffee shops of Amsterdam. He spoke of a "Magic Bus" which had taken him from Amsterdam to the Khyber Pass, of converting to Islam to follow a girl into Saudi Arabia. He sounded like a man alive in a way that I had never been.

In one communiqué, Banahan simply forwarded two excerpts in French torn out of a book titled *Bourlinguer*, penned by an author I'd never heard of named Blaise Cendrars. The two excerpts were heavily annotated with Banahan's script. I imagined him in Tangiers, strung out on heroin, his glaucous amphibian features pushed up against the page as he attempted to decipher the meaning of the message. I placed the two passages inside a day journal I was keeping, giving no further thought to their contents. They possessed talismanic, not literary, value for me, and the proof that I would keep my vow to escape the prison of family.

As I had a plan, overnight my marks improved, and both my teachers and my father, while at a loss to explain it, decided I was finally finding my way after a brief period of rebellion and lacklustre performance. I could have just fled, but I feared the risk of returning penniless and defeated. I wanted to bury this beast in one coup. My opportunity arose at one of the formal Sunday dinners over which my father, a Supreme Court judge, presided. I announced that I was leaving the country for Europe.

"An ambitious scheme and one that requires an equal dose of planning," decreed the judge, looking over his half-moon bifocals as he reached for another glass of the Portuguese Mateus that he favoured. "Have you picked your country yet?"

I answered simply that I was leaving the following day to read history at the Katholieke Universiteit Leuven, the great mediaeval institute and alma mater of Erasmus. I laid out the confirmation of registration from the university; following the judge's advice to the letter, my paperwork was in perfect order. The shock was too sudden and the time too short for them to react. I shall never forget stepping into the taxi waiting for me in front of the family home, and the lot of them standing on the driveway, raising their hands limply in farewell like a Rockwell painting. Pathos.

On the way to the airport, I was seized by a terrible guilt—at having escaped prison camp and left others behind to their fate—and the power of it nearly convinced me to turn back. But I held firm and, once on the plane, the die was cast. I have no idea how the matter was discussed. Maybe they filed my conduct under the safe label of a gap year, a convenient myth harboured by parents in 1974. But I knew from the first minutes when I saw their faces recede and then disappear that I'd never turn back.

In a matter of days, I stepped off an inter-city train in the mediaeval city of Leuven in Brabant province, Belgium. I was greeted by a dowdy, near-vacated waiting area and a shabby set of exit doors leading onto the main street which bore an indecipherable name—Bongenootenlaan. I reached inside my pocket for a city map but found myself looking at the scrap of paper containing the excerpt from *Bourlinguer*. I decided to save it for good luck.

Several months later, I was still in Leuven, shivering in my one-room flat with only cold running water, a Turkish toilet out in the hallway and a torn excerpt of *Bourlinguer* as company. I reflected back on Banahan's Chelsea Bohemia, then laughed at my earlier fantasy. The sparse solitude of my new life did nothing to discourage me. On the contrary. The right place, the only place, to make sense of Cendrars was in a miserable, unheated flat while drinking red wine warmed up by my Bunsen burner.

> The international trains passed through the station from 4:30 pm onwards. There were usually five or six of them, running in both directions. I had time, all the time I needed ... at precisely four o'clock, I threw my suitcase and jacket out of the window, and risked my neck on the narrow corniche, shuffling down it until I arrived at my sister's bedroom. Once I penetrated her room, I swiped twenty or thirty hundred sou coins that my sister kept in the drawer of her commode. Then I slipped into the office of my father, and grabbed a few packs of smokes perched on the furniture ... in the dining room, I spotted half a dozen sets of silverware, stuffed them into my pockets and, in my mother's study, I pried her secretaire open, and stole a few hundred franc notes.

Although my departure was more conventional, I felt an immediate attachment to Cendrars as a brother vagabond, someone who had fled in order to escape the confines of a provincial bourgeois family with nothing but security and prestige on the brain. I proceeded to the following passage, the effect of which was even stronger on my mind:

So, there I was in the train. Everything had gone as planned. I had been cool, as if I'd prepared the coup for a long time, when in reality, everything had been improvised on the spot and it was only at the last minute that I yielded to an impulsion. *Obviously, I had been in a dream state for the four or five days previous, feeling intermittent desires, but it would be wrong to see any meditated plan and still less an act of will. In short, I climbed out of that window like a somnambulist, and that's probably why I didn't break my neck. I felt vertigo on the train and was stunned to find I actually had left for good. I felt a sudden malaise at the prospect of having turned my back forever. It was the first time that I had obeyed this need for evasion which so often took hold of me, and has pushed me into such eccentricities, taking endless extreme resolutions, as sudden as they were without reflection, risking everything, even death, to emerge from the trance shattered, but ecstatic, in a state of ravishment, in the absurd, at the end of a cul-de-sac, or in full flight, but never regretting anything, or anybody, and always extraordinarily content and proud of what I had just sacrificed, while laughing at myself and, although intoxicated by the sensation of being lost at sea, or approaching a new world,* still maintaining a healthy disdain for myself at continuing to believe in life.

I concluded that my recent departure was totemic, that it had not been a rational decision at all, but something containing only contours which I was yet to fill in. I felt that I was being reborn in my lonely digs and dwelt in an intermezzo, fluid phase while my new self annihilated the old. And then I discarded the thought. This Cendrars had nothing to do with me. He was a bum, a gypsy and a writer, from other places and times, and I had my own destiny, and nothing to justify. If I had escaped and severed the links with my past, that was my business and mine alone. Or so I thought at the time.

III

There is no truth ... there is only action.
—Blaise Cendrars

The Katholieke Universiteit Leuven was originally a theological college founded in 1435 much in the mould of the Sorbonne, its 13th-century precursor, where I would eventually find what I was looking for. Nothing can possibly convey the mediaeval terror which reigned at this institute during the years of my attendance. It combined the austere tyranny of the madrassas with the bullying of the British public schools. With the Christian brothers, we had the consolation that we had been sentenced to that stockyard without having committed any crimes, which freed us up for rebellion. But in Leuven, the problem was one of voluntary servitude. None of the students had faced up to the fact that, in the unlikely event that you survived running its gauntlet, your only reward would be the right to torment others by taking your own place in the hierarchy.

The tyrants of Leuven were a group of elderly men for the most part, the majority of whom came from the clergy or the secular ranks of linguistic nationalism. When I moved into my sparse digs perched on the fourth floor of number 53 Arendstraat, or Street of the Eagle, I had no premonition of the sadistic mentors who exercised absolute, invisible, unaccountable power over the lives of Belgium's future leaders. Had I been on the street side, I'd have enjoyed a view of the Grand Library of Leuven, one of only three buildings which survived the ransacking by a Furor Teutonicus in August 1914, when the Germans shot two hundred citizens in cold blood and torched over a thousand historic buildings under a barbaric policy known as *Nicht ein Stein auf eineme anderen,* or "Don't leave a stone standing," but whose major result was the confection of the notion of a just war.

I attended classes where I listened to Professor Leopold Genicot, the emblematic champion of Wallonia, pontificate on the Carolingians and the Visigoths or sweated through Chanoine Aubert's classes on *Heuristique Générale,* a drab repetition of the hierarchy of sources which somewhat resembled evidence courses I would later follow when reading law. It was tailor-made for archivists working six floors beneath the ground at the Bibliotheek and, in principle, hard going for someone issued from the rowdy backwaters of British Columbia. But I took to it well. During the day, I listened to the professors drone on without understanding a word.

During the evenings, now safely alone, I pored through French-language texts and, to provide relief, read the Russians in English—Tolstoy, Dostoyevsky, Gogol, Turgenev, Solzhenitsyn, in no particular order. My deprivation was self-imposed. I was reinventing myself—as what I had no idea. Each name I heard in the classroom—Van der Weyden, Kirk Bouts, Mathijs de Layens, Erasmus, the ultra-Montagnards—filled me with a sense that I was building a strange and archaic building myself on the rubble of my not-so-distant past, my own *Nicht ein Stein auf eineme anderen.*

The austerity of my living conditions only heightened the sense that I was now an orphan of the continent that had produced me.

After a few weeks, I was well into a routine—reading and studying during the day, and at night exploring the niches and corners of that strange, mediaeval city. Under the tutelage of the Vlaamse, I was learning the art of drinking Belgian style in the Oude Markt cafés, particularly three holes known respectively as De Werelt, De Delper and Den Allee, where you could swallow Maes Pils or Jupiter for a dime a glass until the sun rose.

Leuven suited me all right—it was ancient, baroque, Teutonic, macabre. There were no fights in pubs or cafés or even out in the street. And no hallucinogenics. In Leuven, everyday life was hallucinatory and could test your sanity to the limits, so my former attraction to mind-bending hallucinogenics died a natural death upon arrival. In Leuven, reality appeared to be palatable. And despite my rough New World beginnings, I looked forward to entering more fully into the life of the mind and its myriad representations.

De Werelt, which was frequented by roadies for a local band, became my home away from home, as I'd struck up a friendship with the drummer for the band, a Dennis Hopper look-alike named Eddie. During one of our all-night forays, Eddie recommended I check out West Flanders, a place where he said the students congregated in mediaeval student clubs and, in Eddie's words, "pretty well anything goes."

I took a train out to West Flanders on the weekend and looked up Eddie's Tante Blanche, a friendly, middle-aged woman who ran a grocery store in a village named Wingene on the flatlands between Ghent and Bruges. Tante Blanche had purchased her store after selling her piggery to someone named Uncle Seff. Tante Blanche seemed pretty happy to see me, despite not knowing me from Jan Peter. She introduced me to Madeleine, an old lady who moved through the room glumly in an ankle-length black crinoline dress while massaging a crucifix hanging from her neck. Madeleine would spend my Saturdays filling me with *stoofvlees* or witloof and generally looking sour.

The previous year, another Canadian had made an entrance in Wingene—an Italian from Winnipeg named Sonny. Blanche's living room was littered with photos of Sonny. Particularly against the bland furniture and the crucifixes hanging on the walls, Sonny, with his curly black hair and his gold neck chain under an open-necked Greek blouse, looked like some kind of Vegas star doing one-night gigs at the Sands. There was no point trying to live up to the act of Sonny the Winnipeg Italian.

It was a village, and people were curious about the Canadian newcomer, whom they called *De Canadese,* as if I were some kind of Javanese bastard just off the boat, who came to learn to live like a Belgian. Which wasn't that far from the truth, when you think about it. Within a couple of days, two atavistic-looking identical twins named Carlos and Ignace dropped by.

"You know how to drink, *Canadese boyka?*"

"I think it's rude to refuse a drink," I responded.

"You come with us, we'll learn you how to drink. Fifty, sixty beers per night."

Later the same day, a slick looking, pug-faced character named Gerrit came to pay his respects, arm in arm with a tall, black-haired Vlaamse beauty named Magda. Gerrit drove a used gold Mercedes-Benz and managed a hotel in nearby Bruges. During that evening and many to come, Gerrit would take me out to the local haunts and ply me full of wine while I tried to figure out how to fuck Magda. Gerrit was a Flanders version of Mister Manners and, pretentious but exquisitely coiffured son of a bitch that he purported to be, he decided to pass on a few of his hard-earned trade secrets to me while keeping my glass full at all times. That gave me an angle on Magda, whom I had fallen in love with, and so we started spending our Saturday evenings together. During one of our outings, we got to talking about books.

"You ever read Henry Miller?" Gerrit asked.

"Never heard of him," I said, which was true.

The fact was, I'd read Dostoyevsky, Tolstoy, Pushkin, but I had no overview about reading at all, because I didn't discuss the books that fell into my hands with anybody. The next day I found a copy of *Nexus* waiting for me on a coffee table in Blanche's living room with a note signed by Gerrit, saying: "Try this." I opened the book by Henry Miller, skipping the introduction by Erica Jong. Oddly enough, the first page opened with a dog barking.

"WOOF! Woof woof! *Woof! Woof!*"
The sound of that dog barking inside my head was to change the entire course of my life.
Barking in the night. Barking, barking. I shriek but no one answers. I scream but there's not even an echo.
"*Which do you want—the East of Xerxes or the East of Christ?*"
Alone—with eczema of the brain.
Alone at last. How marvellous! Only it is not what I expected to be. If only I were alone with God!
Woof! Woof woof!

Old Madeleine, miserable old slut, hunched over, fatalistically churning a marmite of mustard soup with unidentifiable remains adrift on its surface, to be followed by the inevitable beer stew. Her spindly legs reminded me of a rotting oak tree's roots. Another glass of thick brown table beer, the ambient mumble of a red-nosed Vlaamse priest while he allowed Blanche to pour more cognac into his snifter. I thought I could smell excrement on the thick boots worn by the priest. I glanced back at the page. A propos of nothing at all, Miller was listing some names he claimed were old friends—Whistler, Lovis Corinth, Breughel the Elder, Botticelli, Bosch, Giotto, Cimabue, Piero della Francesca, Grunewald, Holbein, Lucas Cranach, Van Gogh, Utrillo, Gauguin, Pieranesi, Utamaro, Hokusai, Hiroshige ...

I laid the book down and closed my eyes, savouring these mellifluous names, each of which seemed to suggest a thousand stories.

The priest was fumbling around for his pouch of tobacco stuffed like a handkerchief in his pocket and sniffing at his cognac like some kind of a dog. I looked at the cover again and at this writer with the shoeshine-boy name and the look of a Mongolian with dubious plans.

Well, I thought, if they are your friends, then they are also mine! If you please, Mr. Henry Val Miller, let me also meet this Lovis, and this Breughel fellow, and this Holbein. Blanche had placed an LP 78 record on the turntable for the priest, which was playing the theme song from *Un homme et une femme* and Lara's theme from *Dr. Zhivago*. He looked ecstatic. I wondered whether his daily vespers gave him the same high that he was obviously getting out of his Zen moment in Blanche's living room.

WOOF! Woof woof! Woof! Woof! To be sure, I knew instantly that I wanted more of whatever this strange codified message from Miller delivered me. I would do anything to get it. I found myself making secret vows, like some autistic shepherd boy struck dumb by a vision of Christ.

Men like Miller and Cendrars, who was partially introduced to me by Miller, attract first the vilification and then the morbid curiosity of the establishment, who seek vainly to understand what could possibly motivate a man to write in this mad, formless way. He was a runaway, says one. A nonconformist, says another. Crude. The king of smut. A sexist, say the feminists. None of the above. All of the above. An enigma. *Inclassable*. A bug on a wall. A guru. A good man at a party. A man who stood on his own two feet, and enjoyed life and hung out in the street. If there was any doubt in my mind about being a lifetime exile, that day in front of *Nexus* settled it. I wasn't going anywhere near kin, and I wasn't going home.

Within a few months I was fully integrated into Belgian life, such as it was. During the week, I studied and played rugby with the French-speaking Walloons. On the weekend, I fell in with my cronies of the Flemish-speaking Schreveke student club, led by the identical twins Ignace and Carlos, and Geert, a loyal regular who looked straight out of Van Gogh's *Potato Eaters* and whose plump girlfriend had a roving eye for something. During the raucous evenings in that hamlet, we'd salt away *pentjes* by the dozen and sing ludicrous Vlaaamse songs like a chapter of grizzled legionnaires, except we were all under twenty. Maybe it was the table beer from birth, but the Flemings seemed to travel from wide-eyed childhood to bug-eyed old age without the usual interval of puberty.

One morning, I stumbled out of the Schreveke in the predawn and spotted Magda sitting inside the gold Mercedes-Benz on the Tieltstraat, smoking a cigarette and, as far as I could make out, Gerritless. By that time, Miller and my dawning life as an exile had moved guile a few rungs higher than scruples on my hierarchy of values. Since closing the last pages of *Nexus*, I had vowed that I would fuck Magda some day. And now, there she was. High cheekbones, angular, tall beauty, dressed in black, waiting. An apparition, looking as bored as Bacall behind the wheel of that Mercedes-Benz. It was the chance of a lifetime and the work of a minute, taking her up to my room over the grocery store.

Making love to her was like stepping off a cliff into an abyss of ecstacy and despondence. I fell asleep, amazed and grateful to the gods that such a stunning beauty could be languishing in a prison of her own and that I would ultimately be the beneficiary of her disconsolate fate. Later, I was awoken by the sound of angry voices in the grocery store and could hear the word *Canadees*, one of the very few I could demarcate from the as yet indecipherable, saturnine phonetics of the Vlaamse. I quickly ushered Magda down the stairs under the shadow of Madeleine's scowling face in the rear kitchen, where she was already stirring some unholy concoction while soaking beets through a white rag. Beets for breakfast, for god's sake! After successfully pushing Magda out onto the Tieltstraat, I poured myself an acrid coffee and returned to my room to plan my next move.

A while later, I decided it was safe to make an entrance downstairs. Blanche was playing cards with three old ladies in the living room as I came in and, upon seeing me, all four looked shocked about something.

"Return to your room, *boyka!*" Tante Blanche ordered.

I retreated up the stairs in a state of confusion and sought refuge in the bathroom, where I caught a glimpse of myself in the mirror. I recalled Magda the previous night saying she wanted to see what was concealed under my beard. After stumbling up the stairs, drunk with Duvel and Leffe beer, I'd started shaving it but only made it halfway through.

Later that day, I was on a train passing through Ghent towards Brussels and noticed Geert, the guy out of the *Potato Eaters* canvas, locked in an intense set-to with his plump girlfriend. He was banging his fist on the table. He was very upset, crying about something. I couldn't make head or tail of these people. One minute they seemed frozen into a lifeless stare, the next they were weeping with no sign of what triggered their emotional states. I quickly retreated to a sleeper car, found the beer wagon, and spent the remainder of the trip salting back Maes Pils until I arrived safely back in Leuven.

The next weekend, a Peruvian friend took me along to Paris for the weekend. I had the number of a friend's older sister who could lodge me on the *rue Séguier* in the fifth. Coming out of the Porte d'Orléans/Clignancourt line at Place St. Michel, I wandered into the *rue St.-André des Arts* and instantly fell under the spell of the calm effervescence which permeates the Latin Quarter. Before the week was out, I had enrolled at the Sorbonne, found a flat in the ninth and defaulted on my contractual obligations in Belgium. My brief sojourn in Leuven had been eventful, but here was destiny writ large upon the walls of the city. From the instant of my arrival, my transient days were over. I was home—home at last.

IV

The hand of a man ... is useful to him, because man is intelligent. In and of itself, the hand is nothing ... did the hand create machines? The intelligence of man exceeds infinitely his limbs, mere extensions. Intelligence submerges them, demands of them the impossible, the absurd. And so we have railways, the telegraph, the microscope, all these instruments which multiply the power of mere limbs, which have been reduced to their rudimentary functions due to the demands of the brain, our true master.
—Rémy de Gourmont

My in-depth discovery of Cendrars the writer came about at the age of 21, shortly after my own return from three years spent in Paris during the mid to late seventies. At that time, it was possible to live in the city on nothing—or close to it—and thus escape the yoke that crushes virtually all humans for the better part of their existence on the planet. It is perhaps useful to reprint the costs of what I considered to be the staples of monthly existence required for a young man of my inclinations:

Two litres of Nicolas red table wine per day at FF 1,10 per bottle	*FF 132,00*
Ten pouches of Drum tobacco	*FF 20,00*
Sixty CROUS Resto U tickets for student restaurants	*FF 180,00*
Rent for flat at 9, rue de la Victoire, Paris 9ième arrondissement	*FF 205,00*
Total	*FF 537,00*

If you were disinclined to work, and only a fool would work for a boss as cruel and miserly as the French *patron* when Paris beckoned, you could live and live well in the former neighbourhood of Henry Miller for 120 CAD$ per month. This placed me in an idyllic position which the great masses of *successful* humanity failed to achieve after a lifetime of bashing their heads and scraping their knees along the road towards imagined material wealth. Most died en route, some upon the very day of completing their 40-year corvée and, of course, these were the success stories. The heavy underbelly of mankind expired anonymously in lean-tos, cawing and bleating as those less unfortunate refused to share the fruits of their own desperate efforts. Early evidence, as I sized it up, reinforced my intimate conviction that my philosophy of fatalistic attraction and avoidance of responsibility was as good as anything else being offered up.

It is impossible to replicate the feeling of ekstasis which seized me randomly during my daily walks from my one-room chambre on rue de la Victoire to the Sorbonne, passing by the Folies Bergères, the punt shops of the Faubourg Montmartre, the old Bouillon Chartier, a grand old belle époque restaurant with skylights embedded in high ceilings, where you could be served *pommes à l'huile* and *oeuf dûr mayonnaise* by rondin-clad waiters, all for a fair price. I moved across the *grands boulevards* under the shadow of the old Stock Exchange and from there into les Halles, which still had the old slaughterhouses and butcher shops emitting their rancid fumes, having only a couple of centuries previous been the site of the Cimetière des Innocents, where 2 million wine-soaked Parisian corpses lay until the toxicity of their decayed bodies poisoned the drinking waters of the city and threatened to bring the remaining living underground to join those who had preceded them.

Every day, until it became a wondrous, internalised, banal quotidian, I strolled past the early morning whores of rue St. Denis, the detrital alleyways of the rue de la Grande Truanderie and the rue des Prêcheurs, where Villon and his cronies stole, harassed and molested, occasionally murdering a priest and without fail squandering their ill-gotten gains on drink. I then crossed the Seine into the Latin Quarter, where during May '68 the students had gone on a rampage of anarchism and sexual fraternizing which resulted in the downfall of no less than President De Gaulle. Arriving at the Place de la Sorbonne, I passed under the statue of Auguste Comte, the positivist philosopher, whom my own professor, René Poirier, a co-founder of the Oulipo school of absurdity, loved to mock humorously. Poirier liked to mimic Comte's arrogant sense of mission, the great philosopher pompously announcing to his looking-glass as he rose from bed each morning, *Il y a de grandes choses à faire.*

Poirier would then direct our minds to the antics and mind-bending tricks of the word wizards of French literature, particularly Alfred Jarry and Raymond Queneau, the Gallic Lewis Carrolls. Poirier's Oulipian asides shared from the erudite benches of the Galérie Richelieu rescued me from the subterranean muck and stalactites of my Nicolas wine hangover, and brought me back into the world of ideas. I have no idea what effect Poirier had on the 20-odd other students in his class, but I had found the antidote to the petrifaction of my former life. My corruption was reaching noxious intensity. There were days in the courtyard during the break in Poirier's three-hour lectures under the shadow of the statues of Pasteur and Victor Hugo when I thought I would explode with joy. I had tasted infinity and surrendered to its spell. But alongside my ecstasy, as the end of my three years approached, I felt a creeping dread of my impending return to the New World and wondered what punishment awaited a man for having committed the crime of finding true happiness.

V

> *Then Chagall returned to Russia, fought for the revolution, fell into misery. More drawings, more canvasses which are sober and splendid. In Paris, he was considered a dead man. When he returned in 1922, his studio had been broken into and his pre-war works resold. He suspected Cendrars of having a hand in it all. End of a friendship.*
> —Philippe Lançon,
> "Blaise Cendrars et ses amis de bohème"
> *Libération*, July 28, 2009

In fact, my return to the New World proved even more catastrophic than I had anticipated. No one in the Vancouver of 1978 appeared in the least interested in Paris, let alone the immensity of riches it had to offer. My enthusiastic renditions of day-to-day life in the City of Light met with blank stares or snorts of disbelief. The only questions on the minds of family or acquaintances concerned the names and dates of my interviews with prospective employers. I initially enjoyed taunting these apostles of income with mock earnestness, safe in the knowledge that I'd be leaving them behind sooner rather than later. As my resolve to depart hardened, I adopted a social veneer of gravitas as if considering seriously the various career alternatives being offered up at the family dinner table, each of which privately appeared as the door to a separate Dantean inferno. The effect of maintaining this hypocrisy while every part of me ached for fugue began to tell, and within three months my health broke down, eventually causing my physical incapacitation and forcing me to endure the charity of a man who saw his offspring as an extension of a principle utterly foreign to me —that of prairie Catholic conservatism. My father's strong point and my weak one coincided at the quadrant of will. Like the Europeans before the discovery of the concept of zero, he saw my worldview as nihilism, whereas I felt I held the key to infinity. Our courteous but relentless stalemate nearly killed me morally and physically, and none of the dangers I later ran into—from the perils of Hong Kong in '89 to those of courting the daughter of an Antibes mobster —put me closer to death than this brief period of return into the supposedly safe embrace of my family.

Lying face down on the bed of your childhood sorrows gives you plenty of time to mull over these things. Although the thought of suicide occasionally hovered on my mental horizon and the rational consideration of murder offered me periodic solace, neither held my interest for long, and both seemed rent with hidden complications and contingencies which would make my present plight appear trivial in comparison. Coincidentally, I came across a newspaper article around that time which reported that a man had pointed a shotgun under his chin "apparently in an attempt to take his life," as if there might have been other intentions on the poor fellow's mind. In any event, he only succeeded in blowing off part of his jaw. I am not sure what motivated the reporter to include front and side photos and a graphic sketch showing the trajectory of the bullet. Summer is a slow time for the papers anywhere. In any event, it put me on guard that, while things weren't looking good, they could always get worse, and it convinced me that a fair dose of social hypocrisy was a necessary strategy under what I identified as conditions of extreme duress.

The day which followed my reading of this article, Stanton dropped by with a copy of a book titled *Moravagine, Idiot* by Blaise Cendrars. As I was more or less being treated like Moravagine, the criminally insane idiot-genius sequestrated in the Waldensee sanatorium near Berne, Switzerland, and since the frontispiece reported that the author had narrowly escaped the mercantile prison erected by a Scottish mother and an Anabaptist legal father, it looked to be an appropriate read. A few pages into the book, I came across the following passage which discussed the nature of sickness itself:

> *What is conventionally referred to as health is in fact only a momentary aspect, transported onto an abstract grid, of a morbid condition, a particular case which has already crossed a threshold, and been recognised, defined, finished, eliminated and generalized for the common usage.*

From the outset, the narrator and accessory to the criminally insane genius, rapist, murderer and terrorist Moravagine denounces the advent of junk scientists and charlatans who classify as mutant that which is simply different.

> *Pursuant to what law, what morality, what society do they hand down their exactions? They intern, sequester, isolate the most remarkable individuals. They mutilate physiological geniuses who carry within themselves the prophetic genomes of a future time. They proudly proclaim themselves princes of science, and as they suffer from a persecution complex, they easily wear the mantle of victim. Sombre, obscurantist, they clothe their language of defrocked Greeks and having donned this apparel, they insinuate everywhere in the name of a boutique-style rationalist liberalism. Their theories are jaundiced, fetal, dejected. They are the henchmen of a shameful bourgeois virtue, formerly the exclusive domain of sanctimonious hypocrites. They have delivered up their knowledge to a State Police and organised the systematic destruction of everything that is fundamentally idealistic, i.e. independent. They castrate those convicted of crimes of passion and even attack the lobes of*

the brain. Senile, impotent, eugenic, they fervently believe in their power to eradicate and uproot evil. Their vanity is only equalled by their deceit and treachery. Only their hypocrisy prevents them from levelling the ground before them—hypocrisy and their sexual obsessions.

Moravagine certainly wasn't a novel in the traditional sense. He was the protagonist, Dostoyevskian, but without any redeeming feature. The book read like a charge sheet against the rule of sanctimonious hypocrites and what he labelled a *fureur nivellatrice*, or levelling frenzy. Cendrars *J'accuse* took on intellectuals and scientists —whom he clearly saw as war criminals—through the eyes of a nihilist physician and an anarchist serial killer. Through the musings of the narrator, the book prophesied everything that would happen in our times, when good men would be purged throughout every sphere of society, always in the name of a greater good—the most sinister, Stalinistic utopia being that of equality—impossible to define, impossible to refute, and therefore a preferred weapon of the Kafkaian *nivelleurs* that have led us to the present impasse.

Outside of its harsh polemic, *Moravagine* is a eulogy to action. At one point during my reading of *Moravagine*, I fell across a sentence which stood apart from the tale itself, as if written in graffiti.

There is no truth. There is only action.

I confess that during my convalescence, I was piked to the eyeballs with an experimental drug that would later claim several hundred lives, and thoughts and discoveries came to me in fits and seizures as well. So, I seized that phrase to give me the strength to survive my own ordeal. That a whole series of disasters followed is a detail. I rose from my bed, showered up and walked down to the local manpower office. The first posting on the jobs board advertised for a kiln loader. Within the day, I was on the assembly line at Crane

Pottery Works, loading units into a 2400° Fahrenheit brick kiln. That I endured that Dantean inferno for 17 hellish months is a footnote. My recurrent discovery of Blaise Cendrars—poet, adventurer, immoralist, brigand, legionnaire, precious stone dealer, friend of Chaplin, Braque, Picasso, Modigliani—gave me the knowledge that now, no matter what misadventure or folly I concocted (and my follies would soon become the rule of my existence), every one of them would appear as flecks on the screen, silhouettes faded against the infinitely larger chiaroscuro of this man who had achieved the greatest of feats and become human, just a human.

There was another problem disclosed to me by Cendrars, expressed in the way of a koan by one of his heroes, Gérard de Nerval. *Je suis l'autre.* As I mulled over this riddle and how the difficulty of the problem had resulted in de Nerval being discovered hanging from the bars of a grate which closed off a sewer on the *rue de la Vielle-Lanterne*, my predetermined life, the one which my father had charted for me in advance, was already a fading memory, and the new challenge of living up to the monster who was Cendrars/Moravagine became my sole and abiding obsession.

VI

You have to understand that what is important is ...
locomotion. What I mean is progress, getting on with it.
What you put into the machine is of little consequence
provided it can move. There has to be a raging hellfire within.
—Blaise Cendrars

Near the end of my sojourn in Paris, I took on a temporary assignment triggered by a chance encounter. Short of cash and ready to try anything that came my way, I agreed to act as an interpreter for a Californian who had come to the old continent to purchase vintage French automobiles for resale in America. Steve was a San Francisco North Beach man who had served two tours of duty in Vietnam and then returned with his body intact but his mind shattered. Just another kinetically overcharged, strung-out surfer boy with a smile on his face and the memory of napalm and Agent Orange lurking just beneath the surface.

When Steve arrived in Paris, the infectious laugh, curly hair and jaggedly handsome features of the born-and-bred North Beach boy, reinforced by a thickly padded wallet and a healthy stash of Quaaludes, made him an instant hit. Steve was looking for early 20th-century Citroëns and Peugeots which were selling for dirt cheap prices on the strength of a robust US dollar and a temporary public lack of interest in older models. A young ex-paratrooper named Florent, an Argentinean refugee known as Chuchi and I joined Steve for his car tour of the Côte d'Azur.

Each afternoon began with tours of garages, checking out the old Citroën Traction models, Panhards and Peugeots prior to seeking out the beaches and bars. As evening fell and the cocktail of Quaaludes and beer kicked in, our fates became random. After one pleasant evening in Aix-en-Provence, things degenerated when a Marseillais entered the bar with his curly haired, miniskirted woman friend, and Steve made an obscene gesture, clucking his tongue and groaning obscenely: "Boom boom, baby, boom boom." The man stood up, along with half a dozen other Latins seething with offended honour. Steve put on a lazy grin, but his eyes were dead. "Boom boom, motherfucker," he said, slicing through the air. The Marseillais decided to leave off and left the bar muttering and shaking his head. Steve caught the eye of the bartender, a burly, bald man with a big belly who was staring at the proceedings.

"Uhh, gimmee some BA MA BA, motherfucker," Steve said, sounding half asleep. Steve was cradling an empty glass in his hand, leering. The bartender was wiping out a similar looking beer glass from behind the brass counter. He gave no indication that he'd heard the remark one way or another. Steve shook his head at the glass in the palm of his hand, stood up and threw it over the bartender's head.

"I said more tiger piss, motherfucker!"

The following day another incident occurred. Outside Villefranche-sur-Mer, an idyllic village on the cliffs of the French Riviera, we stopped for petrol. We were the sole customers. The dark-eyed Italian youth manning the station made his way out to the car after making us wait 10 minutes. The station was perched on a high cliff with a spectacular view of the Mediterranean, but Steve had a way of attracting your attention. He was perched on the gas pump island, chewing on a toothpick as he leered at the swarthy youth shuffling towards us in no particular rush. Steve shook his head, grinning.

"Look at this shithead. He thinks he's the man."

Steve stepped off the island and moved past the gas jockey, disappearing behind the gas station.

"What's he doing now?" Florent asked, uneasy, after a few minutes.

"Taking a leak. I'll check."

Steve was standing outside the door leading to the toilet area out back, grinning at a fifty gallon drum of petrol he had just tipped onto the ground. A thick tarry pool covered the floor and now was spreading over the asphalt outside. Steve studied the results of his work. He held a Zippo lighter in front of him at eye level and was swivelling it horizontally in a wide arc, like a periscope surveying the ocean surface.

"Put that away, Steve, or we all go up with the building."

Steve's face was empty. We were both captivated by the blue flame of the lighter.

"That's the whole idea, motherfucker."

"C'mon man, let's go buy some cars. We're on a mission."

He flipped the cap of the lighter downward and smiled.

"Sure, man. Buy some vintage fucking metal," he said, his voice lazy and drifting.

While descending the coastal road called the Basse Corniche, a winding ledge of a highway leading into Monte Carlo, Steve spoke for the first time.

"You ever get in Stevie boy's way again, motherfucker, you're body parts, you hear me?"

As our travels went on, our nerves ratcheted up or released depending on the arc of his mood swings. For the most part, I drove, keeping a wary eye on Steve in the backseat as he emerged from semiconscious states, mistaking us for former comrades, telling us to "lock and load" or "lay chilly" or warning about "Charlie up ahead under the dust cloud" with a blank look in his eyes, ordering me to go for cover while I fought to hang on to the wheel at 200 km/h. Somewhere on the road between Cannes and Nice, the traffic bottlenecked, and up ahead we could see something bad had happened. A semi had crossed the road onto the wrong side, hit about 20-odd cars and flipped. A good half a dozen had caught fire. We moved past at a crawl, seeing the charred bodies of cars that were still burning out of control, and the police had not yet arrived. I caught sight of Steve in the rear-view mirror gauging the whole scene and repeating, "Adios, motherfucker," or "Fubar, man, fubar." Later I asked him what *FUBAR* meant.

"It means 'fucked up beyond all repair,' my friend. Just like Steve."

When he said that, that boy-next-door look disassembled into a Braque collage, eye over here, mouth stretched into a diamond, torso upside down. In those moments, you could see that good ol' boy Steve the surfer and gook-chaser had to retrieve his facial cubes off the floor in the morning and piece them together in no particular order before he stepped out the door.

Our arrival in Italy coincided with the *Brigate Rosse* kidnapping of Aldo Moro, the Italian president who was executed after 40 days of captivity. But my sense of immunity was such that being held at gunpoint by the Carabinieri, even while those six officers searched us and waved their Beretta 9mm Parabellums at us recklessly, was recorded in my mind as a tale I would later recount to similar-minded cronies I knew back in Paris and other ports of call. Later, I noticed that the cubist image of Steve had a way of paying unexpected visits to the mind's eye.

Years later, when I received the *San Francisco Chronicle* article in the mail from a mutual friend which reported on the bodies in the yard of his Big Sur property, it wasn't so much a surprise as a confirmation of the seemingly multiple forms contained within his facial features. Multiple, geometrical and pell-mell.

Somewhere between that time and the present time, I would acquire my own backlog of experiences too sharply delineated and turbo-charged for the mind to process. These memories became catalogued as a visual slideshow which displayed itself at unforeseen moments—usually provoked by minor, everyday stresses during quiet phases of my existence—and no doubt made those within proximity keep their distance from me just as I had once feared Steve. When the crises passed, I would take pen and paper and jot down lists of the images which made their intermittent appearances during my mental breakdowns in no particular order.

Some experiences were buried somewhere beneath the reach of recall. Rationally, I saw these images as the products of a mind weakened by the juxtaposition of intense introspection with impulses of violent, tempestuous action. All of this was borne of my hunger for experience. But my internal engine room, which pushed me impulsively towards Cendrarsian action, was countered by something in my fibre which resisted the forging of the inner steel that some men develop. Cendrars suffered, and he claimed to have still loved the world, but there was a hardness which was undeniable, forged through his trials. But somehow, despite having survived the ordeal of China in '89 and everything that followed, I failed to develop the enduring mettle of earlier generations of men whom I revered and resented.

These memories of experience I had been unable to digest had a way of returning to the mind like an unpredictable companion. From a mental standpoint, it felt like the reopening and cauterizing of a deep wound. Somewhat like the fish in Hong Kong markets that are sliced open and whose organs continue to pulsate, the last convulsions of life served up as evidence of recent capture for the predator. Those exposed fish in their death throes were the clearest metaphor for the China of '89, where life was not a sacred thing—and where no man could retain the illusion that his person counted for anything within that mosaic of a billion people transforming themselves into the China of the 21st century.

Being FUBAR didn't stop Steve from carving out a healthy share of the California market for French vintage automobiles. If you removed the moral component, Steve's system struck me as fairly Cendrarsian. When FUBAR became my own governing reality, I turned to the two men who had been there and done that—Steve the surfer and Cendrars the one-armed poet. We're all a little bit FUBAR in the end. It's just that, for me and Steve the surfer and Cendrars and the rest of my FUBAR cronies, getting de-FUBARed didn't look like a viable option.

VII

What's the use of documentation?
I surrender to the impulses of memory.
—Blaise Cendrars

I arrived in Quebec City on a red-eye flight from Vancouver on a sunny September day in 1980. The hack driver's name was Marcel. Around 8:00 a.m. Marcel drove me through the arches of the Porte St. Louis under the shadow of the Plains of Abraham. On the upper side of the *Grande Allée* stood the bunker of the PQ separatist government and on the lower side a string of cafés for politicians and civil servants. The old city was half empty in those days. Rent was dirt cheap, and there was nothing to do but drink and scout out dark-eyed Québecoise women wandering the streets in their mothers' fur coats, their hair tied back in ponytails. I hadn't really considered the fact that I was the enemy. I hadn't considered anything except that the city was filled with bars that stayed open all night and it didn't look like they cared about the outside world.

Quebec offered the opportunity to shatter the premise I found intolerable—that my father had proprietary rights over my life. It's one thing to rattle your chains, but if you are going to escape the jail of a great clan, you have to be capable of planning and prepared to delay gratification, and I was the typical product of a generation incapable of either. I had a heavily charged libido, two sheets of white blotter acid and I'd just landed in a hotbed of Québecois nationalism, which made the whole game board fluid and multi-dimensional. My sympathies were with Quebec, but my education was antipodal, the product of history, of British parliamentary democracy sprinkled with the folklorish sentimentality of our family, who had been every bit as dangerous as the Québecois at an earlier point in history.

Geography once again separated me from my father, but it was impossible to eradicate him from my memory, and the steel-blue of his critical gaze always penetrated into the mind's eye to devastating effect. All of this created a double helix effect, like the two enormous foundations of buildings grinding against each other or a cape vessel pushing against a dry-dock designed for smaller vessels. It was the irresistible force of my vitality pitted against the immovable inertia of the judge's entrenched dogmas. Our relationship degenerated into periodic skirmishes where we did our best to avoid open conflict, but we remained unable to move beyond caricatured versions of each other.

After a brief stint teaching English, I enrolled in the law faculty at the local university. I was still young enough that I hadn't entirely discarded dreams of glory, and this route presented no particular difficulties. Whereas for others the law was a mystery, any half-sentient Fingon had the judiciary embedded into his mental, social and spiritual template from birth onwards. Fingons breathed the law. Even the idiots, drug addicts and plumbers could expound on promissory estoppel or the Hedley Byrne principle.

I approached law school from a mathematical and time-management standpoint. Ten thousand cases had to be read over three years. Shortly following enrolment, I recruited nine other students of like mind, and we divided up the case load between us for the entire three-year span. Within sixteen weeks, we had summaries for three years' work, which left us free to pursue other interests. During the day, I listened to sharp-minded men and women explain with calm certainty the principles of personal property security and the formation of contracts. Canada's finest constitutional experts described passionately the construction of a great pyramid of rights and obligations born from the ashes of endless wars.

The greatest minds of the Enlightenment had rejected the mediaeval justice of the star chamber courts in England and drafted their new vision, which they had entrenched in the Magna Carta, the Bill of Rights and the Declaration of Independence. I pored over the feudal legalese of the *Coutume de Paris* and learned how the Revolution and the Terror had erased a thousand years of history and in its place superimposed the Napoleonic Code.

At night, from the confines of my flat inside the walls of the old city, I left off with nemo judex and the law of negligence, cracked a beer, and settled into my readings of Bukowski, Cendrars, Miller, Hunter S. Thompson, Rabelais and the like. These plain-speaking men, of equal erudition and far more hands-on experience of life's turmoil than my law school mentors, had quite another version of the truth, although it was based on the same set of facts. Their words crackled with spite, violence and humour and contained a message I felt was directed towards me: that the entire edifice underlying my indoctrination into the law was at best a well-intentioned plan gone awry and at worst an elaborate fleecing operation designed to skin the common man.

If I had failed earlier, things would have been less complicated. My graduation from law school with *magna cum laude* honours did nothing to resolve this inner conflict. My success in meeting the formal requirements of the noble profession threw my family into an uncharacteristic and temporary rapture of enthusiasm. It cast me into a black despondency, knowing that I was a bad fit for the world I was about to enter and that only one of these two competing world visions could possibly survive. The answer wasn't long in coming. The year was 1985, which marked the advent of a new class of business predators known as the Masters of the Universe. I had been summoned for a job interview before a committee representing one of Montreal's international megafirms, Ducasse & Jarndyce, who wanted to discuss the future of one Jack Fingon, recently Esquired.

I found myself sitting on the 72nd floor of a shiny high-rise by the stock exchange, facing a triad of lawyers led by Gérard Mayotte, a squinty-eyed man wearing a bow tie, an Armani suit and a put-on, cutesy smile that implied that he might have enjoyed sticking butterflies into wet cement as a child.

"What can you tell me about mortgaging ships, Mister Fingon?"

"Nothing."

The two other lawyers, junior partners named Poliquin and Alliot, wore a quasi-permanent smirk, but this bland response caught their attention. Mayotte was higher up the food chain. Bloodless after feeding off clients.

"Maybe I haven't made myself clear, Mister Fingon. What do you know about ship liens?"

The boardroom was massive, overlooking the St. Lawrence River and the old sugar and textile concerns from another era. I noticed that the windows were hermetically sealed. There was a large painting of peasants scuttling around in the Quebec snow by Cornelius somebody or other. I already had an offer in my pocket from Deloitte Perkins one tower closer to the stock exchange, and I didn't feel like sucking up to this dude in a bowtie.

"Not a thing. Honestly, couldn't tell you a damn thing about ship liens."

"That's all you have to say," Mayotte responded.

"No disrespect meant, Mr Mayotte. My aim is to be a trial lawyer. If you want a paper shuffler, my class was filled with them."

Mayotte emitted that crispy, sadistic smile and closed up the folder he'd brought in as a prop.

"That'll be all for today, Mr. Fingon. You'll be hearing from us."

Mayotte left the room first, and the lawyer named Poliquin laughed.

"Strategically, I'm not sure you took the wisest tack."

"True enough, but I didn't read ten thousand cases so I could fill in forms. I'd rather work in a pool hall. Matter of fact that's where I'm headed right now."

"Well, we enjoyed meeting you. Good luck."

We shook hands and I left for a smoked-meat sandwich and an afternoon of nine-ball in a pub on the Main. The next day I received a phone call. It was Poliquin.

"You got very, very lucky. We told Bourque, our senior litigator, how you handled the interview, just as an anecdote, and he stepped in. Maybe your strategy wasn't so stupid."

"It wasn't a strategy."

Turned out the barristers needed a new man, so I was shuttled to the 73rd floor and the barristers. For a time, I really took to the trench warfare of trial practice. I had nothing against a good punch up, and the Montreal courthouse and its corridors were filled with a rough-and-tumble atmosphere. It was like Philadelphia but in French. Blood is an acquired taste, and it can become an intoxicating one. I was better than decent at crucifying witnesses, having had the trick performed on me from the cradle. For a time, there was a sense of inevitability. Maybe this was my destiny. Samurai barrister. Gun for hire. Then, without warning, a lawsuit which should have confirmed my irrevocable ascension up the ranks of the judiciary proved to be my own undoing.

The case in question concerned a man who was one of the first AIDS victims to file a claim against a hospital. He was gay, but the cause of his fatal condition was blood contamination resulting from a routine transfusion. The man was suffering from a plague-like symphony of syphilitic distress—from crabs to herpes to gonorrhoea. His days were as filled with mortal pain as his physicians' reports were with denials and omissions. While this postmodern leper lay stricken in his bed, I had spotted a fatal flaw in the plaintiff's case. It appeared that he was statute-barred by a mere 24 hours, having taken a day too long to file his claim. His solicitor had attempted to gloss it over in the allegations, but the stamp of the court registry told another story. For three nights, I mulled over my discovery and its probable impact on the poor sod contemplating the end of his mortal existence as those bound by oath to save him all ran for cover. I wasn't given to pity. Maybe it was the mathematical, exponential nature of the disease that caused me to consider for the first time that the cold-blooded treatment of this innocent man had broader implications.

Monday morning, trial lawyers met at 7:30 a.m. for coffee, croissants and some collective brainstorming in the 72nd floor conference room. I felt a little tired, not giving it too much thought. I glanced over at my colleagues. Eric Leduc was recounting a breakaway goal scored by the Canadiens during the previous Saturday night's hockey game in the old Montreal forum. Somebody mentioned that Lebrun, one of the senior partners, was being touted as Court of Appeal material. Poliquin caught sight of me, grinned.

"There he is. What are Maître Fingon's thoughts on *Quebec Medical Association et al. vs Meunier*?"

"I think the claim was filed out of time."

"No, it isn't; we checked that. Look at the statement of claim."

"That's the allegation. But look at the stamp of the date on the proceeding."

Poliquin, bug-eyed Groucho Marx face on a marathoner's physique, marched briskly across the room and peered over my shoulder at the statement of claim on the table in front of me.

"Christ al-fucking-mighty, he's right. Fingon's fucking well right. It's not the same date. What's your conclusion, Fingon?"

"Under the circumstances and given the plaintiff's suffering, the proper course of action is an ex gratia payment to ensure proper care in exchange for a release from the plaintiff."

There was a silence in the room. All eyes turned to Samy Le Bourque, granite-faced senior litigator. Le Bourque lifted up his hands and began slowly clapping. Poliquin grinned and joined in. Remaining counsel, para-legals and articled students broke into a round of applause and the back-slapping started, broken by one or two jaundiced glances from junior counsel in the room. One of them, McPherson, was muttering: "How could I have missed that? How!"

"This baby is barred," said Poliquin, walking over to give me a high five, and then whispering: "You're on the fast track for partnership, pal. This is a game-breaker."

"What about the ex gratia payment?" I asked.

"Fingon, this isn't a charity; it's a law practice."

I recall the remainder of that day in a cloud of freeze frames. Leaving the room in a daze and returning to my office. Closing up my files. Deleting my entire computer. Removing my diplomas from the walls. I felt asphyxiated, but I also knew I had to retrieve my personal effects, as I wouldn't be capable of re-entering the building once I departed. I reached for the key to my filing cabinet but stopped before opening it and slumped back in my chair, feeling the full weight of what I had done with the previous seven years of my life. Not a man standing in that room would have thought twice before defending a dictator, a child murderer, a cigarette concern. We did it every day and washed our hands of it every night. And I wasn't even getting a good cut of the profits.

I knew full well that the colleagues who minutes earlier had been slapping me on the back would turn on me like jackals if I betrayed them. At the same time, I felt a physical nausea at the mere touch of the filing cabinet. I was paralysed. For a good fifteen minutes, the door closed, my head buried in my hands, I tried to think my way out of the mental vice grip where I had found myself.

Finally, I managed to stand up and walk out the door, taking nothing with me but my diplomas. Nobody seemed to pay much attention as I caught the elevator downwards and moved through the lobby, out the door and into the first cab at the line-up of taxis outside. The driver was a young, unshaven man wearing a tracksuit.

"I'm not taking you to Jacques Cartier Bridge, mate."

"Good. That's not where I want to go."

He kicked the car into gear and moved slowly out onto the road, glancing into the rear-view mirror.

"Last suit got in here carrying his diplomas, he says take me to Jacques Cartier Bridge. We get in the middle, he says stop here, and so I do. Then he climbs over the rail and leaps eighty metres to his death. Know what? He even managed to fuck that up. And go ahead and smoke, I mean it's only a fucking taxi, right?"

"Uhh, thanks. How do you fuck up leaping off a bridge?"

"You land on an ice floe. And, Mister Suit brings his diplomas with him." He shook his head. "I'll bet he was never late for an interview."

"Well, he was obviously having a bad day."

"What, you want me to feel sorry for this dude who jumps off a bridge with his diplomas?"

"No. I want you to drive me to Le Biftek."

Le Biftek was a seedy bar I frequented on the Main. It was over—noiselessly, seamlessly, without fanfare. The turnstile barely clicked as I exited, the world of my future success now behind me forever.

A few days after leaving Ducasse & Jarndyce, I was still out and about and happened to find myself in a drinking hole in the east end of Montreal known as the Inspecteur Epingle, where I was sharing stories and drinks with a man named Massicotte. In a casual way, Massicotte let drop that he was part of a cell of terrorists.

"What kind of terrorists?" I asked.

"The kind that kills English Canadians," he answered without smiling.

"Well, make up your own mind, but you won't make much hay out of me, political or coinwise. Nobody cares enough. Plus, I'm not even English."

"Yeah, but you're a lawyer, right?"

"Yeah, I'm a lawyer. Just don't have an office. I'm like the Lone Ranger without Silver. What's that got to do with anything?"

"We can get you an office. I got lots of friends in the Hells, they can front you, no problem. We need a new lawyer."

"I have a couple of questions."

"Sure, my friend."

"I'm assuming this is criminal law."

"Sure. Mostly."

"On what charges?"

"Nothing complicated. B & Es. Fraud. The odd murder. Arson."

"What happened to your last lawyer?"

"What, you talking about René? He died."

"Okay, so what if I don't get you off?"

"No worries. You get to meet René. Any more questions?"

"Just one. Got your chequebook with you?"

I didn't sympathise with the political opinions of my new friends, but I enjoyed their company more than that of my own countrymen. It was also my first sustained time with a group that made no effort to dissimulate the hatred they felt for English Canadians. There was something pure about that, and their acceptance of me was natural despite my background, for I felt the same way they did about my compatriots, who had given me nothing I deemed of value.

Dostoyevsky had given me an insight into the criminal mind, and it seemed to me that my new friends—Massicotte, Bérubé, Sauvette—were a merger of Raskolnikov, Villon and Jacques Mesrine. They smoked joints like cigarettes, they flew hang-gliders, they travelled on dubious pretexts to Cuba, they were on speaking terms with Baader Meinhof and Action Directe, and they had the guts to come up with an entire project to start their own country.

My own compatriots—bland English Canadians obsessed with their diets or their marathons or their wakeboards or the imagined slights of the most self-serving and insipid gender on the planet—the English Canadian woman—held little interest for me, and my conduct and inclinations became more and more radical by night, as if by osmosis. And whatever their personal shortcomings, I never heard a complaint about the size of my retainers or an invoice. Massicotte and his cronies didn't kill me when things didn't go our way in the courts. I had my first taste of a decent living outside the system of corvée labour down at Ducasse & Jarndyce and spent my evenings with a colourful bunch of nasty bastards down at the Inspecteur Epingle, the Mecca for English-haters and losers. I fitted right in.

As I no longer felt any inclination to earn money the old way, I even lost the taste for the relatively easy money of defending Hell's Angels and small-time terrorists. That no doubt explains why during the late eighties, I began frequenting immigration conferences and made the acquaintance of a Hong Kong businessman named Lee Fook Lam. Lee Fook Lam, I was later to learn, conducted business under his fourth pseudonym, Harvey Lee. Harvey Lee persuaded me to move to Hong Kong to take advantage of an exploding market of Chinese itching to get their hands on a Canadian passport, and Harvey Lee had a chequebook with a bunch of blank entries just waiting to be filled in.

My departure for Hong Kong, and involvement with Lee Fook Lam, provoked another schism, and I was a lucky man to escape the Wan Chai district with my life. I was beginning to learn that, if a man changes countries on short notice, it's for a reason. In any event, my escape would prove to be only physical, as my post-China life was spasmodic and jagged, my professional and personal life a series of fits and starts. Without any driving philosophy or life plan, there was no longer any continuous thread to my existence. On the personal side, I had almost haphazardly fathered a series of children under circumstances which even I had to admit didn't resist scrutiny. My ability to construct a normal, day-to-day existence was further complicated by the need to go to ground when it appeared that someone had put out a contract on me. Even had I wished to maintain a semblance of conventional living, the option was no longer open, and my freedom had become curtailed by circumstances beyond my control.

Still, that experience as a trial lawyer had served its purpose. My time served at Ducasse & Jarndyce dispelled any residual doubts I had entertained on the noble profession. By the time I stumbled out the doors of that tower, I had more than enough evidence that codes of ethics and the like were pure cover, *ex post facto* window dressing for a massive mafia operation.

There was no point in sorting it out. Hong Kong beckoned. Nobody knew the intentions of the mainland Chinese, and a euphoric panic seemed to have seized the island territory. Every last man, woman and child wanted to get out. But the kinetic attraction of Hong Kong in those days was irresistible to anyone who had fallen under its spell, and we all kept returning like bees to a hive, trying to squeeze everything we could out of the dying colony. An invisible, rancid fog hung over the city. The stench of opportunity was everywhere.

VIII

I took the path of action. I have killed.
—Blaise Cendrars

China taught me something that had only been hinted at by Cendrars and that has stayed with me to this day—that I was nothing more than a fleck on the landscape of life. It was a lesson of fundamental importance, and I now realise that, when Lee Fook Lam said the West was selfish, he meant not only in its way of business, but as an enveloping narcissism that indeed would lead to our utter downfall. Lee Fook Lam, or Harvey Lee, depending on which side of the bed he rose from, was part of a class of Hong Kong entrepreneurs known as astronauts, as they had nominally emigrated to Canada only to leave their wives and children behind in their elected place of abode, cordoned off in monster houses, while they returned to the hive of activity in the South China Sea, where they could tap into exponential profits, limitless access to high-end whores, the Macau gaming tables and the Happy Valley horse racetrack, which placed more bets every race than the Los Angeles track did in an entire card.

During one of my sojourns, Lee Fook Lam invited me to breakfast at the Excelsior hotel. The Excelsior had the best breakfast in the world, where you could taste the most sumptuous offerings of Tokyo, California and the Dim Sum specialists while ruminating over your next scheme. That particular morning, a Uruguayan diplomat joined our table, made up of businessmen from Taipei, New Territories and Kowloon. The discussion turned to providing papers to immigrants free of charge in exchange for a lifetime services contract with the Kar Wai Company formed by Lee Fook Lam and myself recently in Canada.

While Lee Fook Lam was busy pitching the new deal, I looked out the window of the Excelsior at bustling Victoria harbour, right at the mouth of the Pearl River. Whatever the moral drawbacks of slavery, the mental number crunching was pointing to a high-yield product, very low overhead and a captive client base, literally. On the other hand, if Suzy Fat Kow or her sick aunt ever complained, I already knew of a couple of law society benchers and human rights commissioners who would be happy to string up an errant solicitor. My thoughts were interrupted by the inquisitive smile of Lee Fook Lam.

"Do you have anything to add?"

The man from Kowloon was Jimmy Ho. Jimmy Ho had swum across the South China Sea aged 11, only to be sold into slavery. But by 1989, he owned six metalworks factories and employed seven hundred workers in Tuen Mun in the New Territories. Jimmy Ho wanted to branch out. Canada was a new and exciting opportunity. A start-up sort of people business, as he put it, earnest, serious as hell, chain-smoking as he laid it out from his side. Did I think, as an expert in such matters, that Lee Fook Lam's plan was feasible?

"Well, Jimmy, at first ogle, I'd call it more than feasible. Might even take wing with the right nurturing and guidance. But I'm fresh off the tarmac, and I don't do deals in the first 48 hours."

I pleaded jet lag, excused myself and set out to return to my office on foot. That took me through a basketball court where a pick-up game was being played by a dozen or so young men. I had stopped for a cigarette when I noticed a man I was sure I had seen before. When I picked up the pace, he seemed to also. I moved around the corner onto On Lok Lane and then ran through a restaurant to another road leading back to the office. When I arrived at the office, there was the usual line-up of "business" refugees with their doctored diplomas and five sets of accounting books preparing for their big schmooze as Canada's immigrants—ready to talk about their tofu factories or whatever the civil service had dreamt up in their inane plan to create wealth when in fact Canada already had the wealth but just lacked the balls to exploit it properly.

With half a dozen interviews concluded, I left the office earlier than usual, returned to my flat on Jaffe Road, brought up some Carlsberg and some smokes and gazed out over the water. Everything moving, the Star Ferry, Jumbo restaurant, the Tate's Cairn and Kowloon peak visible, and just on the other side, Guangdong province and a ruthless regime that still saw Hong Kong as a spit in the ocean. I was staring into a future ripe with Cendrarsian possibilities. All I had to do was rubbish what remained of my reputation and sacrifice a few neo-Canadians on the altar of my ambition. A no-brains, ground-floor opportunity at a time and in a place where even the teenagers glittered with gold. On the risk side, outside of the law societies, there were other intangibles to deal with. Some bad feng shui, a look in the wrong set of eyes on the street, the number four turning up in transactions, and you might get a knife in the guts or find some heroin planted in your suitcase at Canadian customs. But the day I had brunch with Jimmy Ho, end of the empire Hong Kong looked good—better than good.

After a few hours, I wandered down to a massage parlour and spent an hour or two there, then left for the Old China Hand for a couple, spotted a strip bar with Philippine girls and a chintzy version of a Las Vegas stage and wandered inside. There were no more than half a dozen customers. Two men walked in. One of them was a lanky, sinewy type, about six-foot-one, with a low-rooted nose which gave his light green eyes an amphibian aspect. His buddy, a thick-chested, slack-jawed type, sat down beside me and greeted me in a Down Under accent.

"Keep your distance," the newcomer said, nodding in the direction of his friend. "My buddy's ex-Serb army regular. And he wants to take somebody out tonight."

His accomplice had remained on the other side of the bar, having detected a man standing beside a table engaged in casual conversation with half a dozen girls who looked to be off-shift dancers. The Serb flashed a set of jagged canines, then crossed the floor towards the man. At the table, he executed a kung-fu scissors kick, barely grazing the man's chin. Like leaving a calling card. I had had one eye on a Filipino girl showing some serious leg up to a minute and a half earlier, but centre stage had shifted and was mobile. I set to work on my beer and ordered two more while I mulled over my next move.

"I'm bad, man, I'm fucking bad!" the Serb said to all assembled, performing another kung-fu kick for anyone who hadn't yet noticed him. Anybody looking for trouble in Wanchai was suicidal. Maybe he'd lost his brother. Maybe he'd flunked his driving test. He was now moving my way to rejoin his friend. The old madam running the joint was shaking her head and waving two or three girls off-stage and into the dressing room. The buoyancy of the show had vanished, and we were moving into slow time.

"Hey, what the fuck are you doing in here, beard man?" he announced as he arrived at the bar.

"Beard man is having a beer," I responded.

"You got too much hair. What are you, some kind of hippie?"

I stood up and reached for my jacket, and smiled at him while I pushed my beer glass under it. I'd have one chance and then it'd be over for me. "Guess I'll be movin' on."

"Stop right where you are there, hippie boy."

"Beg your pardon?"

I was a step away now, lifted my jacket up, and pushed the beer glass hard upwards into his chin, which worked about as well as I could hope, splitting his chin open into an ugly gash and knocking him off balance. I ran forward into him and tore the glass sideways, ripping open his cheek.

The Serb lifted his hands upwards like claws, and I knew I was dead. Behind him, the man he had been tormenting lifted a chair and smashed it onto his head. The off-duty cop went down and, as he shook his head, a dozen of Hong Kong's finest streamed in, looked down at him, dragged him out the door, and he was gone. One remained behind, talking with the old madam, who quietly described what had just ensued. The man who had saved my life came over and invited me to his table for a drink.

"Hi, I'm Jason Fitzpatrick, own the Texan Grill up the road."

He couldn't have been more than in his mid-20s. Broad-shouldered, jowled and baby-faced, thick hair, a young Orson Welles. We wandered down to Mes Amis, a discothèque, and stepped inside. The music was deafening and the dance floor reverberated with knock-out Eurasian women sliding in and around what looked like the day shift of the trader's floor on the Hong Kong stock exchange. The glitter of rolexes, diamonds and strobe lights. Chock full of a dying breed—the white, Hong Kong born taipans, whose resemblance with Europeans ended at the physical.

I noticed a couple of golden boys in Armani beside a bevy of women who could make a priest go agnostic, but they only had eyes for their own images in mirrors provided for the purpose. Both blond, typecast for *American Psycho*, coked to the eyeballs, glued to the narcissistic perfection of their own delusion, utterly oblivious to the women—Indians, Eurasians, Chinese—who were all there for the taking. Jason Fitzpatrick shouted out something I couldn't hear, then waved towards the exit. We returned to the Texan Grill, took a table and ordered up filet mignon and a couple of Carlsbergs.

"Even a little crazy for Wanchai tonight."

"No shit."

"This quarter used to be the R & R stop-off for Vietnam veterans during that war."

"Uh-huh."

Jason Fitzpatrick snapped his fingers, and a waiter arrived with more Carlsberg.

"You reacted well earlier on."

"I didn't have much choice."

"Piece of advice?" he said, all business now.

"Sure."

I reached for a Marlboro Light, my head buzzing. Before I could find my matches, I was looking at a small black dress and red lipstick through the flame of a lighter being offered by one of Jason Fitzpatrick's staff. A quick smile, and then she evaporated.

"If I were you, I'd shave off that beard tonight. You stand out like a sore thumb around here. Then, I'd catch the first flight out of here tomorrow. That Serb won't come for me. He knows who I am. But he won't rest until you're in the Victoria Public Mortuary."

I considered that for a moment.

"I think you're right."

A couple of days later, I left for Tokyo and stayed in one of the Prince Hotels in Minato-Ku, my usual stop-off and jump-off point for Shibuya district or Machida down at the end of Shinjuku's Odakyu line, where I had some faithful names and places where I could drink all I wanted for a couple of thousand yen and finish the night in good company. But this time I stuck to the hotel. I was developing China burnout. So I played it safe and spent the early evenings in the Fukusa tempura restaurant, then wandered to the Windsor main bar and drank Glenfiddich straight up until the manager pointed me towards my room.

***

It was the dead of a cold winter upon my return. I decided to give Massicotte a call. Massicotte picked me up and we drove up into the Portneuf region to his cabin on a lake in the middle of a forest. It was forty below, and during the first night we drank and watched the fire, loading it with logs, and tossed back beers. Nothing had to be said, and that suited me. The next day, we were out cross-country skiing. There had been fresh snow, and the temperature had dropped down to minus forty again. Massicotte lost me quickly, and I continued at my own pace, looping onto a trail that had been made by a snowmobile earlier that morning.

I stopped and stared at the ice forms hanging from the leafless maples. Thoughts of Wanchai were racing across my brain as I gazed at these frozen, hexagonal prisms. Spoked wheels, columns, and then my eye caught a dendrike snowflake, like the sceptre of a Russian Orthodox starets. The clarity and piercing beauty of it were pushing my senses up against a private wall of my most acute terrors, a charcoal backdrop to my memory of the stink of Wanchai, and a voice spoke to me in hyper-real terms in the tones of a man giving a class seminar. He was saying something like: "Snowflakes and snow crystals are made of ice, and pretty much nothing more."

I felt myself panicking as this voice out of nowhere continued: "A snow crystal, as the name implies, is a single crystal of ice."

It was cold, dead cold, and I had to get back to the cabin, but the voice kept speaking to me in its didactic neutrality: "A snowflake is a generic term; it can mean an individual snow crystal or a few snow crystals stuck together or large agglomerations of snow crystals that form puff-balls that float down from the clouds."

I continued skate-skiing, whoosh-whoosh, in rhythmic strides, and in a quarter of an hour I'd arrived at the cabin, but my mind was not in order at all. I kicked the clip out of my shoes, stepped up the stairs into the cabin, shut the door, set up the woodstove, and reached for beer. By the time Massicotte returned I had finished three Pilsner Urquells while staring into a wood fire, wondering whether I shouldn't stick a hand into the flames or something, anything to stop thinking.

"Where'd you go? I thought you'd dropped into a snow bank."

"Yeah, I'm not sure myself."

"I'm sure. You look like somebody just been in the yard for the first time."

"You know this pristine wilderness, Massicotte? It doesn't seem so pristine anymore."

"Exactly. What the fuck does pristine mean?"

Massicotte looked at me funny when I didn't laugh.

"The centre isn't holding. And, guess what. We're not the centre. We're the outback of the middle empire."

Massicotte reached inside the fridge and poured me out another beer.

"You had a good, simple gig before. I don't understand. Why don't you just come back and work for the Hells again?"

IX

> *I am the first man to bear my name since*
> *I invented it, assembled its constituent parts*
> —Blaise Cendrars

At some point during the early nineties, without being able to pinpoint all the causes, I stopped thinking of myself as being fully alive or thinking that anything mattered. I turned to trekking along mediaeval pilgrimage routes to sort this out, beginning with a three-day walk from Paris to Chartres. I felt that unless I took a pause to reflect on why, whatever the cost, I was doomed to repeat the same patterns and come to a bad end in ways not even I had anticipated. Paris was my traditional escape route; my hideout was the Hotel des Alliés, a well-kept hotel in the fifth run by an Auvergnat couple for 40-odd years. The Hôtel des Alliés contained everything I needed in the world—a bed, a shower and a desk. During the night, I tended to drift towards Mouffetard and begin my drinking there. On the night preceding my departure for Chartres, I made the acquaintance of a South African journalist named Chad in the American Bar on Mouffetard. Over Guinness and single malt whisky, Chad began expounding on apartheid and wanted to know my opinion.

"My opinion. I dunno. It sounds Dutch."

Chad the South African mentioned in passing that he had also lived in Vancouver but had left the place, because there were "too many slant-eyed bastards moving in and taking over. They're fucking up the Zen of a cool city, ya?"

"Yeah?" I said. "How do they do that?"

"Walking into people's private homes, offering cash down, building monster homes, and nobody does anything about it."

"Well,"—I paused for gravitas—"contrary to your neck of the woods, it's a little bit difficult to set up apartheid when you're a hundred-plus nationalities."

At that point, Chad called me a lefty cunt. I stood up and punched him hard in the jaw and the fight was on. Some time later, I found myself lying on the street, forehead grazed, knuckles swollen and scraped. I stood up, weaved my way down Mouffetard, which by that time of night seemed no different to me than an endless corridor of the hotel, turned up rue de l'Arbalète, pushed upwards past the police station and crossed Claude Bernard, which landed me onto Berthollet and the Hôtel des Alliés.

After a few hours, I woke up and packed a walking rucksack. My walk took me up boulevard Montparnasse, past Le Select and the rest of the twenties cafés—Le Dome, La Rotonde—and kept moving on right through the Porte de Versailles, and upwards towards the Meudon forest, Céline country, with a pounding head but not much else on my mind. Around the outskirts of Issy-les-Moulineaux a pair of young black thugs detached themselves from a gang of 40 or so and started moving towards me. I carried a Bowie knife and let the blade flash under the streetlamp I was passing under. The two kids hovered on the bank of the square. A police car came by, slowed to a crawl, flashing its headlights and then moved on. The distraction gave me the opportunity to move out of sight of these youths.

It wasn't so clear at the time that our society was at some kind of breaking point, and that things would worsen, as the savagery of a new Middle Ages was almost upon us. I continued into the Meudon forest. By dawn I was coming out of the forest and away from the bands huddled around fires with their dogs, shouting and dancing like wolves. I walked down the rue Royale right past the Palais de Versailles and continued straight up into the Vallée de la Chévreuse.

By late morning of that first day, I found myself walking through the Vallée de la Chévreuse. I was thirsty, and the hard edge of my hangover was biting into me, but at the same time, with nothing on the programme but more walking, things started returning to me, older thoughts, thoughts that had lodged themselves somewhere in the psyche, waiting for a time such as this. There are roads leading to Chartres, but there are also rights of way leading through farmland and forest, the tracking grounds of Racine and Pascal, so provided you have a compass and follow a direct south-southwest line, you'll get onto the Beauce plain sooner or later.

I was a few kilometres outside of Trappes at the edge of the valley, and my mind turned back to the way I had fallen across *Crime and Punishment* at the age of 12. It had appealed to me straight away. I liked its fatalism, and the examination of life through the moral prism of the poor student Raskalnikov planning his murder afforded me no little solace, for reasons I didn't care to delve into. That being said, it left no indelible print on my mind, just enough to push me to select *The Brothers Karamazov*.

On the day I picked up *Karamazov*, while returning from the library, I had the bad luck to come across a group of young thugs from the public school looking for trouble. One of them approached ahead of the others. He was a year or two older, smoking a cigarette; his five or six cronies were half a step behind.

"This park is off-limits, Catholic boy."

"It's not your park."

"Not my park, says the dogan."

My short remark earned me a hard punch in the chin, which knocked me to the ground. As I tried to get up a foot came down on my ribcage.

"Did you call me a faggot, Catholic boyo?"

"I didn't call you ..."

When the next kick arrived and the other boys joined in, it didn't seem a good idea to fight back. So I covered up as best as possible, and after what seemed like a long time, I got up again and walked home alone. My eyes felt hooded and, though I felt pain, there was something else in my now clouded view of the park. I wiped my face with my shirt sleeve. It was covered in blood. When I arrived home there was shock, stupefaction and tears. *How could this have happened to you?* But I had no explanation for it. My tormentors were anonymous; they had evaporated, and I was alone again, with a park still to cross the next day and nobody to help me get through it. That evening, I had begun reading *Karamazov*. After a few days alone, poring through the pages of Dostoyevsky's work in complete isolation, I fell across the following passage:

> *I'm a Karazamov ... when I fall into the abyss, I go straight into it, head down and heels up, and I'm even pleased that I'm falling in such a humiliating position, and for me I find it beautiful. And so in that very shame I begin a hymn. Let me be cursed, let me be base and vile, but let me also kiss the hem of that garment in which my God is clothed; let me follow the devil at the same time, but still I am also your son, Lord, and I love you, and I feel a joy without which the world cannot stand and be.*

That long phrase of Ivan Karazamov struck me as a message from somewhere, as if someone were showing me the two sides of good and evil. Good was a permeating presence; you could feel it in certain people, and it was not confined to their physical or mental borders. When a person was good—at least this was my thought as a 12-year-old, they acted as agents or vessels of good. But the good transcended them and was greater than them. They participated in it. It seemed to me translucently clear from my vantage point, and it was manifested in the stories of certain saints whose lives I had also begun to read—St. Francis of Assisi, Joseph of Cupertino, Teresa of Avila—who had a childlike belief in the essence of goodness.

A day went by, and my eyes, both black, began closing, but not enough to prevent me from reading *Karamazov,* which I read day and night until completion, leaving me drained and room-bound for another three days. Two decades had passed, and now, I had the rare luxury of another trinity of days to consider my fate once again. I had brought this old tattered page with a Charles Péguy poem, titled *Présentation de Paris à Notre Dame,* to keep me company, a wine-sack, some cigarettes, and a compass. After two days I was beyond Rambouillet and into another forest, mulling over a passage from the Péguy poem that had caught my eye:

> *And we will arrive in the Sea of Sargasse*
> *Dragging along our useless and grotesque carcass*
> *And the English will say: they put nothing inside*

That struck a chord somewhere. I'd turned my back on the law, on some friends, on my first wife, and I was just getting warmed up. That's the way you feel when you're alone with your thoughts on the Beauce plain—like a grotesque, useless carcass. The liberating part of that first pilgrimage was that I felt no compelling need to resolve anything. Paris was close by and would be beckoning after the ritual purification in Chartres. That was enough for the time being.

X

The important thing is to sharpen one's gaze.
—Blaise Cendrars

There's not a lot you can do in a church, outside of pray, gaze at the icons or go to confession, and when you're on a pilgrimage and you don't collapse in a heap along the way or get otherwise distracted, sooner or later you'll find yourself exhausted and inside the object of your journey. And so it was that, after stepping over the celebrated labyrinth of that pre-Renaissance Gothic vault under the dark-eyed gaze of the Madonna of the Underworld, I drifted towards the confessional, thinking about my first son, whom, to all intents and purposes, I had never met.

So, after three days walking through the Meudon forest, Céline's old turf, by the Palais de Versailles, through the Vallée de la Chévreuse, alongside the paths trod over countless times by Pascal and Racine, and across the Beauce plain, my mind alternated between philosophical regret for abandoning my son and the more practical reflection that, if I had left him to his own devices, it must have been for a compelling reason.

I didn't see where he gained if I showed up and his mother and I started acting out the Kama Sutra while throwing cutting instruments at each other. Nor was I in the least inclined to get involved in an even worse form of self-abasement and slave away for his food in exchange for weekly visits. My entire youth had been a corvée of listening to the judge drone on with his *stare decisis* and his *non volenti fit injuria* and his promissory estoppel, and damned if I was going to re-enter a new life of slavery so soon after having escaped the old one.

Nevertheless, Chartres is beautiful and mystical and preliterate, and its intense and direct explanation of creation impressed me deeply. Standing at the foot of the steps outside, I faced the central entrance to the building, containing the entire, condensed history of the world in the Christian vision through a series of symmetrical, intricately carved figures in its indented, arched entry, as if the entire edifice was abjectly retreating or coaxing you surreptitiously to enter its vaults and crypts.

God created man in his image, promised him salvation, and the beatitude of Mary, Mother of the Church, symbolises the realisation of the promise. The creation portrayed before the Crowning of Our Lady recalls that Mary, Mother of God, is the *sedes sapientatiae*, the throne of Wisdom. But it is the ancient images of the Virgin—*Notre-Dame de la Belle-Verrière, Notre Dame du Pilier, Notre Dame de Sous-Terre*, the Black Madonna—showing the Virgin in her simplistic, oriental iconography, which struck me deeply and embedded within me that certainty that my life was worthless and microscopic, and the realisation offered me far more solace than the earlier torment that I somehow had to make my mark and "change the world for the better."

Two men can make the same observations about their creation by God and state of original sin without coming to the same conclusions at all as to how to best apply those lessons to the remainder of their lives. I walked into Chartres Cathedral in a state of deep humility but not feeling any of the defeat which had been plaguing me. The labyrinth appears immediately to the visitor upon entry—a magnificent floor mosaic inspired by the Greek myth of Theseus and the minotaur, which Christianity in its genius had converted to its own ends. Man, to follow the Chartres labyrinth, was cast out of paradise and wanders in a state of confusion, threatened by the minotaur of evil and ignorance within the labyrinth which is life on earth. I had with me an account by the 19th-century archaeologist Rodolfo Lanciani titled *Pagan and Christian Rome*:

> Theseus killing the Minotaur in the labyrinth of Crete, and labyrinths in general were favourite subjects for church pavements, especially among the Gaols. The custom is very ancient, a labyrinth having been represented in the church of S. Vitale at Ravenna as early as the sixth century. Those of the cathedral at Lucca, of S. Michele Maggiore at Pavia, of S. Savino at Piacenza, of S. Maria in Trastevere at Rome (destroyed in the restoration of 1867), are of a later date. The image of Theseus is accompanied by a legend in the 'leonine' rhythm: *Theseus intravit, monstrumque biforme necavit* [Theseus entered, and killed the bi-form monster].

The labyrinth, in the Christian remake, cannot be escaped except with the help of "Ariadne's thread," spiritual grace, or the help of the woman, Mary, who leads us from the pits of Hell by pointing us towards her divine son. It is hard to convey the deep impression when you see the labyrinth fresh on the heels of a three-day pilgrimage with nothing but your thoughts to guide you. I admit that when I walked into the Church I had every intention to continue straight up to the confessional and cover the entire gamut of *delectatio morosa, gaudium and desiderium* and might even have gone through with it had I not been seized by a sudden thirst for a cold

Kronenbourg beer, brought on no doubt by the sight of a café right across the street from the church and a hole in my belly which turned out to be even deeper than the pit of my sins.

Ten minutes later, sitting alone contentedly over a glass of cold Meteor beer, one of the last of the authentic Paris-brewed *bières blondes*, I reached into my pocket and pulled out once again the passage that had attracted me from the Charles Péguy poem. Péguy had composed it while walking across the same Beauce plain I had just covered, in order to thank God for saving his son from a mortal illness:

> *And we will arrive in the Sea of Sargasse*
> *Dragging along our useless and grotesque carcass*
> *And the English will say: they put nothing inside*

Pilgrimages are like that. The tempo of walking alone with nothing but your thoughts to disturb you along roads travelled on foot for a millennium leaves other landscapes, physical and mental, behind and brings to the forefront of the mind things hitherto passed over or ignored. I had come on this pilgrimage without any preconceived notions, and I had finished it with an unexplained message from a poem randomly discovered. Nevertheless, in accordance with the laws of attraction that had always governed my restless soul, I immediately knew I would follow this direction, regardless of its significance, its source or the consequences of doing so. If it was madness, it was a madness I could call my own, and that was a matter for me and nobody else. There was less and less holding me tethered to what was commonly referred to as the conventional world anyways. As to the final destination, that was now clear; that I felt that with a calm certainty. I knew that I would someday be dragging my useless and increasingly grotesque carcass in the direction of the Sargasso Sea.

XI

It wasn't an easy task, picking and choosing the elements of my father's philosophy which I wished to apply to my own grid of life. Emulation would highlight me for certain defeat and worse, as my own pro-forma and half-hearted attempts at replicating his ideals of golf, God, country, community and family, in that order, were universally sneered at by a slew of acolytes in just about every walk of life. Even the criminals he tried felt he at least listened to their side of the story before sentencing them just as harshly as anybody else. However, two hallmark qualities seemed sufficiently arbitrary and open to definition that I took to them readily: the first was his defence of the underdog and the second his performance of deeds invisibly, without any need for recognition from the community at large.

I was all for discretion. Nooks and crannies were my natural habitat. As for the love of the little man, I felt fairly certain that I could embrace this philosophy unreservedly and even take it a step further. The little man, I recall thinking, would give me a fairer hearing than the big man had done to date. That eventually led me, with a lot of in-between, to write *The Imbecilic Quantum*, my antihero take on a world ruled by a thirst for money, a theme that the reading committee of Editions de la Lune gave the green light to. If all houses in the world were built on the Parisian model, there would be a lot less urban strife, and if all publishing houses had the layout of Editions de la Lune, books would be better, authors would be happier, and the evil, bland, kinetic internet would assume its rightful place on the back shelves of offices, and people could start enjoying life again. That pretty well sums up my rosy view of the literary world right up to the day I walked through the doors of Editions de la Lune.

The layout of Editions de la Lune, one of Paris' and the world's last surviving literary houses, was all dust and cracked walls and disused furniture. Not a bustling assistant or fashion statement in sight. Just prior to my first meeting with the powers at Editions de la Lune, I had been sitting on a rickety chesterfield, which forced you to look upwards at a poster advertising volume 12 of Cendrars' collected works, *Anthologie Nègre*. When you're that close to the Golden Fleece, it's a bit of a dream; you're not thinking about numbers or sales, any of those things, just being indoctrinated into the cult and getting the holy tar, or whatever they used, brushed over your body and making whatever human sacrifices are deemed necessary to show that you're one of the new elect.

So, in this half-baked state of mind, while gazing up at old Blaise in an exquisitely slow delirium, it occurred to me that if she were still around, I wouldn't mind crossing paths with Celestine Cendrars. Once again, it was purely the laws of attraction entering into play—thinking of him and thinking of her and being connected to them. If anything, it was a sexual reverberation, and what is sex if not a return to the familiar, a connection with a place where you want to be without knowing why you want to be there?

I was guided upstairs to the director general's quarters by a friendly secretary and found myself in front of Xavier Hirsch, legend of Paris letters and maker or breaker of the lowly scribes. Francesco was already seated at a round table and motioned me to join a dead-eyed, stooped rail of a man I'd noticed wandering down the corridor upon arrival. His name was De Coligny. Hirsch paid me a compliment about having an eye for Paris as an outsider that was acute and original, and I thanked him for that.

"We're thinking of marketing you as the next Henry Miller with a splash of J.P. Donleavy. How's that sound?"

"Sounds good. Real good."

"Any objection to us putting a girl on the front in a suggestive pose?"

"None at all, so long as it sells books."

De Coligny looked at me from what seemed a long way away.

"How do you feel about editors?"

"That depends on the editor. Who do you have in mind?"

Hirsch interrupted at this point.

"We want your input on a title, say by tomorrow. The release date is September 11."

"September doesn't work for me."

"What do you mean it doesn't work for you?"

"Got some tickets booked for the Indian ocean for a half year. I'm uhh, pretty sure they're non-refundable."

De Coligny's anaesthetised eyes glanced over at Hirsch briefly. He stood up and closed his notebook.

"Nice meeting you, Mister Fingon."

Francesco shook his head either at me or De Coligny, somehow mixing negative with noncommittal. Xavier Hirsch managed a smile, shook my hand, and Francesco and I walked downstairs and onto rue des Cannettes in a northerly direction towards Aux Deux Magots. All credit to Francesco, he knew I'd blown my future before it even began, and yet he allowed me the token recognition of a lunch in the holy of holies. I'm sure there's nothing wrong with some recognition in the world of books but, in the meantime, it wasn't bad sitting over some *gigot froid mayonnaise* with a half bottle of Givry Champ Nalot, la Saulerie in front of me. Watching the manager throw out an American woman who complained about Francesco blowing his Cuban Cohiba Splendido smoke in her face was all right, too.

Francesco was pretty high on me that first day, god bless the old bugger, what a class act. He welcomed me as a future star, personally escorted me to the inner circle—Café Les Deux Magots, where his personal table awaited him as Chairman of the Deux Magots literary prize, created in 1933 as a literary *salon des refusés* to counter the orthodoxies of the right-bank Prix Goncourt. And since its inception in 1933, the year when Raymond Queneau the word-wizard took honours, Francesco was only the second chair of the committee.

He showed me pretty quickly that the genteel veneer was just that—a thin cover of surface material to keep intruders from wearing down the inner essence. We stepped out on to the rue de Rennes, and as we arrived on boulevard St.-Germain, a woman stopped him and engaged him in a five-minute conversation. He handled it with flair and begged off so he could take care of "his author." The moment she walked away, he turned to me and said: "I have no idea who that person was."

I could have said the same thing about Francesco. Between his anecdotes on the left-bank scene and his dog named Rabelais and that chin-up bar in his office as if he were Rocky Marciano and his desiccated powder-blue lips, and yet—he was something so refined, so exquisitely simple in his sense of old world decorum, and that something was an accessory to a man who I learned had plenty of hardness close at hand, ready for use at a moment's notice. That son of a bitch really had mastered something. A shield of manners and a sword of ridicule and exclusion. A forgotten art.

It wasn't really a problem from my end. Something strong was pulling me towards the Seychelles. Beneath the superficial blurb on paradise, it sounded like a real hornet's nest of crooks, arms runners and terrorists. I hadn't been anywhere meeting that description since Hong Kong, so it just wasn't to be missed. When I returned in the fall, *The Imbecilic Quantum* was on the shelves, but so were 660 other books out for the fall season. The closest I'd get to the big time for a while would be *gigot froid, salade verte mayonnaise*.

Beneath the intoxicating sensations which dulled my senses that day, the old doubts were biding their time, knowing that things would go awry with Editions de la Lune, but I also felt that Cendrars, or anybody who knew him, held some answers for me. Attraction and intuition were coming home to roost. Whatever they were, whoever they were, we'd all be having a big reunion to discuss the man who had lured us into a cult devoted to futile endeavours and the worship of unfathomable labyrinths and tangential quests. It was a form of dementia, Dementia Cendrarsia, and the knowledge that we suffered from the same condition would do little to unite us in holy matrimony. Or maybe, then again, we'd all share a laugh and a drink over a one-armed poet and become hard and fast friends. There's no way of predicting these things in advance.

PART II
Leptocephalus

1

Art is a profound reality which is difficult to satisfy.
It is a phenomenon as complex as life itself. And to live,
one has to struggle, to love and to suffer.
—Blaise Cendrars

2003 was the summer of *la canicule*, when a drought-like heat wave was responsible for ten thousand deaths in Paris alone, and both Francesco and Celestine had lost their best friends. During the first half of August, the temperatures failed to fall at night, and poor ventilation systems in the buildings triggered peak rates of nitrogen dioxide. The first estimate of the *Institut de veille sanitaire* delivered to the Health Ministry disclosed 11,435 deaths August 1-15. The official causes were medical—heat exhaustion, heart failure—but the underlying reason was the French habit of abandoning their aging parents, forcing them to live out their lives alone in Paris flats and, for those without the benefit of lifts, trapped inside their cramped quarters. By August 24 in the Paris region, there remained three hundred bodies unclaimed by families, awaiting inhumation in fridge trucks parked for the purpose in Ivry-sur-Seine. Francesco and Celestine had escaped the debacle, as they spent summers at their retreats, respectively at Palais sur

Mer in Charente Maritime and at Kerliou in Bretagne Sud, only spending the odd weekend at her Boulogne Billancourt flat.

While driving along the Quai Voltaire, Francesco recounted the story of the end of Cendrars:

> He spent his final days in a windowless ground-floor apartment wedged between a small courtyard on the rue José Maria-de-Hérédia, which ironically was located under the shadow of the UNESCO building. Cendrars was emaciated, impoverished and had suffered a stroke which left him paralysed. His daughter, Celestine, and Raissa, a Parisian theatre actress in Louis Jouvet's troupe and the love of his life, attended to his needs with a Doctor Chabrol, cousin of Raissa. A tiny coterie still visited, comprised of Nino Franck and Bernard Privat, the director of Grasset Editions. But the outside world of modernity which Cendrars had so extolled had left him to his fate. Francesco was smiling, but his voice conveyed depth of feeling as he described the last minutes of the poet's life on earth.
>
> It is a vivid scene; *imagine, donc*, such pathos. Cendrars dying in the arms of the daughter he had abandoned for so long, while Raissa knelt on the floor and prayed.

Francesco parked. We entered a building, and he sounded the name Celestine Gazon-Cendrars over the intercom as he continued to fill me in.

"Celestine is the daughter of Marzena, a Polish Jewess. Gazon was her husband. A military man, devoted to her, and then he was killed in an absolutely senseless, random incident."

"What happened?"

"Shot dead outside his house. An untold and unresolved story. This family just attracts tragedy."

The lift doors opened. Several paces from the end of a short corridor, Celestine Cendrars stood. She smiled.

"*Eh bien*! You have come. Welcome."

Celestine Cendrars ushered us into her living room, where she invited us to sit down on a couch before a long teak coffee table. A set of layouts of cover concepts for the Cendrars collected works series were displayed before us on the table. Celestine Cendrars introduced herself and sat down.

"Have you come to do Xavier's dirty work? If so, the answer is no to his last three proposals."

She smiled warmly at Francesco.

"Imagine, you and I the last men standing, Francesco."

"Oh, there are a few others. But it seems, present company excepted, that only the bores have survived."

"I've never been accused of that at least," she laughed.

"Mr. Fingon, Francesco has been telling me about you," she said, turning her attention towards me.

I nodded.

"You seem like an exceptional man, very much in the mould of Mr. Miller. And my father."

"I've been accused of that. I take it as a compliment."

"It is intended as a compliment."

She was sizing me up, but in the friendliest way, like a crony.

"Francesco told me not just about you, but also about your project. This project you have come up with seems to have come out of nowhere."

"That's how I feel about it as well."

"I think the idea *magnifique*! There is genius in it. Transporting the ashes of my father to the Sargasso Sea to fulfill the terms of the quatrain. Only one small detail to work out, and we can get on with it!"

"Great! What's the detail?"

"Where do I start?" she asked Francesco.

"As I told Jack, at the end."

"When Cendrars died, no one had planned for it. So, then a friend ... Lamberjack was his name, I believe. Yes, Lamberjack informed us he had an unused chamber in his own vault in Batignolles, in the seventh Division. So Cendrars remained there for 33 years. Do you realise that Cendrars had 33 books in the making at all times?"

She seemed to pause after referring to her father as "Cendrars," gauging the effect of that, prior to continuing her tale.

"Then, during early 1994, we were informed by the mayor of Tremblay-sur-Mauldre that they wanted to give him a burial ground *en perpet*. So we went to Batignolles, and for some reason the cemetery was not open to the public that day. The *gardien* refused us entry, do you recall, Francesco?"

"Yes! Yes! You must tell Jack about the police officer."

"The police officer, of course! While trying to explain the situation, a police officer arrived and demanded to know what the problem was. We showed him our *permis d'exhumation* delivered from the conservateur, and the officer exclaimed: 'What! Is it true that you are the daughter of Cendrars?'"

Francesco nodded. This is what he wanted to hear.

"When I nodded, this police officer removed his cap and genuflected in front of me. 'Your father is a hero,' he exclaimed. 'At the *préfecture*, we keep a framed photo of him on the wall. The police officer turned angrily towards the municipal employee, who was scratching his head trying to figure out who this Cendrars was. 'You're blocking the daughter of Cendrars! Open the gate and let her proceed!' Shortly after, two employees arrived, picks and shovels in hand, and we made our way to the vault. They descended into the vault, beneath the ground, and we could hear them clear as day. 'I've got his foot! *Tiens, j'ai trouvé le fémur! Et le tibia! J'ai l'autre! Eh bien, j'ai la crâne! His skull. La crâne de Cendrars, imaginez-vous!!*' They had dismantled Cendrars from bottom to top. So, Mr. Fingon, that is the story of how we were given the remains of Cendrars, and so we undertook our journey across the city for cremation at Père Lachaise."

For a moment, she remained silent.

"But, as we were to learn, someone had been tracking us the whole time. We were cut off by three cars as we drove onto avenue

Batignolles. Someone forced their way into the car, and removed the urn."

She looked at me.

"We had no choice but to go through with the pretence of the ceremony. My father's remains were never buried. There is an empty urn in his tomb at Tremblay-sur-Mauldre. And, then, a year later, we learned the reasons behind this unusual act of larceny. The stories started coming out about unknown Cendrars' works. And, the claim of this Bibi Cendrars that she was Cendrars' daughter, born on the Normandie passenger ship during his trans-Atlantic travels to America and the worst of it, all kinds of details on me. So, here I am, the daughter of Cendrars, and I have no way of proving it against this scheming madwoman. And, now my own life coming to an end."

Celestine Cendrars removed her sunglasses, stood up and crossed the room towards me. Tears welled up in her eyes as she stared into mine.

"Mr Fingon. I haven't much time left and this is a poison with me—because it dishonours my father. I believe …"

She stopped, choking up, and then regained her composure.

"I believe you have been sent to help me. Please. Consider my plea."

Once again she stopped.

"This is not theft. It is desecration of the family name."

She grasped my hands in a surprisingly strong grip and held my gaze. What felt like an electric shock coursed through me, and I had no doubt that I had received a message from Cendrars himself.

"This problem will go away," I heard myself say.

"Make it go away," she said, "kill her and her cronies if you have to, but make it go away."

She paused.

"And then the rest will follow."

"As day follows the night."

11

In my dreams, I am a sightless raven at the top of a Celtic totem pole. The pole is perched in the midst of a cemetery in the highlands of my home country—British Columbia—and I sense through the clawed out orbits that once held the lens of sight, that I oversee the very field of death towards which we all gravitate. Outside of time, a mist hovering over this field, death everywhere, and the sense that what is happening has always happened, and that my life was a brief and unhappy interlude before this return to the fields of grey dreams.

De Nerval and Cendrars were obsessed with "Je suis l'autre." In my dreams, I am the other. Some days my other is the raven, my death mask, and in my waking hours, it is you, through the oddest and most random of destinies. My seed swam up an estuary in abeyance to the erratic and electro-magnetic rules of attraction that have governed my life, and parked inside a uterus, being carried by a soul circling like another bird—a falcon prior to the kill.

I cannot cure your condition of chagrin and resentment and I cannot improve your material position. I learned almost immediately upon hearing of you that there is no wisdom I can impart that will be of use to you. Who am I to pretend to such moral heights when I left you to fend for yourself under the control of a criminal? And, come to think of it, who are you anyways—a waif, an oedipal agent sent to wreak revenge and ruin once again what I have built up? To do your mother's bidding?

And, yet, I have to consider the opposite, that you may be good in an imperfect way, because half your blood is mine, and that somewhere within the labyrinthine workings of the Creator, you will be able to see what I see. So, let's go back to the day of this strange tale, where I sat in limbo, considering what a writer must consider, which is everything at once and at all times. While my mind weighed up the possibilities of profit with this hoaxster claiming to be Cendrars' daughter, and the reasons why people would be repelled by a man, and then suddenly worship him upon his death, I had been continuing a lifetime project of investigating the creative methods of painters, and the possibility that Cendrars' technique of writing, because of his proximity to visual artists, and his careful hiding of his creative sources, drew certainly from three painters whose techniques resonated in Cendrars' work:

- Durer's grid through which a three-dimensional scene could be depicted with accuracy on a flat plane. By partitioning the picture plane into distinct frames, he could focus on local proportions and lines.
- Hokusai's revolving technique for woodblock prints, as exemplified in his 36 views of Mt. Fuji.
- Van Gogh's technique of "quickness" or "on the spot"—rapid-fire execution of canvasses in as little as 20 minutes per canvas.

Craft was the governor of Van Gogh's painting, but he was driven by a passion to penetrate a mystery, which he described as follows:

> *What is drawing? How does one arrive at such a thing? It is the act of punching a passage through an invisible iron wall, which appears to divide what one FEELS, and what one CAN. How does one cross through this wall, for it serves nothing to hit it hard, one has to make it crumble, file it down bit by bit, slowly and with patience, that's how I see it.*

In order to understand the approach of an artist, one also needs to examine how he sees life, not just life generally, but how he perceives his own life. Van Gogh looked to Hokusai, striving to make his life "more and more like a Japanese painter's, living close to nature like a petty tradesman."

Cendrars' method belies entirely his reputation as a "character" or a fabulist. Nor was there any mystery in it, for Cendrars made no mystery of his reflections on the craft of writing. In one of his essays, in which he relates the writing of *Moravagine*, he describes his technique for writing, portraying thought as a wild horse that must first be captured and then tamed:

> There are three stages or states, which also imply a variety of other aspects—condition, spirit of approach, country, mood.
> 1. *Formulation*: immersion in *thought*. A state of mind. I stare out at the horizon, I trace a given angle. I capture thoughts as they pass, and cage them alive, pell-mell, fast and in great volume: *sténographie*.
> 2. *Modulation*: immersion in *style*—tone, resonance, images. I sort my thoughts. I caress them, I wash them, I train them with the whip, before bringing them harnessed into the corral: *calligraphie*.

3. *Fixation*: immersion in the *word*—correction and new detail, the proper term—*mot juste* acts like a whip causing them to rear up in surprise: *typographie*.

Cendrars allotted himself one year to write each of his books based on the time it took him to write *Transsibérien* and *Panama*. On his "most beautiful night of writing," he claimed to have written 18,000 pages.

And Cendrars identified climactic conditions as crucial to an artist: "And, there also has to be the warmth of the sun ... that's in my blood."

But the crucial precondition for the writer is to belong to no one. Although Cendrars never says so, this is a separate question from the existential issue of freedom which he addresses in the following way:

> *My position is very special and difficult to maintain to the end. I am free. I remain independent. I belong to no country, to no nation, to no social class. I embrace the entire world and I scorn the entire world. This is no paradox. I scorn the world in the name of Poetry in Action, because men have crossed the line and become too prosaic.*

Cendrars also took the time to describe the most secretive and taboo zone of writing, that of finding a subject worth telling. This is contained in the postface of *Moravagine* and penetrates to the very heart of this oracular, mysterious zone which writers are loathe to discuss in open terms:

> *I don't believe there are any literary subjects. Or rather there is only one: Man. But which man? Well, the man who is doing the writing, by God. There's no other subject possible. But who is that exactly? For sure, it's not me. It's the other. 'Je suis l'autre' wrote Gerard de*

Nerval under one of the rare photographs taken of him. But, who is this Other? Doesn't matter. You meet somebody accidentally and you never see him again. Then, one fine day, the same fellow reappears in your consciousness and harasses you for ten years. He's not necessarily extraordinary. He could just as easily be bland, amorphous, even neutered.

Cendrars' Moravagine, the fictional monster, was in reality a dejected and broken child rapist who had just completed serving a 25-year prison term. Cendrars came across him sitting on a park bench, eating a plate of roasted potatoes and drinking coffee out of a bowl. He invited the wretched idiot into his home: "... he didn't have any bread, so I bought him a small *miche*. He had no place to sleep, so I offered him a bed."

Much later, Meunier—his real name—returned to dwell in Cendrars' mind, as if "he'd flopped into an easy chair." Bit by bit, Moravagine took possession of Cendrars the man, himself a virtual creation of a man once known as Frédéric Sauser. It was as if six people dwelled in the foreground of Cendrars' mental space:

> *Frédéric Sauser*
> *Meunier*
> *Virtual* Meunier
> Blaise Cendrars
> *Moravagine*
> The Other

Behind the men, forming a choir singing inside Cendrars' brain, a multitude of Others through time. A virtual choir composed of Rémy de Gourmont, de Nerval, Catullus, the Marquis de Sade and the organic vine of Others synthesized within the mind and spirit of the man-phoenix, Blaise Cendrars, who in turn had allowed himself to be possessed by the virtual Meunier—an abject child rapist and murderer, whose alter ego refused to leave the antechamber of Cendrars' mind until Moravagine was unleashed upon the world:

> *It was a horrendous drama. Over time, I began to notice that this Other began to appropriate everything which happened to me in my life, and that he began to take on all the traits and features of everyone and everything I observed. My thoughts, my favourite studies, my way of feeling, everything converged towards him, became part of him, allowed him to live. I fed and raised a parasite at my own cost. In the end, I no longer knew which of us was plagiarising the other. He travelled in my place. He made love in my place. But there was never any real identification because each remained autonomous, me and the Other ... That's why all great books resemble each other. They're all autobiographical. That's why there's only one literary subject: Man. That's why there's only one literature: that of this man, this Other, the man doing the writing.*

Written on August 13, 1917, in Courcelles, less than two years after losing his hand. And, now, during this consideration of the Other, suddenly you return as an apparition, this ghost that I saw on the periphery of my life, the child I had deserted in order to save him. A ghost despite my certainty that you are still alive. Aye, there's the rub. Only a man in my position could know that when you came into the world, there wasn't a hope in hell for a foreigner to take what is rightfully his, his own flesh and blood, when the blind madness of passion disallows a quiet settling of a matter. And, so you were left with her, and I with myself, and the gods left you and I each to suffer in our own ways, particularly you, having to bear my name, as part of the curse.

III

What disappears over my horizon by travelling towards the Orient
Is what Christopher Columbus discovered by travelling towards the West
It was in these waters that he first sighted that black and white bird
Which brought him to his knees, exalting and thanking Almighty God
With such emotion
And then improvised this Baudelairian prayer which he recorded
In his log book
Where he asks forgiveness for having lied daily to his
Companions by charting false points on the ship's navigation chart
So they would never find his route again.
—Blaise Cendrars

Bretagne is reminiscent of Ireland—grassy knolls, menhir stones, dismal skies and signage in an old Celtic language. It all sounds so inviting in the travel brochures, but the oppressive grey of the cloud cover, the long grisly days, the menhir stones push the local lunatics and shamans to court perverse practices and to allow irrational grudges to take hold of their souls. We drove up the D783 through Pont-Aven, Gauguin's town, where he founded the Ecole de Pont-Aven with Emil Bernard before he left for Tahiti, turned onto the D77, taking us through another series of Celtic-sounding towns: Kergrouez, Kerfany les Pins. Kerliou was nowhere on the map, so we stopped and asked directions at the Office de Tourisme in Nevez. At Kersacouet, a small hamlet of thatched cottages, I dialled Bibi Cendrars from my mobile phone, and she guided me as I arrived within proximity.

"Ah, *bonjour*! You are in Kersacouet? Drive through the hamlet, between the thatched cottages, it's only for local residents, but you can take it. Come out of the hamlet on the other side; you will arrive at the head of a road with a cream-coloured house. Take that road, and when you get to number 16, take the dirt road, follow it along until it branches right, keep going until you see a woman on a mobile phone. That's me who you see; I'm waving."

She was standing out on the driveway when we arrived. She looked barmy all right, as if the seaside and the brackish air had dragged her to her natural zone of madness, that had gone into brief remission in Paris, or was less visible against the Lutecian tapestry of maniacs, psycho killers and neurasthenics circulating in that pleasant corner of hell. She was dressed for the part—a wide-brimmed straw hat, knickers, and a coquettish, Charleston-style pageboy cut that issued a *pronunciamento* to the world that she was loco-coco indeed. My entrance up the driveway was ushered in by a flock of oversized seagulls swooping down in formation over us, offloading a few white turds prior to executing a seaside landing in V-formation on the front side of the house. As if the folle du Chaillot had suddenly won the lottery and went out on a shopping spree.

"Do you see the size of those gulls? Reminds me of D-Day. I'll show you the pellets I use to shoot them with later," she said, her eye returning from prey.

"Come in, come in," she blathered cheerily, ushering us inside.

Bibi Cendrars wasn't alone. Three men were visible on her rear terrace as I arrived. One of them had crow-like features, his lined face partially obscured by hair hanging like a venetian blind shutting out the sun in mid-day. The second, raising a glass of rosé in a toast, was a heavy-set man with thick lips sporting an earring and a headscarf. The last had his back to me. A busty, black-haired woman sat with the three men. She looked to be a recent import out of the Balkans. The three men glanced indoors, then turned back to their discussion. After a few minutes, the entourage disappeared, and we took a seat on a crimson divan in her sunken living room, offering us a wide view over an expanse of grass and behind, the grey North Sea waves hitting the shore a hundred metres further on.

The heavy rain sweeping across the wide expanse separating the house from the sea gave it a savannah look. The mantel of the room was bric-a-brac, with the flavour of objects picked up at flea markets and antique stores—a kitsch sculpture made of papier-mâché, a gold-tinted bird, scraps of cast iron crafted into various irregular shapes—the casual asymmetric decor of a beach cottage. Nothing visible which showed signs of tributes to her father.

"So, Monsieur Fingon. I imagine you're here to talk about my father. What's the interest in a carcass fifty years dead."

"I'm here to recover something."

A sound of a car skidding to a halt on the gravel driveway. A dark, frizzy-haired woman entered the house, walking like a waitress, with submissive purpose, but it looked to me like a posture she'd acquired or put on for the day and not one she was born into.

"*Je vous présente Maria Alvares, mon assistante.*"

At first glance she struck me like some kind of unemployed diva, maybe a stand-in for one of those off-off Montmartre plays running down by the flea market in Clignancourt, but more than eager to serve the higher cause of art for an hourly wage, subject to future considerations. Bibi laughed during Maria Alvares' breathy introduction to the Life & Times of Maria Alvares. Alvares enthusiastically recounted her epic journey from a squatter's flat in les buttes de Chaumont to Villa Cendrars. The conversation turned to Maria Alvares' artwork, particularly her recreation of Genesis in a biblical tapestry. Money. Then to how the two women had escaped Paris.

"It was no longer possible to be creative under the climate of fear which reigned in Paris. It's become like that for everybody. The anxiety in the metro, on the streets. Here, I can walk the entire night alone. I came to Pont-Aven on an artist's sabbatical, but I never turned back."

"I'd always thought of Paris as a city to escape to, not from."

Bibi Cendrars interrupted. "Paris has become a museum, and we are the artefacts. The Paris you refer to is gone forever."

"So you've left permanently?"

Bibi Cendrars shrugged.

"I still have the apartment, but Maria is correct. We are refugees of a sort."

"How do you pay the bills, Maria?" I asked.

Maria Alvares assumed a theatrical wince at my invasion of her safe space. "I am a poet, but also a visual artist. I am expressing weaving as a modern medium."

I grinned.

"Come off it. The only thing you're weaving is a tale about yourself."

Bibi cackled cruelly, and the cackle sounded genuine. There was guile to her madness.

"Touché! And, you, Mr. Jack Fingon, how do you pay for *your* vices? Tell me more. You have caught my interest."

"I don't pay for my vices," I responded, directing my gaze at Bibi. "Other people do."

"How do you survive then?" asked Alvares.

"Putting together deals."

"Deals? What kind of deals?"

"All kinds. But my cash flow is 100 per cent private sector. How about you?"

"I provoke images."

"I'll bet that's not all you provoke."

"Provocation; it's a form of manipulation. Maybe that's my calling: manipulation."

"Duly noted. Another growth sector. Wouldn't mind getting in on the ground floor. So to speak."

The rain was still pouring down heavily—visible through the solarium, granting a broad view of the Atlantic.

"I think someone else should pour the tea. Otherwise, there could be *dégats*."

Maria Alvares poured the Darjeeling out of a samovar through a strainer.

"Stir the leaves in the pot a bit," Bibi Cendrars instructed, showing her impatience. "I always take milk and sugar. Or whatever else is available; you never know. But, you know, I adore appliances. Convenience is a wonderful thing. Maria Alvares, of course, is a Luddite. All wood stoves and weaving. You should get a television some day, Maria. They're really quite useful." She watched Maria Alvares again for a moment. "Stir the leaves in the pot a bit; bloody hell, *provoke* them if you have to," she repeated, then seemed to forget her assistant. Bibi Cendrars removed her glasses, exposing a glaucomatous fish stare.

"What are you doing here exactly, Mr. Fingon? I don't believe for a second that your reasons are literary."

"I'm here to talk about a poet's ashes."

"It's the first day of rain," answered Bibi Cendrars, non sequitur. "We are indifferent to the weather here. Tahiti is for Gauguin, not Bibi Cendrars."

It was all a picturesque scene—the devoted and loyal personal secretary, the magnanimous executor of the immortal poet's heritage, and only me to disrupt the Zen moments and toss some holy water onto the literary succubus that Bibi had temporarily tamed. Except it had nothing at all to do with the three people in the room. Like anybody else, we had agendas, and those agendas would cross like perpendicular axes on a co-ordinate plane. It was inevitable and mathematical. But for the time being, we were not calling things by their true names.

IV

The post-modern mind has become so cluttered and levelled that even the simplest, most discernible of motives are missed, regarded with suspicion, contempt and derision or ignored. Only money and its offshoots, sex and power, trigger a reaction in the species and that is Pavlovian, grovelling, salivating or all of these simultaneously. I felt the drawing impulse towards the final act in my own drama, the same forces of attraction that had governed me. And, know that if you consider your life as hitherto useless, you now have the opportunity to vest it with deep meaning. You cannot retroactively confer love upon a life, but in its absence, what counts for me, if we are to be realistic, is your hatred and your seething resentment. That can be used. Together that can be turned to advantage, and bring me to my natural, incorporeal state as a sightless raven. That will be our sole, but concentrated "quality" time together, and you will usher me to the edge of this vale of tears. And the matter will be concluded, but for reading this epitaph. And, then when you read this, you will see it was my only act of love left, just as my abandon was the only act of love possible two decades ago. And, you will understand that this story of a hoaxster and ashes had nothing to do with these harlequin figures, but with a very real other. But, for that, you must understand the most formidable of adversaries, as she operates under the opposite law of that which governed she who spawned you—the law of good.

The setting: Kermeurz'ach, south Brittany. The sun had emerged after weeks of cloud, but the air remained unseasonably cold: March temperatures in May. A red robin crossed the terrace every evening. Out on the cliff, a bric-a-brac of menhir stones served as a reminder of the Druidic beliefs of the locals. This is the backdrop, and the rehearsal is being conducted by Carmen, listen carefully, because if you don't you will never make it to your target.

I had spent the better part of the day building a makeshift target with a 2 × 4 and a 4 × 8 sheet of coarse plywood so that Carmen could do her knife practice with something that wasn't a tree. Carmen used a twin set of Malagasy cutters. The handle of each blade was carved palissander hardwood with something written in Betsileo and served as the scabbard for the other twin blade. When you fit the two together, it looked like a nunchuk stick, which she said the Betsileo used to hit zebus over the head. The blade itself resembled a stiletto blade, thin and lethal, multipurpose. It was a gift of Rakotomela during the time when he was courting her in Maravato. He'd taught her to throw, and she had maintained the unorthodox underhand style which she used during her practice sessions in our large yard overlooking the cliffs. Every morning and afternoon, she marched out by herself, stood for a time praying on her knees in front of the target. Then she'd stand up, walk three metres, her back to the target, stop, about-face, and with a short cry, launch her knife. Thwack. Then she'd walk up to the spot she'd hit and say something in Betsileo dialect, a high-octave, mellifluous expression of wonder or contemplation, and finish the move by tracing her finger around the spot, remove the knife and march out the same three or four paces. After a time, she would repeat the process at five, seven and finally ten metres.

The Malagasy knife missed the board entirely and planted itself into a tree trunk. Carmen walked barefoot up to the tree, said something. "*Tady*," she uttered, as if talking to the tree.

"You ever consider that's a transferable talent?"

"I've found enough use for it."

"Next time we're up at Cendrars' central, why don't you do a William Tell, and throw a knife through Bibi's straw hat, and I'll growl, 'gimme the fucking ashes' or some such thing?"

Carmen launched another knife, but before retrieving it, asked me this:

"What's with the eel, anyways?"

"Got any better ideas? Home invasion? Seduction? Actually never thought of that. Wonder what insurance she's got. Plus, there's the issue of jail."

"Since when have you been worried about doing time? You've lost your nerve since we came back to the first world."

"No, the eel's necessary. Anglo-America is anaemic. We need a shot in the balls. Needs to grow some gonads, the old ones have atrophied. France is the reverse—top heavy with brains, balls and poetry. We have to frack the shit out of the French psyche. We have to pulverize some fucking shale."

The cliffs and the sea formed a natural study in perspective, one picked up unconsciously by the eye. I decided to use Durer's grid to mentally chop up the images which I was seeing every day. The goal of my experiment would not be to use any specific tool but to examine scenes from our rear terrace as if looking through Durer's grid.

Carmen arrived at cliffside carrying a bottle of Rosé d'Anjou and a pair of stemmed wineglasses. She sat down beside me, uncorked the bottle and poured out a glass for each of us.

"Where are you?"

"Just mulling over form. And forms. How a thought becomes an image."

"Now, are your thoughts the same as one minute ago?" she asked as I placed the now half-empty glass on a flat rock to my left.

"No idea. One minute ago is ancient history."

We watched the cove again for a few minutes. I didn't want to know her thoughts. They seemed better whole and untouched, unreleased. Carmen had returned from Madagascar, but something almost stigmatic in her experience on the red island had remained within her and set her apart from others. The few who had known me from past lives had stared in disbelief when they first met her. They knew little or nothing of her, only that she shouldn't be with a man such as myself.

"You know," I said, "Cendrars admired men who were builders, so surely he sensed that modernism represented the destruction of craft. Nothing was invented after 1900. Nothing. People forgot invention and moved on to the means of production. The patron saint of modernity is Henry Ford."

"This is the only place I ever see you without pen and paper."

"When you look at Durer's theory and his work, you see how truly impoverished our era is. We live in a material and spiritual wasteland."

"Very few people can see what's happening right in front of them," she said. She crossed her legs, sat face to face with me, held up the glass of rosé and looked through it at me.

"What do you see?" she asked.

"The last remaining hope for civilisation."

"Ah, yes. Civilisation. An ancient concept."

"A fleeting one, disappearing into the firmament. Cendrars saw that. So did Miller."

"You always mention those two in the same breath," she said, not really an echo of my earlier adulation.

"Miller is the flip side of Cendrars, because he was his opposite. Miller was not a vagabond; he was an exile. Very sedentary, very attached to places. But that is what allowed him to describe in his best work the spiritual death of Western civilisation. Miller's most brilliant exposé on this is in *Nexus*, in the monologues of John Stymer, the suicidal lawyer who has lost the ability to distinguish between criminal and citizen."

The afternoon sun cast a silhouette of shadows through the birch leaves and bramble pathside. I broke four branches off a tangle of bush, stripped off the leaves with a cutter, making four sticks.

"All right, small game. What do you see?" I asked, pointing to the path.

"A path. Dirt. Pebbles. A lizard."

I took the four sticks and formed a grid of nine sections, which split the shadow and formed a chiaroscuro jigsaw of earth, rock and vegetation. Carmen stood up and circled the new configuration. She stepped back and examined it from a step away.

"*Mampiomehy izy.*"

"Meaning?"

She was still examining the grid I had constructed. "It's funny that an even number of sticks produces an odd number of spaces."

"This is how the Durer grid works, Carmen. He borrowed the idea from the Italians, who understood how to use light better than anyone. Da Vinci called it the geometrical construction of shadows. Think about it! The *geometrical construction of shadows.* My mind boggles when I hear that phrase. It's as if a superior civilisation from another planet were showing us a glimmer of their infinitely greater knowledge before enslaving us."

"When you talk of the death of our civilisation, I see traces of light in you."

"Durer also used a technique called the *camera lucida* to superimpose human figures on the page. And then it fell right out of use for two centuries."

"You're becoming untethered. The centre's no longer holding."
"You're right."
"Why?"
"Old memories."
"You've forgotten. Life isn't what is taken from you. It's what you take and protect for yourself."
"A dead poet's ashes."

She considered this. I wondered whether she could see what had consistently evaded me.

"Look into my eyes. Tell me what you see there."
"I see a nine-part geometrical construction of shadow and light."

V

We are in Villa Cendrars. Celestine is showing impatience today. Carmen says nothing. She is listening, as she says, and she can hold that posture for hours if necessary. I am curious however, and wonder why someone like Bibi Cendrars would even develop such a hare-brained and high-risk scheme.

"She's not the only one. They seem to come out of the woodwork."

"Really."

"About six months ago, someone from the United States contacted the press and told them she was Cendrars' daughter. A woman calling herself Marcelle Cendrars. Needless to add, a hoaxster, and not a sophisticated one."

"What did she want?"

"She is some kind of activist, seems to be embarked on a Steinbeckian crusade against unnamed enemies. Ultimately too quirky to hold the public interest. She appears to have gone back to her causes and left off with Cendrars. Outside of her claim of filiation."

"False pretenders, illegitimate heirs. Executive assistants on the hustle. To be expected."

Celestine Cendrars laughed.

"There's an itinerant circus that comes through the region every year. Apparently there's a flame-swallower who says she's Cendrars' daughter."

"Ah, that's good. It's not entirely surprising, though, is it, given his notoriety?"

"Frankly, there are times I tire of people coming to talk about Cendrars. My mission ..."

"Your mission," I interrupted, "and I apologize for this, but isn't your mission to get the ashes to the Sargasso Sea?"

This sparked a flash of real anger.

"Are you as mad as the rest of them? My mission is to save Cendrars' work."

She stood up and disappeared from the room, returning with a forged metal tool of sorts, which resembled a rake with only the stub of a handle. The prongs of this rake were shaped like long sorrel leaves.

"This is a *fouêsne*. Do you know what a *fouêsne* is? An eel rake." She held it up.

"May I examine it?" I asked. I was beginning to get her. She was strange, but she was a believer. I could deal with crooks and shysters, but eccentrics were outside my zone of comprehension and their sincerity didn't make them any less dangerous.

Celestine Cendrars was crossing the mezzanine, up two steps, and into the kitchen. I examined the eel rake, then glanced out the window. I could hear Celestine Cendrars' voice from the kitchen, talking to somebody on the phone: "Yes, of course. Yes, he is here. No, I haven't told him yet. Yes. Yes. I'm showing it to him right now."

I checked out the metallic leaves of the *fouêsne* while looking through the window at the flat grey Atlantic, just south of the trajectory where my own father had flown 50 feet above the waves to avoid German gunners and tracer fire. What a hash we'd made of things since. All of us, left, right and centre. I noticed, for the first time, the large number of African fetish art pieces in her house—a Chokwe fetish mask, a couple of primitive rhinoceros, a serpent mask, fertility carvings from Guinea, Upper Volta, from tribes with strange phonetics like Kplekple, Guro, Bobo that resonated like First Nations peoples I knew from British Columbia such as the Gitxsan Wet'suwet'en. We were good, the lot of us. Good at pillaging, and we'd all pay for it someday.

Celestine Cendrars re-entered the room, now carrying a long scroll which appeared to be made of parchment. The book was composed of a series of four sheets glued roughly together in an accordion style binding.

"Cendrars self-published 125 copies of *Easter in New York* in 1912," Celestine Cendrars explained. "Do you know how many sold? Not a single one. That didn't stop him. He went ahead with publishing the *Prose of the Trans-siberian* and had it illustrated by his friends, Sonia and Robert Delaunay. If you were to unfold the book, it would measure just under two metres. The original idea was to publish 150 copies. If you were to place them end to end, they would equal the height of the Eiffel Tower."

She was a bit in Berne institute mode, but it was information and might lead somewhere.

"This edition is a masterpiece of both visual art and literature. A premonitory work of genius. I once had 33 copies of it. This is the last one in my possession."

"Where are the other thirty-two?" I asked.

"Stolen. From the Paris apartment. It's invaluable."

"That depends on the whereabouts of the other thirty-two."

Our very brief honeymoon was coming to an end, and at that point, there was still plenty of time to call it a day.

"That's a matter of indifference to me. What do you take me for, some kind of street-hawking *faussaire*?" she said.

The eel rake, which I was still clutching, was cold to the touch. I noticed towards the base of the handle was a barely legible mark carved into it with a knife. Two letters, possibly B.C.

"How about this? Significance?"

"I wonder whether I'm not deluded sometimes, having thought you could help me. Why would you indeed?"

"If she has the ashes, I'll have them back with you."

"When?"

"You know where she is?"

"She is close by."

"Give me a day."

"Fine. In the meantime, let's get the charts out, shall we? I've a mind to go to the Sargasso Sea myself."

VI

The wild and woolly field of drift bottle research included scientists, dilettantes and quacks, and the discoveries emerged from as many nooks, crannies and ship decks as there were experimenters sending messages or trying to gauge the tides, gyres and currents of the great oceans of the world. The leading experts of the traditional world of science were Runciman at the National Institute of Water and Atmospheric Research Ltd., New Zealand; J. Yamimota of the Ocean Research Institute in Tokyo; Casamajor of the Institut français de recherche pour l'exploitation de la mer (IFREMER); Dr. Rainer Hartmann of the University of Bremen; Dr. Hendrik de Witte of the Netherlands Institute for Sea Research; and Dr. Fraser Cavanagh of the Bedford Institute of Oceanography in Nova Scotia. The dilettantes were led by a certain Dr. Curtis Ebbermeyer, retired oceanographer, who literally was a quack, as he spent his productive hours tracking 30,000 rubber-duck toys, glass balls and other paraphernalia which had fallen into the ocean.

After a preliminary glance at the credentials of these scientists, I settled on Fraser Cavanagh—a man with an old pedigree, whose forefathers were among the early settlers of Pictou County, Nova Scotia. Cavanagh came through in an unexpected way in his June 17, 2008 e-mail:

> Our institute has a research vessel going south from Nova Scotia to an area about 100 miles north of the Sargasso Sea in late September. There would be a good possibility of drift from this area into the Sargasso Sea, but it would depend on the winds and ocean currents during the subsequent weeks. I don't know whether an arrangement for our vessel to help would be possible, if it were of interest to your friend.
>
> —Fraser Cavanagh

The following day, I received additional information. In addition to recommending other ocean expeditions sailing for the Sargasso Sea being led along 48° north by the Bremer Institute, he provided further threads into the Netherlands Institute for Sea Research and the French Research Institute for the Exploration of the Sea. On the issue of success of the drift bottle arriving at destination, he stated as follows:

> We can provide some further information on currents and wind at an appropriate time, but it will not be firm. The ocean circulation (including the boundaries of the Sargasso Sea) vary in time in a similar way to weather patterns that we are all familiar with. The currents cannot be predicted with any level of certainty; rather, only rough probabilistic type estimates can be made. The flip side of this is that, if one releases something in the vicinity of the Sargasso Sea, one cannot be certain

that it will not drift there (in a case like this, it would be in nature's hand and one would probably never know the fate). I will get back to you after discussing with our management.

—Fraser Cavanagh

The following day, I telephoned Dr. Cavanagh and followed that up with a missive to Celestine Cendrars setting out the progress in investigating Bibi Cendrars and how I viewed the mission once we retrieved Cendrars' ashes.

Log Book Entry

June 20, 2008
Telephone conversation with Dr. Fraser W. Cavanagh over Skype mobile
Head, Ocean Circulation Section
Ocean Sciences Division, Fisheries and Oceans Canada
Bedford Institute of Oceanography

Fingon: I'm really getting the sense that we're moving closer to making our mission a reality.
Dr. Cavanagh: It's slightly premature to label it our mission.
Fingon: Oh, of course, no doubt, and nothing will move forward until both parties receive all necessary guarantees. Maybe I should give you a few more particulars.
Dr. Cavanagh: It sounds a bit unusual.
Fingon: The man whose ashes are to be disposed of was the co-inventor of French modern poetry—as well as being a man of the sea, legionnaire, veteran of circuses, war journalist and aviator. Indeed, he felt very comfortable perched on the cusp of navigation, poetry and invention, and saw them as necessarily complementing each other.
Dr. Cavanagh: Are you telling me this is Apollinaire?
Fingon: No, actually, and this is under confidential seal, it's Blaise Cendrars.
Dr. Cavanagh: Hmm. I'm not familiar with the name. You say he is the inventor of French modern poetry?
Fingon: That and much more.
Dr. Cavanagh: Hmm ... (inaudible fade)
Fingon: I intend to follow up on each of your suggestions, but personally, I would very much be in favour of your closing suggestion concerning your research vessel leaving from Nova Scotia in late September.

Dr. Cavanagh: Well, our current expedition is an oceanographic survey of the Scotia shelf. The continental slope. Part of that expedition involves oceanographic moorings and getting into deeper water. Moorings portion will be seven to eight days at sea. The whole thing is part of a Canada/Europe oceanographic project related to climate change.

Fingon: And, that's ongoing?

Dr. Cavanagh: Are you familiar with the Gulf Stream?

Fingon: Yes, to the extent of my research … (coughing, inaudible)

Dr. Cavanagh: It comes within 100 km of the shelf, and then it meanders, which means it may contain remnants of the Sargasso Sea. The Sargasso doesn't really have clear contours. It's shoreless.

Fingon: What about these claims that it's not a sea?

Dr. Cavanagh: A sea is a sea because of the water, not the land around it.

Fingon: Makes sense.

Dr. Cavanagh: There are three legs to our particular mission: September 2008, spring 2009, September 2009. (Pause) It occurred to me, your family name is known around these parts. Do you have connections out here?

Fingon: Couple of generations back, around Antigonish, yeah.

Dr. Cavanagh: What about the Quebec component? Would people be interested in this man? Do they know who he is? As a Canadian institution, we have to incorporate the Quebec component, maybe invite one of their scientists.

Fingon: Would you be interested in the oceanographic component: it is tailor-made for our man, a seafarer who made navigation the bedrock of his story telling.

Dr. Cavanagh: So, the questions from my end are: 1) Does the department want to get involved?; 2) Security clearance: police five-year clearance.

Fingon: Well, in terms of involvement, it depends upon how well your department can handle all the media attention you'll be receiving. And, of course, you'll need to seek advice on how you protect yourself.

Dr. Cavanagh: How so?

Fingon: I'm talking about copyright, royalties and the like. If all goes well, it could be lucrative, but only if you are prepared for what will seem like a tsunami of attention.

Dr. Cavanagh: You really anticipate this?

Fingon: Let's get the baby steps right first, Fraser. All right if we proceed on a first-name basis?

Dr. Cavanagh: I don't see why not, uhh. Let me see if I understand you correctly. You're suggesting you pass as a volunteer, and that we cover meals and berth?

Fingon: Unless you have a better suggestion. It's not really a stumbling block.

Dr. Cavanagh: Hmmm. Is there anything you need to disclose that could potentially embarrass the Canadian government?

Fingon: Not per se. But seeing as we're on topic, I have to stress that from our end, we have some confidentiality concerns as well. I'm not worried about them, but they need to be addressed. It's a fine line we're walking, but a worthy one. But we also have concerns on the success of delivery. Are you able to provide us with projections on winds, tides, currents and gyres, which could convince the principal contemplating the mission that the ashes would have a good chance of arriving at their destination?

Dr. Cavanagh: I suppose Donald Massey could help us here. Donald is our lead scientist on this trip.

Fingon: There remains the issue of ensuring safe transport of the bottle itself. Due to the sacred, irreplaceable contents of the cargo, measures would have to be taken to ensure the bottle is safeguarded until the very moment of release.

END OF TRANSCRIPT

VII

> *"There is no truth, there is only action."*
> —Blaise Cendrars

*E*arly January. While driving up a rising crest out of Pont-Aven, Carmen is frowning, reading aloud a recent Bibi Cendrars note:

> ... *so relieved you're back in the civilised West. I look forward to seeing you again, loaded down with your usual treasure chest of oceanographic maps, lithographs of tides, lunar calendar and of course your next expedition proposal. We can look at this whole issue of ashes and sea currents.*

Carmen knows me better than I know myself. I am attracted to shit like a fly, and follow the imp of the perverse. She reasons with me until it is no longer possible. And, that's where we're at.

"We've been up against it before, but the evil came from without, and wasn't of our doing. This misaligns us with the gods. You know it and you ignore it."

"Let's just case out the situation."

"I don't like it."

"If she's got the ashes, this train leaves the station."

"And you're basing that on?"

"A hunch."

"None of this adds up. On any front. Even if you do squeeze a book out of it, who will care? An old heir and her delusions. People are over the idea of caring. They've moved on."

"But I haven't. I care."

"You care about yourself. It's care without compassion. And what does that make you?"

"The world's last Christian?"

"What if she doesn't buy into your version of Christianity?"

"Doesn't matter. I'm gonna turn her upside down and shake out her pockets. Blaise is coming home where he belongs."

"That's not a plan," she said, lighting up a smoke. "Do you want me to help you?"

"Don't worry about it. Let's just feel out the situation. I'll react."

Bibi Cendrars stood on the rear verandah of her house. It looked like a well-practiced welcome posture. She ushered us into her living room, and we exchanged civilities until I got to the point and laid out the plan exactly as I had to Celestine Cendrars and to Cavanagh.

"I've been offered a berth on the CCGS *Hudson* on its next oceanographic survey to the Sargasso Sea. A string of oceanographers at University of Bremen, the IFREMER and the Netherlands Institute for Sea Research had expressed interest in the topic, but Cavanagh is the only one with a serious proposal. The next departure will be in the fall, a few months from now."

Bibi Cendrars let the silence linger, then pushed forward in her chair towards me.

"Well, that was a mouthful. Almost brought Blaise Cendrars back from the dead. Maps, dreams, trajectories. I can see you won't be easy to outdo."

We were interrupted by the arrival into the room of one of the three men who had been sitting on the terrace, a curly-haired, roebuck-eyed man who kissed Bibi Cendrars and then retreated a step without sitting down.

"Thomas," she said, greeting him warmly, "I'm pleased you've arrived. Come and join us for a minute, why don't you? This is Jack Fingon. He says he has a plan for us, and for Cendrars."

I shook Tommy Bayou's hand. He said nothing but remained in the room. I turned my attention back to Bibi Cendrars.

"I have a plan, but it can't go forward without your father's ashes."

"Go speak to the authorities at Tremblay-sur-Mauldre." Tommy Bayou said.

"That won't be necessary," said I.

"Thomas, what's your view on the idea of fulfilling your grandfather's wish?" interjected Bibi.

"I'm the wrong person to ask," Tommy Bayou replied, giving me a hostile stare.

"Let's continue our discussion in the kitchen over tea, Thomas," his mother suggested.

"Mind if I admire the view from the solarium?" I asked.

"Why not? Don't be too long. Thomas will be talking to your lovely wife and he might just spirit her away."

The two of them watched me as I moved towards the rear solarium, which provided a panoramic view of the Atlantic. An arrangement of three objects had been placed on a shelf running the length of the windows. The first was a metallic, cylindrical receptacle with a lid on it. A two-handled urn had been placed on the flat surface covering the receptacle. Either a pitcher, a goblet or an urn in pewter decorated with artificial copper-plated flowers. Beside that the bust of a lion, mouth ferociously agape. And, oddly enough, in the corner of the solarium, an eel rake similar to the one shown to me by Celestine Cendrars. I heard Bibi's voice from behind.

"Whatever you're looking for, it's not in the solarium, Mr. Fingon."

She stood rigidly a few paces behind me, leaning on her ivory cane.

"What's with the eel rake? Curio item or something more?"

"The eel rake. I would have thought that's obvious! Eels, as you surely know, spawn in the Sargasso Sea."

"Seems to be a big topic these days."

"Come now for a cup of Darjeeling. We'll return to the topic another time, shall we?"

Tommy Bayou poured out the tea in the Moroccan style, lifting the pot high above the glass.

"The first time I ate an eel was in Ostend," I said, grinning at Bibi Cendrars as if she'd just come out of an estuary. "Marked a turning point in my life. Ambled into Willie Van der Donck's brasserie, Le Grillon, and never looked back. Spent many an afternoon sampling eels and Trappiste beer by the half-dozen."

"Are you serious?" laughed Bibi Cendrars. "Well, in those days, I admit there was no shortage of eels in France."

"You mean in the government."

She smiled. "Tell me, Monsieur Fingon. Whatever brought such a maverick to the dreary port of Ostend?"

"An interim err, humanitarian project, assisting Chinese and Vietnamese nationals in their quest for freedom.

"You were a people smuggler," said Tommy Bayou.

"Only thing worth selling these days is people. I don't recall any clients complaining."

"If they had wanted to, were they really in a position to do so?"

"PR was a no-brainer after Tiananmen Square. It was like having the Chinese government do all the work for you. A regular money-printing operation, provided of course you could stay alive. As for the food, best Texas steak I ate in my life was in Hong Kong. Not sure about the eel. Eel wasn't really on the menu in those days."

"Do tell us more," Bibi said.

"I was a facilitator. Transferable skill for a solicitor. I used to work out of Hong Kong in the old days—before the lease expired with England. Things were more fluid then. You either adapted or you changed direction, did something else."

"And how did that land you in Europe?"

"Actually, around the time the EU was getting its first legs, I was invited to set up something similar by a friend of a friend working out of the Belgian customs and excise office. It was gold rush time. They set up a gig with a couple of British and Flemish truckers. Good lads. Very skilled at putting out fires and reaching accommodations with the local authorities."

"So how many of these *clients* were you fitting inside of each lorry?" Tommy Bayou asked.

"The Channel's a short trip."

"Answer the question."

"Are you speaking as a human rights activist or as a potential investor."

"Both."

"A hardened refugee family could swim it, give or take a younger sibling or two. "

I stopped smiling.

"Right, let's stop pretending here. I've come for the ashes."

Tommy Bayou sneered, but said nothing.

"If I walk out of here without that urn out in the solarium, and what's in it, your problem only gets bigger."

"If you walk out of here," Tommy Bayou said.

"Bibi," I said, turning to her. "Up until now, this is an idea. A lousy idea, and luckily an idea we can make go away. It's better than the alternative."

Bibi Cendrars waved Tommy Bayou silent.

"Better than what?"

"I'm glad you asked. You're too old for the alternative, Bibi."

Carmen was watching Tommy Bayou, and he was watching Carmen right back.

"I'm taking back something that doesn't belong to you," I said, standing up. I took my time strolling back into the solarium, removed the urn, then returned.

Carmen kept her eyes on Tommy Bayou.

"Stay where you are," she said to him, then spoke to me.

"Put the urn back."

"No, this comes with us."

"There are no ashes in the urn. And these people are not who they say they are. That's all I can tell you."

Then she turned back to Tommy Bayou.

"I don't know who you are or who sent you, but what you are doing is wrong. It dishonours the dead and it offends the ancestors."

"*Putain, c'est pas vrai,*" sneers Tommy Bayou. "Now we get this magical bullshit."

And then something unexpected happened. Bibi Cendrars began crying.

"I'm sorry. I can't do this anymore. It is wrong, and I am too old. We'll do what you want; just leave us alone."

Carmen sat down beside her, and held her.

"It's all right. It's over."

VIII

It was while looking out over the sea that a buried memory of my time served in Nice returned to me after a 10-year blank. I had walked into her life because the hues—reddish purple and a leafy green—of her clothing had drawn me close enough to take a seat at the neighbouring table in the *Bar des Oiseaux* in the old city, where I'd stopped in to catch an evening jazz performance. She had been pencilling an image onto a page in a notebook. The image was of an exotic plant characterised by two lobes running along a rib and follicles on the inner side. Later, that image would appear in my dreams, and I was dominated by the sense that I was enveloped in a cocoon of sorts and that gradually I was being coagulated by unguent enzymes coating my outer body, breaking down my defence mechanisms and bit by bit decomposing me.

One particular day, we lay together in bed on the second floor of that *pavillon* with a panoramic view of the sea from a chalky 18th-century terrace. I was recovering after some stab wounds incurred during our previous set-to. She had tracked me down in the harbour area a couple of nights before and cut me up badly. She pleaded with me to return. She didn't know what got into her; she'd never pulled a knife on anyone before. I had pushed her too far and then she had become *folle*. But she forgave me, although to ensure I didn't do anything unpredictable, she appropriated my credit cards and my wallet after my return.

"Otherwise, you just might do it again."

We moved together in a solemn procession towards our lair, me wounded but more than ready to feed the host body. There was no pretence any longer. She could reveal what she was, and I recognised her need, which was purely physiological. I was fucking her like my life depended upon it, because it did. Feeding the beast. Our organisms symbiotically linked, but no room was left for personality. When she was satiated, she fell immediately asleep. I lay still, watching her pigmentation alter noticeably in slumber. She appeared to be sucking energy from a phantom world. For the entire night, I contemplated this life form while knowing that somehow I had become tethered to the walls of her dungeon. In the morning, she awoke with a start and gripped onto my arm.

"I shall nurse you to good health. We are together again."

"That we are."

"Do you love me?"

"Undoubtedly."

"Say it."

"*Je t'aime, bébé*. I'll love you forever. Wait here. I'll be right back."

I walked downstairs, car keys on the buffet. I stepped out rapidly into the garage, opened the door. Pushed the keys into the ignition. I backed up onto the street. Thought I spotted the door to the rear garden opening. The road took me back towards Villefranche-sur-Mer. I parked near the beach, off the road behind a grassy knoll, walked into a restaurant and had dinner. Racing into Nice would be fatal. If I were found, that would be the end of me

—of that I had no doubt. The next morning, I drove into the train station and took the first train out towards Paris, managing to make my way to the north by talking some conductors into letting me continue. Once there, I found my way to an old hotel in the fifth where people knew me. While I mulled over my next move, I recalled someone whose existence was unknown to anyone in the world but me and who proved crucial to my short-term survival.

IX

Whether you are uneasy or not about revealing the self is irrelevant. You take whatever you need to create.
—BLAISE CENDRARS

Chuchi the Argentinean had turned up in Paris during the early seventies when her brother disappeared under the Argentinean government's first Dirty War, waged by the military and police allies against dissidents, when somewhere between 10,000 and 30,000 people went missing. During her first years she became Salmon's mistress. Salmon was a Rouen businessman who struggled for years with the idea of leaving his wife prior to patching things up on the home front and leaving Chuchi to her fate.

A five-year relationship followed with Dany, a Parisian social worker who liked Amazonian flute music and had participated in the May '68 riots and talked a lot about going to Buenos Aires some day to track down Chuchi's missing brother. When that died down, Chuchi met Steven the Nam veteran, and Chuchi fell for him hard. Steve, during our hair-raising business trips, fed Chuchi's illusions with cocaine and Quaaludes while he stopped at every town to phone and mail postcards to swear undying allegiance and passion to four ex-wives and girlfriends before swaggering back to the car.

So by the time Steve finished with her, Chuchi's teeth had darkened, her hope was shattered, and she retreated to a life inside her second-floor flat on rue St. Honoré in the first, smoking Gauloises and drinking espresso coffee and more or less keeping her thoughts to herself. I called her from a booth on the *rue Claude Bernard*, then made my way to her flat, taking care not to follow my usual paths, going rather through the *Jardin des Plantes* and crossing the Ile St. Louis to the third arrondissement, then moving down *rue de Rivoli* towards Chuchi's.

"You show up just like that. Must be a big problem this time."

I sat down at the table and watched Chuchi from behind as she brewed coffee on her Bleuet Coleman stove. She still wore those faded jeans tight around that low-slung Buenos Aires cowgirl ass of hers. She poured out the coffees, lit up a Gauloise and sat down opposite me.

"You're running away from this person, aren't you?"

"Running, hiding, whatever."

"Is there any chance she knows you're here?"

"No chance of that."

Chuchi weighed that one for a minute, expressionless.

"So what happened this time?"

Chuchi stubbed out her Gauloise and lit another. The light-blue soft packaging triggered a recollection of nausea from another time, which I couldn't place.

"There was a guy named Dmitri. A Georgian. She was running some kind of racket with him. Caviar, she said, but I think it was hand weapons. What's the fucking difference, Chuchi?"

Her features were granite.

"Who, she? Does this she have a name?"

"Mimi."

"*Putain*," she said, disgusted. "Go on."

"Dmitri's dead. In the Lot River, somewhere in the Tarn Gorge region. I was in bed and she carelessly tossed the morning's newspaper onto the bed. With Dmitri's photo."

The look she wore made Chuchi's next words redundant. "You can stay three days."

"More than enough. I'll be leaving for Prague by then."

Deal concluded, but Chuchi still looked hard. "I wouldn't be in the least surprised to see you do just that, *pauvre con,* you're so pigheaded. But you'll look like even more of a fool. When that turns bad, you can expect even less sympathy than you have now. *Voilà ce que je pense. Point à la ligne.*"

"I didn't realise the jury was already deliberating."

"They have been for a long time. You have to make amends. You've hurt a lot of people."

"That's a bit on the overkill side. I lead my life. I don't bother anybody."

"There's a child involved."

"Yes."

"There's a child involved and you are telling me you don't *bother* anybody?"

She stamped out her cigarette in the tray between us."

"*Je déteste les américains.*"

It came out like sandpaper, filled with decades of abuse.

"I'm not American."

"You are worse. At least Americans *assume* for their actions, vile as they are. On top of everything, you've become dishonest. *T'as vraiment rien compris, pauvre con.* Maybe it's just in your nature."

Chuchi stood up and put on some more coffee. My heart was beating fast. I knew I had to have lodging or I'd be out on the street and easy to find. It felt like energy, that one wrong move and I'd be gunned down or run over. I watched her from behind, understanding for the first time how little I knew about her. Chuchi turned round, looking like she'd decided something. "Jack."

"Yeah." I wanted to give Jack Fingon three days notice too, but it doesn't work that way.

"This person, this Mimi, just is what she is. She is a possessed devil. But you're divided. You're doing all these wrong things, I don't care you want to rob banks, go ahead and rob them, but quit dragging other people into it."

I didn't know what to say. I wasn't entirely sure what she was talking about or who she was talking about. Somebody named Jack.

"Go home. Pay your dues, pay your debts. Wipe the slate clean. If you do it right, maybe you'll see a day when you come back. As for the child, you're no use to anybody now, let alone a child. When he's ready, he'll track you down, and then he'll do what he has to do. You have no control over that anymore."

"You're right. I'll deal with it then."

"Sure. You'll deal with it then."

What she said was true, but it was too late to do any good. And she was right: I had always done honesty on the instalment plan. It was only later that I realized that Chuchi didn't help me as a friend. She was decent, and I was like others. I'd thrown common decency out of my repertoire.

PART III
Estuary

1

One of the mysteries of the animal kingdom is the long-distance migration (5000-6000 km) of the European eel Anguilla anguilla L. from the coasts of Europe to its spawning grounds in the Sargasso Sea. The only evidence for the location of the spawning site of the European eel in the Sargasso Sea is the discovery by Johannes Schmidt at the beginning of the previous century of the smallest eel larvae (leptocephali) near the Sargasso Sea. For years it has been questioned whether the fasting eels have sufficient energy reserves to cover this enormous distance.
—Van Ginneken et al.,
"Eel Migration to the Sargasso: Remarkably High Swimming Efficiency and Low Energy Costs,"
Journal of Experimental Biology 208, 1329-1335 (2005)

In the year 350 BC, Aristotle stated in his *Historia Animalia* that eels "are produced from the so-called 'bowels of the earth' which are spontaneously produced from mud and moist soil."

In fact, this English translation is belied by he original expression *ges entra*, which does not mean bowels of the earth, but "entrails of the sea."

Satellite photos of the Sargasso Sea show the extent to which the algae there in fact resemble entrails.

Unable to determine the eel's origins through observation, Aristotle concluded that "the male is neither male nor female, and is procreated from nothing."

During the times of Aristotle, there were not such clear divisions between the thought processes of science and art, and the state of unknowing proposed by Aristotle in no way inhibited conjecture. This marriage of physiology, sexuality and knowledge has only survived in the vulgar poets and artists of the French nation—Villon particularly—who see that the rutting of an animal is much closer to beauty than the witticisms of the salon. It is a wisdom born of *le terroir* and entirely absent from writing in the English language with the exception of D.H. Lawrence, and so there remains an unbridgeable chasm between the two worlds.

In AD 77, Pliny the Elder in his *Natural History* recorded his belief that eels rub their skin against rocks, which then break off and metamorphose into baby eels. For the most part, these ancient beliefs survived until modern times. Twenty years prior to the writing of the quatrain, a Danish biologist named Johannes Schmidt asked himself why, during his observations of the estuarine waters of Denmark, he had never seen a baby eel. Like Cendrars (a disciple of de Gourmont), who intimated that life itself originated in the Sargasso Sea in a sort of automatism, and like Celestine Cendrars who followed the laws of attraction when she purchased the *fouêsne*, Schmidt's hypothesis was based upon reason, but it was intuition which pushed him towards his discovery of the smallest eel larva near the Sargasso Sea in 1923.

Schmidt's discovery coincided precisely with the 1923 production of Cendrars' *La Création du Monde* at the Théâtre des Champs Elysées, which also immediately preceded Cendrars' departure for Brazil on the ocean-liner *Le Formosa*.

Cendrars may well have crossed the path of Schmidt's vessel, the *Dana II*, as he sailed towards the equator. The best conjecture as to a possible crossing of the two men's trajectories may be posited as being at 26° north latitude and 56° west longitude, Cendrars moving at full ship speed on the *Formosa*, Schmidt somewhat stationary while tracking his own prey—a five-millimetre *leptocephalus* larva—to confirm his thesis that the European eel, *Anguilla anguilla*, spawned in the Sargasso Sea.

It seemed fitting that a man who dwelled on the origins of the earth throughout his life and expressed the wish to have his remains dropped into the Sargasso Sea could potentially play a role in drawing attention to the plight of the eel. The metaphor looked promising. I could loop it out easily enough. It fit a theme of Cendrars' hero and mentor, Rémy de Gourmont, who in *Physique de l'Amour* had argued that our advancement as a species, which we give the high-minded label of purpose, could be more easily explained by nothing more than our sexual impulses.

What is the aim of life? The perpetuation of life. But the very idea of purpose is a human illusion. There is neither commencement, nor middle, nor end in this series of causes dividing and multiplying without contemplation of what lies next. What is was caused by what was, and is the cause of what will be. There is neither a place of rest nor a start point. Born of life, life eternally engenders life. It must do so, and it wishes it so. Now, life is characterised on earth by the existence of individuals regrouped into species, i.e. having the power, a male joining in unison with a female, to reproduce their likeness. Whether this is the internal conjugation of protozoa, of hermaphrodite fecundation, the copulation of insects or mammals, the act remains the same. It is common to everything that lives, and not only to animals, but also to plants and maybe to minerals limited by a constant form. Causation appeared on every horizon. Hokusai-style wood blocks stamped out my life history in a trajectory of fate, all of it leading inexorably forward to a horizon I could not yet discern:

1. The discovery of Cendrars while in convalescence and still shackled by the clan into which I was born.
2. The irrational urge seizing me to leave the world of law and to follow ancient pilgrimage routes.
3. The reading of Peguy's reference to the Sargasso Sea.
4. The discovery of Cendrars' quatrain in *Bourlinguer*.
5. The publication of my book by Cendrars' publisher and subsequent encounter with Celestine Cendrars.

Destiny, I reasoned, occurs in segments or vignettes. So went the syllogism, and yet these traces or clues of my derivative life were nothing but a baroque blindness, self-induced, because every path I took, every turn was leading to my ultimate destination, predicted in advance, bound by the impersonal forces of DNA, and turning to farce every single pretension I harboured of being a free man.

When Celestine Cendrars held up the *fouêsne* in her Kerliou living room, the strange forged instrument would seal our fate—yours and mine. The words of Cendrars immediately presented themselves as a koan puzzle. Little did I know that it did not refer to the vagabond poet but to me, to you and to our fateful encounter.

> I will be a man fulfilled if, when my time comes,
> I can disappear anonymously and without regret,
> At the originating point of our world, the Sargasso Sea,
> Where life first burst from the depths of the ocean floor towards the sun.
> *Se Deus quiser, amanhã ...*
> Yes, *Se Deus quiser*, tomorrow, we shall arrive in the new world.
>   Already the waves have changed in hue ...

11

While considering the meaning of a mucky, iron instrument used for culling catadromous fish out of estuaries with two initials on it, a passing comment of the Judge returned to me, uttered cryptically and with respect to events borne from his distant past: "All life is a series of traumas."

He'd uttered the phrase for the first time in the immediate aftermath of his brother Geoffroy's death in a hotel room in Mexico City. Geoffroy had been the only one of the four brothers eligible for military service who had chosen not to enlist in the fight against Nazi Germany, opting instead for the rarefied air and confined security of a Jesuit seminary. After reading history at Oxford, Geoffroy worked his way up to being chair of a mediaeval history department at an Ivy League university. But Geoffroy was a Fingon, prisoner to his sensual appetites and privately despairing that he had not followed the path of true sacrifice like his younger brothers.

His life became a succession of impersonations—whisky priest, socialist revolutionary, possible spy for the Soviet Union and, in the family tradition, always ready to take up a lost cause. Whether it was cloak and dagger or another form of clandestine activity would now never come to light. He was found in a sitting position tied to a chair and strangled to death and not a peso poorer for the experience. That left my father with a police report written in Spanish, an indifferent embassy and a bill for thirty grand to retrieve Geoffroy's body. And still no answers.

In theory, I should have been a Geoffroy sympathiser. He'd hung out his shingle as a charismatic local hero, but there was too much posturing and belligerent pontificating to keep me onside. Juxtaposed with Geoffroy's Jesuit predilection for belittling and erudite bullying, my father's silences looked dignified. The seeds of regret were being planted within. I probably sensed already that, despite being his son, I would never come to fully know the man; the gulf between our respective lives was too wide. But I was curious all the same and determined to come up with information, or failing that, at least get a better sense of what had happened.

As an adolescent, I had tried to pry some details on his war years out of him, but he and any others who had survived were closed books. One day though, we found ourselves together on the rear patio behind the family home. For no particular reason, he related a story about being inside a cramped cinema on Main street of the prairie town of Shaunavan, Saskatchewan, during 1940, watching a newsreel showing Hitler's troops goose-stepping in perfect unison down the Champs-Elysées shortly after the fall of France. The sight of it, he confessed, had moved him to angry tears and hardened his resolve to enlist.

"But you were in the middle of Canada, 10,000 kilometres away from events."

"Yes, I was," he responded.

"And still a child," I observed. He looked out over our backyard lawn. The old man had kept his aviator's moustache trimmed in the same style since the war. He wore even his casual apparel with purpose. A well-pressed Lacoste golf shirt and knee-length shorts, white socks and casual shoes. He retrieved this leisure gear systematically upon his return from chambers, emerged on the rear patio to an awaiting tumbler of Glenfiddich Scotch whisky.

Two Douglas firs towered at opposite corners of the yard, each of them a good 150 feet high and several hundred years old, the survivors of the original rainforest which had covered large swathes of Vancouver as recently as the early 20th century. A persistent tangled vine climbed the thick trunks of the Douglas firs, but something about its patterns prevented him from pulling it off the tree. During the nightly happy hour, he sat in his pine lounge chair, sipping his Scotch and waiting. As if on cue, a flock of a hundred or so black starlings would descend upon the tree, their buzzing chatter making human conversation all but impossible. Most of the neighbourhood considered the starlings pests, but the judge revelled in the spectacle.

"Wait," he would unfailingly whisper, and after a pause, the birds now invisible within the evergreen foliage of the Douglas fir suddenly fell silent.

My father stood up quietly, then firmly clapped his hands twice, which sounded like the crack of a whip. The birds flooded out of the tree, arced into a massive pentagonal swarm, and moved away in a geometrical mass not dissimilar in shape and colour to a stealth bomber. He resumed his chair and the tale but continued gazing out over the yard.

"In my mind, and I think many others, Paris was synonymous with liberty. The fall of France was a violation of something essential."

"But you don't even speak French. Why would it affect you to that extent?"

"Maybe we'll go back there some day. You and I. I'd like that."

I was cutting to the chase, as I sensed that this might be my first and last opportunity to discuss this.

"You still haven't answered the question, Dad. To sympathise is one thing, but to fight a war for a foreign king and in Europe to boot? Didn't some feel it was meddling in Europe's internal affairs?"

"This meddling, as you refer to it, was a matter of concern for all of us. Sometimes it's right to interfere."

His defensive tone caught me off-guard.

"Sorry, I understand that part of it, Dad, but the actual reality of it dumbfounds me. You were only three years older than me, after all. I mean we're talking about life, right? I can't imagine how Grandma could have allowed it." A thought crossed my mind. "Was it Grandma's idea?"

"No," he replied, still in another place. "We were responding to our duty."

"And did your friends and classmates all go to war like you then?"

"Yes, we all served," he answered, his guard now slightly down.

"So tell me some of the combat roles you all filled," I asked, warming to the grit of the tale.

"I was a navigator on a bomber-dambuster."

"What's that?"

"It's what it sounds like. We busted dams. What they might call special ops today. We, alongside some Aussies and Kiwis, were merged into the RAF for a foray called Operation Chastise."

"Whew. Love the name. Make them feel the pain."

I didn't see any sign on his face that he even registered the comment.

"Our job was to drop something called the bouncing bomb on three dams on the Ruhr in Germany. Later I became a pilot and flew reconnaissance from the Shetland Islands with Royal Canadian Air Force Squadron 403 out of Calgary. Swede Rosenborg, he was a wireless operator. Ray Bones and Jonny Tillen were bomb aimers."

"What about your classmates?"

"My high school classmates all enlisted, but largely in other services. Army, Navy, Coast Guard. I lost sight of them. The men I served with were for the most part pilots, navigators, wireless operators, gunners. That type of thing. But whatever our posting, our purpose was identical. To seek out and destroy the enemy."

It didn't sound rote but like something felt deeply. He didn't fear mockery or the charge of being over-serious. Now he smiled at the recollection of Swede and Jonny, who he had said were two very funny men, pranksters.

"Did you meet up with them after the war, you know, to share your experiences?"

"Actually, that wasn't possible."

"Why not?"

"They never made it back."

"Well, what about your classmates?"

"They also remained behind. Ray Bones survived, but he was a POW in Japan. He came back a different man."

They also remained behind. I wondered now to what extent that type of phrase had been responsible for my return to the land which he had defended.

I left off with Ray Bones and Swede Rosenborg and my father and returned to the scene of my visit, which had prompted these recollections. The last kilometre out of Kerliou was a road winding through cornfields taking you down to the coast. I was surprised to see her standing alone on the driveway, awaiting me. The moment struck me as cinematic. A Kodak moment with Celestine Cendrars. Like walking onto the set of *Casablanca*. How do you improve on Ingrid Bergman? Simple. You don't. A sublime apotheosis of style.

"Come in, Jack."

It occurred to me as I entered Villa Cendrars that it contained the intended irregularity of rooms and furniture that you view in the canvasses of Cézanne and Van Gogh, what the Dutch refer to as *gezellig*, the quality of the inner *binnenhaert* or inner hearth, where in privacy the denizens of a house breathe in the blissful indolence of their cosy protection unwitnessed by the outside world. There was an old photo album on the table in her living room opened at a page containing photos of Cendrars at various stages of his life. The first photo on the left page showed Cendrars in uniform with the legend *Soldat de 1re classe* Sauser Frédéric, *engagé volontaire, affecté au 1er régiment étranger.*

The year was 1914. On July 29, Cendrars signed with the Italian writer Ricciotto Canudo an "Appeal to foreigners residing in France," exhorting them to join up: "Any man worthy of the name must act today, and cannot fail to act while the most terrible conflict in history rages on ..." Sauser sets the example by enlisting and is assigned to the *3ème Régiment de Marche de la Légion Étrangère* garrisoned in Paris. Within a few months, he reports to Rueil, and from there takes the path of the Somme in November 1914.

The conditions are chaotic in the Somme valley, but Private First Class Sauser is a natural leader, engaged in guerrilla warfare on the margins of official forays. On Christmas Eve, 1914, Cendrars and his men leave a booby-trapped gramophone designed to act as an improvised explosive device. At midnight, the gramophone begins playing the Marseillaise, attracting the attention of German soldiers, and when several soldiers approach the gramophone, the device explodes. He leads an expedition behind enemy lines through the marshlands of the Marais by boat, capturing a convoy and plans from German headquarters. Nominated for the *Legion d'honneur,* he is disqualified for nonconformism and insubordination.

I now examined the hand which he was about to lose to an artillery shell during the attack on Navarin farm on September 28, 1915, a matter of months after the photo was taken. The thumb, index and middle finger visible, disproportionately large, powerful. His left hand holds a clay tobacco pipe. Possibly some of the smoke is drifting out of his mouth, or it is the aged grain of the photo. I had read enough first-hand accounts of Canadian infantrymen in the first war to know that these men had not gone to war joyfully, but they hadn't gone blind either. That being said, the next photo, when juxtaposed as it was in the album, came as a shock. He is still in the navy blue uniform of the Foreign Legion infantry. The greatcoat hangs loose from the shoulders, disclosing two citations, undoubtedly from the *IVième armée*, the remaining left hand evocative of Picasso—angular, outsized, as if grafted on from another body.

The right eye is lifeless, the intensity of the right greyed out, obliterated by the fateful trajectory of the shell that removed the right hand. The left eye also is witness to the terrible event—the iris, contrary to that of the right, dark and widened, still frozen in contemplation. I had seen eyes such as these, stared into them, wondering why I had provoked this gaze of distant accusatory reproach, for 15 years, until I fled the family home. It was only during my scrutinising of the photograph of Cendrars that it came to me that the cause of my father's distant, aloof gaze was not disapproval of my mores but rather the recollection of the insanity of the war he had endured on European shores.

I managed to track down these photos at a rue de Seine Agence de Presse and placed them at my desk on the second floor of the Kermeurz'ach house. The two photos stood like two pillars marking out the illusion of glory, quickly extinguished by the reality of war. Behind them, day-in day-out, I stared into the steel blue-grey of the Atlantic skies. The presence of Cendrars did nothing to conjure up the surrealists or the cubists, acting rather to bring to the fore of my contemplations the image of my father, who like Cendrars had sacrificed his innocence for the cause of freedom. The only difference being that somehow, Cendrars had found a way to speak of the horror, while my father had been reduced to observing that life was a series of traumas. Both, however, had found their way to acceptance of their fellow man, such as they were, putting them on more than an equal footing, and leaving me to my own devices.

Log Book Entry
Re: the transmigration of Cendrars' ashes by way of *Anguilla anguilla* or otherwise in accordance with the sidereal and Oulipian angle of vision

I. Drift bottles and oceanographic expeditions

Note from Dr. Fraser Cavanagh, Head, Ocean Circulation Division at the prestigious Bedford Institute was the first to respond to my overtures:

> "... prospects of drift to the Sargasso Sea from a release off the Brittany coast very low."

Confirmed by: Institut Français de Recherche pour l'Exploitation de la Mer (IFREMER) and Dr. Hendrik de Witte of Nederlands Instituut voor Onderzoek voor Zee who dismissed my hypotheses as "far-fetched and improbable."

Expedition along 48° north towards the mid-Atlantic: Dr. Rainer Hartmann of the Institut für Umweltphysik du Universität Bremen, Kufsteiner Strasse tells me to bugger off.

Plan: Accompany Dr. Fraser Cavanaugh during the scheduled 2009-2011 expeditions.

II. Transport of Cendrars' ashes inside a migrating eel

99 percent of *Anguilla anguilla* have already been guillotined on the cutting boards of あ り が と う, the Rainbow Roll sushi restaurant and other similar sushi bars and Hibachi tables in the Shibuya, Shinjuku and Tsukiji neighbourhoods of Tokyo. Many of those that have escaped a culinary fate have been destroyed by the parasite *Anguillicola crassus* or swallowed up by hydro-electric dams constructed on various European waterways. That being said, the issue

remains straightforward: where to find a single silver-bellied eel, approximately one metre long, that will find the ashes sufficiently appetising to swallow them?

Specialists on eel: D. Runciman of the National Institute of Water and Atmospheric Research Ltd., New Zealand; J. Yamimota of the Ocean Research Institute, University of Tokyo, Japan; Odile Lamarck, IFREMER, France; Pierre Rousseau, Faune et Parcs Québec, Canada; and P. Truchet, Laboratoire de Systèmes Naturels Modifies, Facultés des Sciences de Beaulieu, Université de Rennes I, France.

Find: Dr. Henri Chauvin, the man in catadromous matters. Chauvin piloted a project conducted under maximum security under the auspices of the Université de Rennes I and *La fédération départementale d'Ille et Vilaine de pêche*. Variously mentioned in the literature as being posted at the Université de la Rochelle, Paris VI and latterly Dinard Maritime Station in Brittany, which has been incommunicado for several days due to a storm lashing the coast.

III

Raymone Duchateau once related an anecdote transcribed by Thomas Gilou for his mother in her book *Blaise Cendrars—La Vie, le Verbe, l'Ecriture* on page 389. The year is 1919:

> Féla was passing through Paris, on her way to England. She was staying with Mme Abel Gance. Blaise dropped Odi off rue du Mont-Dore and during the evenings, he left him with me, because it was too late to bring him back to his mother. So, Odi would sleep with me in my bed.
>
> The next day I gave him a little train. And he said: "No, madam, I need two because I have a little brother."
>
> Then, Féla and the children left for England where Féla had family. Several months later, Blaise asked me to meet him at Léger's atelier in Montparnasse where we went nearly every morning to see him. Blaise pulled a telegram out of his pocket and he said: "Look."

It was a telegram from Féla: I have just given birth to a baby girl. I have named her Miriam.

"Oh!" said Fernand.

And Blaise said: "As for me, I'll call her Marie."

In the *Inédits secrets*, an excerpt taken out of context from the correspondence of Cendrars and cited on page 421, Cendrars is writing to Féla during her England sojourn:

Everything you write to me has distressed me and overwhelmed me. I can't take this any longer. Let me breathe—just a bit— before starting things up again.

Towards the end of June, he writes another missive:

Now, let's talk about you. What you have announced distresses me. We have to think about this seriously and take some measures in advance so we're not caught short at the last minute. What do you intend on doing with the children *when the time comes*? Reflect on this, and tell me everything in good time so I can sort it all out for myself.

Finally, on page 425, we read Cendrars' May 26, 1920 registered letter addressed to Madame F. Cendrars Villa Massiéra Cité Robioni Pont Magnan Nice A.M.

My Dear Friend,

Here is what I have wanted to tell you after much hesitation: **Re Money**: I am doing all I can for you. I hope to improve things in the future. You have to get by on what you have, be patient and have confidence in me ...

Re the children: I no longer wish to see them except from an increasing distance. I had thought about taking them in. That is impossible for the time being. I figured that out in Nice. They interfere with my work which is extremely difficult. Besides, I have a bad influence on them.

Re you: I'm starting a new life; you should do the same. You've got the resources. Don't count on any sentimental reunions. Let's remain friends and leave it at that. Let's wait for the day when you can see me without getting disturbed and without bitterness. *Same goes for me.* I know I am a monster—*a monster of purity*—but a monster. Don't hold things against me which you cannot yet understand. I follow a discipline as in a convent.

Sorry to tell you this and a thousand other things so crudely. I'm in a rush, and it seems to me that you needed to be set straight.

Kisses to all,
Blaise

IV

*D*espite the fact that Miller and Cendrars are often spoken of in the same breath, they were vastly different writers and men. Miller was more an admirer than a friend of Cendrars. Cendrars embraced galaxies unknown to Miller, and so triggered the curiosity of the American, who could never resist the attraction of someone who had explored arcane worlds and seemed to sit right on the cusp of experience and fantastical conjecture, but Miller was a pure writer and, in the end, too pragmatic and selfish to risk his own bald carcass on the trail of discovery. The range of Miller's real life experience basically plays itself out in a series of urban flats in New York and Paris, and he scrutinises the world not through the lens of war, adventure or business but through idle conversations with disgruntled losers, or monologues setting out his cosmological world view. His work is the product of a man with too much time on his hands and a taste for beautiful, quirky and equally idle women whom he used to feed the Muse.

In real life, the two men's values were antipodal. Miller once bragged that he would shine the boots of a Nazi if necessary to put food on his plate. Cendrars on the other hand punched out Rilke the pacifist with his one remaining fist in the Closerie des Lilas during an argument on the war. Of all the things that Cendrars has been accused of being—fabulist, thief, vagabond, plagiarist, no one has ever levelled the charge that he didn't bite the bullet or that he spent his time catering to the caprices of femmes fatales.

When this hard man directed his attention to a subject, he stepped right up on the gallows of his past achievements and risked everything anew. When his curiosity was twigged by African tales and fetish art, Cendrars deployed his razor-sharp reportage craft and eye but also wandered onto an altogether less scientific plane, brought on by his willingness to move beyond passive observation to active participation and to befriend and associate with those who engaged in occult practices. It can be speculated that, in existential matters, he also stepped over the line by trying to understand the totemic influences of men such as Fébronio, the sadistic Brazilian serial killer.

Why would a man of such rigour allow himself to be seduced by one of the most facile delusions of the artist: that because the world of science occasionally deploys an impoverished vocabulary when trying to identify the forces of the underworld, the artist's vision can supersede rather than complement that of the scientist?

Cendrars developed a theory that Fébronio was a descendant of an African animist sorcerer—fair enough—but, in doing so, the monster Fébronio's evil is placed under a vase. There is no judgement whatsoever of the man. Cendrars was moving towards phenomena which he understood only imperfectly. That being said, his explanation in *La Vie Dangereuse* is a high display of investigative technique and interpretation:

> The taboo is the talisman of nagualism, which is the religion of dreams and whose baptism is carried out with blood, not

blood which is sprinkled, but blood exchanged, absorbed, integrated, and reincorporated by the initiate who, through this communion of living blood, identifies with the great unity.

This incorporation is the key to the magic of black fetishists who practice incisions, burnings, cicatricial scales, teeth sharpening, deformation of the lips, the gibbosity of buttocks, mutilations of the skull and the sexual organs, tattoos of all sorts, not for reasons of decorative vanity, but for the ends of sorcery, to identify with the Totem: the tutelary Beast of the clan.

This attention to detail is pure Cendrars—"nothing but the facts," he often counselled, "then let the light shine through"—but the next paragraph of this account betrays a degradation of his thought, where he yields to an impulse, and a dangerous one, to defend his *pote* Fébronio by way of attacking modern science, which had labelled Fébronio a "*fou altruiste*" or a "classical serial killer":

But these two labels are derisory and I am of the view that as long as the Law and Science of White Man do not study this figured bass which I note in counterpoint—visions, dreams, voices, gratuitous language and logic, images-force, symbolic acts, which fill the story of Fébronio—we will never learn anything about psychogenesis, morbid mechanisms, the behaviour of mentality, nor anything of repression, imagination, deliria, exhaustion of the souls of the indigenous and drifters.

Cendrars certainly did not entertain the postmodern illusion fostered by our own witch doctors that evil did not exist. Nor would he have been unaware of the colour of evil—a chiaroscuro which blends an artful, alluring combination of truth and sinister deception, bringing the victim closer and closer to the snare. Cendrars knew Fébronio was a devil of the most powerful sort who could subject others to his will to the point that they would accept their fates passively. And Cendrars was not exempt. In *La Vie Dangereuse*, he describes walking into the *confino*, the solitary of Rio de Janeiro prison, where the most dangerous offenders of Brazil were confined. Cendrars first came upon Fébronio sitting nude in the large central cage, locked deep in his own thoughts. The convict was short but with herculean musculature, and he was positioned in front of a fire he was feeding—one straw at a time—from his bed and with newspaper pages which he torqued like rags before tossing them into the fire.

As the guard prepared to escort him out of the dungeon where Fébronio was kept, Cendrars shouted out a remark intended to stir him from his torpor: "You wrote a book, didn't you ... the *Revelations of the Prince of Fire* ... Is that it? So tell me where I can find it. Maybe you'll give it to me ..."

After a long minute of silence, Fébronio suddenly leapt at the bars, cursing, coming so close that Cendrars "felt his feverish breath coursing across my face."

What is the effect upon a man such as Cendrars—a man who had seen firsthand from the trenches what senseless barbarity could be produced by the highest civilisations known to man —when looking straight into the heart of a man such as Fébronio? The following passage, if it had been told by a woman, would be seen as a passive surrender to the seduction of the man:

> To see his feline mannerisms, his supple gestures, his undulating, corrugated hair, his silky goatee, that rare smile, which upon a word naively illuminated his face and lightened what his eye contained as too sad, too deep, too black, how could I believe that I was having a tête-à-tête with a bloodthirsty madman? On the other hand, how could I interrogate him without unleashing the caged beast within?
>
> This brute who admitted the most heinous of crimes without batting an eyelid, this troubled spirit who complained

that he had been beaten and thrashed about by the Devil himself, this suffering soul who said that he had been forced to act, to obey these shattering visions and the voices which came to him from the sky, this ferocious beast who wallowed in warm entrails, barking and lapping up blood, this killer who had no idea of the number of his victims and was unaware of the enormity or the abomination of his crimes, this inhuman sadist bore on himself no external mark of bestiality, nor any indicia of defilement, with the possible exception of his left earlobe, which appeared joined to his head. Then again, come to think of it, his teeth were decayed, a highly repugnant quality for a negro, which transformed his mouth into something disgustingly wizened, stigmatized, obscene.

Is it possible that a fleeting contact—the corrupting exhalation of the feverish breath of possession—was enough to infect Cendrars' fatalistic spirit? Accounts of Cendrars' fugue from the family at age 15 and the manner in which Cendrars approached his entire life indicate the terrain was ripe not for conversion but for hypnosis. Cendrars, and he never lost sight of this, was a man. That meant that he undertook his great adventures, and made his great mistakes, because of a flaw/quality belonging to a man. And I knew from experience that a man doesn't just run away from home or move to China, or in my case desert a fine family, without a reason. The reason lies within the vast uncharted terrain which other mortals loosely call the artistic mind. At its core is not a moral compass but a fate compass which moves the artist at an inchoate stage towards areas that even he doesn't understand. The first and crucial stage is highly destructive and involves a self-inflicted scorched-earth policy, creating a *tabula rasa*, a vast emptiness within, and then allowing your mind, body and soul to lay stagnant, fallow following the fire until something new emerges. Cendrars says:

En Cendres se transmuent
Ce que j'aime et possède
Tout ce que j'aime et que j'étreins
Se transmuent aussitôt en
Cendres.

Into ashes transmutes
Everything I love and possess
All that I love and all I embrace
Also transmutes into ashes.

In French he capitalizes *Cendres* in an obvious reference to himself. The burning of the self and rebirth from the ashes is no random, abstract exercise but a purging of oneself, following which the self remains an empty vessel, an enormous vacuum waiting to be filled by the primeval forces which move the universe.

Our own society has degraded to the point that it denies the very existence of evil, thus making us singularly incapable of understanding the dangers that Cendrars faced. Having embraced and fallen into chasms of sensuality and hatred devised by a she-devil, I had charted some of the terrain. It is like being transported to an arid plateau where you engage in a death dance involving taboo and fetish worship. What is demanded is complete identification with the bestial Totem invoking the animist forces at work trying to possess you. What is at stake is your immortal soul.

A long time previous down in Nice, I had fallen across a journal written in the hand of this succubus who had sunk her claws into my soul. The book described and sketched out practices of incisions, burning, deforming lips, changing the shapes of buttocks, penises, vaginas and even the anus; ritual mutilations described as an instruction manual. I had no doubt about the inspiration for these rituals, as she had a close and cabalistic relationship with two Senegalese sorcerers—a young man and an older woman—and had been involved in initiate rites which she refused to discuss. But now, it struck me as similar to the very things that Cendrars describes in his defence of Fébronio.

Cendrars pointed out, accurately, the failure of Western science to grasp the significance of these lower impulses and how the shock of modernism triggered atavistic impulses and reactions. But in 1927, he was particularly vulnerable to the corruption of Fébronio, having only recently completed *Moravagine*, his tale of the schizophrenic and amoral monster recounted against the backdrop of the early 20th-century revolutions that shook the modern world. This amoral work clearly cannot be dissociated from Cendrars' own confrontation with the senseless barbarity of the nations who had produced mankind's greatest achievements.

We are unable to measure from our comfortable cubicles of life what impact would be felt by a man of Cendrars' sensitivities and idealism as he squatted through the drudgery and dull terror of the trenches. Fine verse and the invention of poetry is somewhat dulled by the constant barrage of artillery fire and the inhuman butchery of one million men. A shell severed a poet's writing hand on an unlucky day during 1915, and it also happened to be the day on which Cendrars' hero, Rémy de Gourmont, left our planet.

When this happens to a man such as Cendrars, the remainder of his creative production appears as random shreds of flotsam —drifting remnants of something which was once whole and which can never again be reassembled. And one must not exclude the possibility of these massive forces causing a certain degeneration of his thought, and one which made his investigations into voodoo, shamanism, fetish art and totemism a highly perilous adventure. It is doubtful that Cendrars could be hypnotised. He had too hard a shell for that. But he might allow himself to be corrupted and to seek a form of literary revenge for participating in the nightmare which has become known under the label of modernity.

Whether the totemic evil of Fébronio eventually possessed the entire Cendrars family, and whether I also might be yielding to the same forces, crossed my mind. The construction of my personal constellations with black Madonnas, pre-literate symbols garnered during my pilgrimages and my own tendency to drift toward nebulous zones was largely unconscious and seemingly independent of my higher rational mind.

While perusing Fébronio's photo one evening, I examined his eyes—lifeless, coal-black, pitted eyes, which put the lie to any efforts to soften the facial expression by tattoos, hair curls, or other lures. They reminded me of someone I had known very well, and I saw in Fébronio a similar use of facial trickery designed to distract or lure the victim further into an inescapable trap.

V

I woke up out of a dream of a different order—a certain day in the extreme southern highlands of Madagascar—an arid plateau outback. I was sitting under a large Baobab tree in Isohy—a southern highlands hideout for zebu thieves. It was late afternoon, and we were waiting as the doctors in the local hospital tried to do something about Maria's husband's cirrhosis. We were halfway to sapphire country, and our eventual destination was Llakaka in Isohy region, where Ratsiraka surrogates were digging out their own ground zero in the biggest and most dangerous sapphire belt in the world.

For reasons unexplained, tension was increasing with Toty, our driver. Toty was part of a mafia clique of drivers who said you had to have a driver and then skinned you the whole way with false invoices, commissions and the like while they cavorted with local thieves and whores with their skimmed gains. We had just completed a conversation, and I had more or less said: "You're telling me a fucking Malagasy gas pedal is different than a Dutch gas pedal?

It's a Land Rover. You gas it. You jake it. What's the big deal? Maybe you need a vacation."

Yeah, Toty agreed, black son of a bitch with his sleeveless down vest and Cat hat, but I didn't think he was going to leave us for long, especially since he'd tried something with Carmen back before I became part of the picture, and she didn't want to talk about it. So we waited in that dusty square while a doctor looked at some degenerate cells and thickening arteries of a man living out his last hours under the dust of the extreme southern highlands plateau. There was the sun, and the shade of that Baobab tree. A man walked across the square towards us. He didn't look at us until he arrived, and then he spoke to Carmen.

"What did he say?"

"He said, there's *fady*. We have to move away from the tree."

We moved on. Nobody defied *fady* in Madagascar. Only an insane man would deny its presence. To do so would put the mark of Cain on you; you'd be nothing but the walking dead after that. I could see there was *fady* also in the waves smashing up against Brigneau cove, a *fady* borne by the deaths of all the men under the sea and the understanding that came with it. It was in the Bretons of Finistère, but it was also in the ground, in the stones, in the inanimate, which carried the message of what had transpired and the curses which governed this land.

The night was coming, as it always did, a grainy background blurring the lines and contours of the day, and one by one, I watched the stars of Orion make an appearance in the sky. I was close to the edge of those Kermeurz'ach cliffs, leading into the sea, the waves beckoning, hope filtering away as the night grew more obscure. I held a half bottle of *Côte du Rhone* by the neck. Something was gnawing at me, tearing at my entrails remorselessly, sucking my energy. Cendrars again. He had brought me from youth to middle age, a crutch of sorts. If a man's thoughts aren't his own by the time he is in middle age, he has failed, and the time remaining will go poorly—a fresco of half-truths, mawkish sentimentality, recrimination, junk thought, half-hearted redemption and bitterness.

I returned to the house and began chopping wood for the fireplace as the night fell. Carmen and the children knew to keep their distance when I did this. It was clean and it suited me. Crack! Like a gunshot, snapping blocks into halves, then quarters, feeling the dull thud of them colliding, then picking them up and trudging up to the living room, allowing the shades of dusk to merge with the grainy textured walls of the mind until I became part of the obscurity. *Mens rea, actus reus.* Criminal and executioner. It was all the same. I was laying out a path, and it would lead me to an end, but an end of my own choosing. I was the solo architect of winding up Ecce Fingon, what more do you want out of life, or death for that matter? And my executioner and progeny, deprived even of the meagre consolation of having conceived the conditions of my demise. So, sorry, nothing left for you, no executioner's song. Acting the crime out is inevitable, and I am ready to pay the consequences, whether life-affirming or life-ending. It was a form of peace of mind.

from: "Henri Chauvin" <Henri.Chauvin@mnhn.fr>
Sent: Wednesday, June 17, 2009 10:04 AM
To: "Jack Fingon" <sargassosea@hotmail.com>
Subject: Re: Mer de Sargasse

Bonjour,

As it so happens, I have made some progress on the subject matter with an English laboratory. Technically, they think it's possible to deposit the ashes inside an "internal beacon" which will cost considerably less. These "beacons" are transported by the eels until their death and then released, at which time they rise up to the surface and go into drift.

For the moment, information gathered allows us to state that solely 15 per cent of eels leaving from Europe succeed in arriving in the Sargasso Sea. It would therefore be necessary to divide up the ashes, a few grams per eel, in at least 20 beacons (and thus eels), if we intend on having a good probability of success.

The sole remaining problem to resolve is that of moral feasibility. The colleagues who manufacture these beacons have to accept the work (handling of ashes, etc.).

There also remains the issue of communication around the project ... Is it necessary to remain discreet, or should it be mediatised? Based upon your desires in this regard, the reactions of scientists involved risks being slightly variable.

In any event, if everything is accepted, we will have to come to a decision rapidly, since the manufacture of the beacons has to be contemplated prior to the end of the summer.

I will be in Dinard towards the end of July, and we can schedule a meeting then.

Bien cordialement,
Henri Chauvin

VI

The Moelan-sur-Mer cemetery had a tribute to men lost at sea and another to any locals who had been caught up in the first war. Back at Villa Nem Dihan, I gazed out over the sea, trying to calculate the odds of return of a Blenheim reconnaissance aircraft flying 50 feet over the North Sea coming in to harass German shipping amidst a barrage of anti-aircraft fire.

The judge had been an aviator, as had three of his brothers and, between the lot, they had collected three DFCs and two bars as well as a slew of other medals. They were all members of the legendary 400 level squadrons of the RCAF, merged into the RAF during the second war and universally admired for their cool courage during a time when the Nazi juggernaut looked invincible. I looked down at some old wartime issues of the *London Gazette* celebrating the feats of the "flying Fingons." One of them was Uncle Archie's DFC citation, reported in the *Gazette* on April 21, 1944:

First tour was ops from 5 June to October 1943, 28 trips (186 hours 15 minutes), all but one sortie in the Mediterranean. Second tour was, when recommended, 18 trips (92 hours 45 minutes), 18 August to 16 October 1944. Since the award of the Distinguished Flying Cross, Flight Lieutenant Fingon has completed many more successful sorties against targets in Germany and enemy occupied territory. His work has been of an excellent standard and his ability to make instant decisions in emergencies together with his skilful pilotage and cool judgment have been an inspiration to his crew. He has displayed fine qualities of skill and leadership. His courage and devotion to duty are worthy of high praise.

The other citations, four in all to the flying Fingons, spoke of "pressing home telling attacks, despite being hit by very heavy anti-aircraft fire," "dogged determination," "skill, fortitude and devotion to duty" and for each of them, fearlessness.

I had met these same men under far different circumstances. They were my father and his brothers. Men who stood around and joked at the family barbecue, each of them sporting clipped aviator moustaches, slicked-back hair and drop-dead beautiful wives, drinking Scotch whisky while they told stories about everything except the war. Uncle Archie, DFC and Bar, was the sole brother who referred to the conflict, but he had been brought home to recruit new pilots, so he had the casual charm of the seasoned public speaker. His anecdotes were many and well-rehearsed, recounting the personalities of the men on his crews, of his parachutes and of aircraft and equipment being sabotaged by the Arabs, who sympathised with the Germans, or of his slight physique.

During one of those endless summer evenings in the backyard, Archie had been expounding on his favourite topic, his slight physical appearance, how he was mistaken at times for a hat rack. Or that he was once saved from drowning when someone tossed him a Cheerio. Or that he was so skinny he had to run around the shower to get wet. The whisky and beer always flowed freely at Fingon gatherings, and the boys in the family grabbed onto any snippets of these stories available and, when nobody was looking, we managed to get some of the whisky as well. We were in our early teens, and Archie held us spellbound. But I had spotted that he managed to deflect any talk of the war by recounting his continuous narratives without disclosing anything of himself. So I interrupted him.

"But Archie, what do you figure were the odds of you coming back alive from your sorties?"

"The odds were good," he responded, his eyes brightening. "They were far better than the odds of not making it."

"How good is good?" I asked.

"Oh, you had a 75 to 80 percent chance of returning to base with your shirt still pressed."

I considered that for a moment.

"The only problem is, you had to fly more than one sortie during the war."

"If your number's up, you only fly one, and back to you, nephew."

"So by that calculation, you were technically toast after five sorties."

"Close, but those statistics aren't very useful on the eve of a mission."

"I don't understand. How could you do it?"

"Well," he said, his right eye slightly bugging as it did whenever he had more than a couple of drinks in his skeletal 115-pound frame, "the principal reason we could climb in the cockpit and taxi down the runway for another round of that shit"—and here Archie would slow down and elongate his utterance of the word shit as shi-i-i-i-it—"is because, boys, we were schtoopid. And, as for the shi-i-i-i-it"—and here his right eye seemed ready to pop out of its socket—"we were swimming in it day and night."

Later in the evening, I spotted Uncle Archie lying back in a lawn chair, looking up at the 500-year-old Douglas firs towering over our gathering, and I approached him. He noticed me, smiled and waved me over.

"Come here. I want a word with you."

Archie was usually drunk after four beers, but his voice never lost its sharp edge.

"I want you to do something for yourself, nephew."

"Sure, uncle."

"Stop thinking of your father as the enemy. He's not."

"I never said he was."

"Well, I'm telling you he's not. You don't yet know the meaning of the word enemy."

"Sure, uncle."

He bristled, and so did I. It was always hard to tell with my father or my uncles whether they were amused or angry, but I also had Fingon blood and knew Archie recognised the flush of anger in my face.

"That's too easy, boy. I want you to go over and shake his hand."

Shaking the old man's hand was no problem per se. And whatever anybody thought, he wasn't any enemy for me. But I wanted something in return for the gesture. "All right, fair enough, I'll go over and shake his hand, but only if you tell me what the war was like. And no bullshit, Uncle."

"Tell you something. I wasn't bad as a pilot, but unfortunately, I was very good, too good, at convincing young men to go overseas to get their asses blown to hell. The fact is only one man has ever told the tale properly who I know of, and he was talking about the first war, not ours. Canadian fellow named Owen. Infantry."

"What did he say?"

"Look it up. 'Dulce et decorum est/pro patria mori.' Between you and me, those few words expose all the bullshit we bought into when we went abroad. I'm telling you, boy, we were schtoopid!" His eyes fierce, bulging out of their orbit, roving towards my father on the far side of the backyard. "Get over here, Gus! Your son wants to shake your hand!"

The next day I walked up to the library and asked for the poem titled "Dulce et Decorum Est," a title Owen had borrowed from an ode by the renowned Roman poet Horace of antiquity, glorifying the concept of dying for one's country. A gas attack is a strange subject for a poem. This is how it went:

Bent double, like old beggars under sacks,
Knock-kneed, coughing like hags, we cursed through sludge,
Till on the haunting flares we turned our backs
And towards our distant rest began to trudge.
Men marched asleep. Many had lost their boots
But limped on, blood-shod. All went lame; all blind;
Drunk with fatigue; deaf even to the hoots
Of tired, outstripped Five-Nines that dropped behind.

GAS! Gas! Quick, boys!—An ecstasy of fumbling,
Fitting the clumsy helmets just in time;
But someone still was yelling out and stumbling,
And floundering like a man in fire or lime ...
Dim, through the misty panes and thick green light,
As under a green sea, I saw him drowning.

In all my dreams, before my helpless sight,
He plunges at me, guttering, choking, drowning.

If in some smothering dreams you too could pace
Behind the wagon that we flung him in,
And watch the white eyes writhing in his face,
His hanging face, like a devil's sick of sin;
If you could hear, at every jolt, the blood
Come gargling from the froth-corrupted lungs,
Obscene as cancer, bitter as the cud
Of vile, incurable sores on innocent tongues,
My friend, you would not tell with such high zest

> To children ardent for some desperate glory,
> The old Lie: Dulce et decorum est
> Pro patria mori.

Out on the cliffs of Bretagne, the world wars had long been concluded and would soon be all but forgotten. Those who had saved the world for democracy and those who had fought to defend tyranny all reached the same destination. In the end, every member of the 400 squadrons went the way of the evil men they had defeated. Outside of a few remaining survivors, every resistance fighter and collaborator, civilian and soldier, was now in another place, or they were nowhere. But behind their tales and the horror of Hitler and the holocaust and all the rest, it struck me that the biggest casualty was the First World War. Nobody remembered what had happened to the millions who had died, and even if we recalled, not even the experts had a clue why that first conflagration had even taken place. No one wanted to know. We all wanted to forget the reason we walked free.

I stared down into the pit of Brigneau cove, recalling a letter by Cendrars complaining that *Moravagine*, his tale against the senseless tyranny of modernity, revolutions and psychology, had been virtually ignored by the world. The world doesn't want to hear truth from a man with one arm. A man with one arm can play the buffoon. The crowds will cheer raucously if he performs in a circus or if they decide he's an artful liar. So much the better. But if such a man begins to claim that what he utters is nothing but the truth, he will be met with either deafening silence or with cawing and hooting, or with derision. Because the last thing the world wants of such a man is to hear what he has to say. And such a man is doomed to finish his life alone. The world cannot love a man without illusions. But if the man has greatness within, he can forgive the world and love it as it is.

VII

The sea also seemed to exercise a gravity of its own, both lunar and submarine. The judge was now visiting me during my solitary nocturnal musings and reviewing together my lifetime of misdemeanours and indictable crimes. He presided over the hearing, but I acted as jailer, sneering prosecutor, jury, prisoner in the dock and executioner. He was handsome, dignified, wore the black robe and scarlet sash of the supreme court with a consummate awareness that his duty was to a transcendent law: the *lex aeterna* of Aquinas, which superseded anything mere man could scrawl onto a tablet.

"You surely didn't harbour the illusion that you would escape the jurisdiction of this court on the ground that death brings you outside the statute of limitations?"

"I hadn't really thought about it."

"What plea do you enter to the charge of dilettantism?"

"No contest."

"And to the second charge of corrupting the minds of the young?"

"Not guilty."

"And to the third charge of harassing and tormenting the daughter of the poet soldier Sauser?"

"I plead no contest."

"Right."

The measure of a barrister in the courtroom was the ability to use one word repeatedly, uttered as a deceptively soft-spoken mantra designed to peel away the untruths and penetrate down to the marrow of a man. For my father, that word was *right*.

"What right do you have to torment a woman who only wishes to preserve the legacy of a worthless man who left her an orphan?"

"The right to expose the truth as I see it."

"Right. Would you not agree, Fingon, that the most abject of humans has his own version of the truth?"

"That's my whole point."

"I haven't finished, Mr. Fingon. You'll have opportunity to present full answer and defence. How is the public interest served by your endeavours?"

"This isn't about the public interest."

"Indeed. If you feel such a compulsion to air your views, wouldn't the letters to the editor section of the local paper be the appropriate forum?"

"I feel compelled to say a little more than that."

"Well, that may be the one point which we agree upon, Mr. Fingon. Now, allow me to draw your attention to the transcript of an examination for discovery dated January 21, 1961."

"The date of Cendrars' death."

"Right. Are you asking the Court to serve a third-party notice on Mr. Cendrars?"

My shoulders sagged. More than any man, more even than God himself, the judge could reduce me to crumbling remains. A punch in the face would have been easier than his withering gaze. Violence is a mercy; disappointment uses love as a weapon to unmettle a man. "May I enter a guilty plea?"

The judge allowed himself the trace of a smile. "We are all of us guilty. The crime lives within us all and awaits only the circumstances to be acted out. *Actus reus* is the original stain, the playing it out only awaits our brief appearance on life's stage. But it is inevitable, and it is universal."

"Why didn't you tell me that during your lifetime?"

"It wouldn't have done you any good."

"You're right."

"Yes, of course I'm right, but not for the reasons you think."

Low tide, the rocks stretched out into a jagged gully. Each crevice descending into a corner of the inferno reserved for a specific subset of the damned. Already, the previous evening, for the first time, she had appeared alongside him in a dream, the two of them taunting figures engaged in a macabre, incestuous dance. What had begun as an inquiry into a poetic quatrain had lured me into the cursed, totemic universe of Cendrars, who had been playing with forces far beyond his control, and then died before he could warn others of their unpredictable patterns. Whatever I was, wherever I was, it was closer to voodoo and necromancy than the literary salons, and I could feel it dragging me further and further downwards.

VIII

"*Tu es plus belle que le ciel et la mer*" is a vagabond hymn of rare beauty, a paradox which describes abandoning the apparent security of the family to embrace the larger world. It is first and foremost addressed to men from a man who followed the principle to its logical extreme. It is the exemplification of the French expression "*d'aller jusqu'au bout des choses*," which is core to the French mindset.

But the experts say it was written for Raymone. Seeing the photo of Raymone Duchateau inside her room doing her make-up at Louis Jouvet's theatre is a real shock for a Cendrars lover. How could this insipid bird who looks like a denizen of a nunnery have excited the great Cendrars' passions? What was the attraction? Francesco claimed it was a *mariage blanc*. Whatever. "*Quand tu aimes il faut quitter*" is much more than a love poem; it is an explanation, a eulogy, an apology, a koan, which should be paired up with Cendrars' statement in Panama, "*l'aventure de mes sept oncles*: 'Je tourne dans la cage des méridiens comme un écureuil dans la sienne.'"

And where did all this spinning in the cage of the meridians land Cendrars—"*confiné à l'étage de la maison de la rue Jean Dolent,*" paralysed, and the holy bird, Raymone Duchateau chirping novenas at his side. His body, at that point flotsam, waiting under the constellation Orion for the great departure, for a trip that even Cendrars had no way of intimating, and yet one which awaits every single one of us, whether we spend our lives accumulating treasury bonds or accumulating experience or raising pigs or racing automobiles. And when you lay waiting for the final departure, Blaise Cendrars, did you call for God, or for Féla, or for Henry Miller? No, you called for a woman whom you had left behind for 17 years and who imagined as a child that she would stretch a rope across the Piazza del Baiardo, her village, from the roof of one house to the house opposite, and that, at the very moment of your arrival, she would dance while balancing on the rope to astonish and seduce her father, the poet vagabond.

IX

I had spent the entire day examining a photo of Cendrars and Léger which frames the two men engaged in intense discussion, as I imagined it, over the relative merits of painting vs. poetry, its similarities, the elements of painting that could be emulated in poetry, the question as to whether the poet uses similar tools to capture form, colour, shade. Or possibly Léger would borrow from the poet's lexicon, such as when he spoke of painting in slang or of using flat areas of colour to create the impression of advancing or receding.

Two men, indifferent to the advance of time on their own bodies and minds, still following the light from beyond, following their instincts ruthlessly, single-mindedly tracking that which is the prey of the artist, using craft as a sort of lens to capture the elusive glimpse of the infinite which they sense more strongly than the common man. I wondered again about the intent behind the quatrain. When a man says he wants to disappear anonymously and then publishes the wish in his most famous work, does he really want to disappear anonymously?

What is a writer, after all? A writer exposes himself publicly; he doesn't seek anonymity. A writer uses an ancient trick to desecrate, to de-consecrate, to unhallow a sacred ordinance. The writer's place is on the stake. A writer is a scapegoat, a public sacrifice to expiate the sins of the body politic. A writer might talk about anonymity, but the intent lies elsewhere. A man who joins the Foreign Legion and drives a Bentley might be looking for a lot of things, but anonymity isn't one of them. And when the daughter pleads anonymity while collecting royalties on his collected works, is the desire anonymity?

Towards the end of the afternoon, I set off on my daily walk alone towards a particular set of menhir stones standing alone in a field nearby. The touch of the stones was cold and eerie and triggered atavistic, inarticulate reactions within that couldn't be characterised as meditation or reflection. More the presence of something undefined, a tumorous mass with a life of its own.

After my walk, I returned to the terrace on Brigneau cove, and we watched the evening descend upon us and the stars become gradually visible in the sky and then form into discernible constellations. During these crepuscular transitions, we said very little. We had first come to observe but now were becoming part of the landscape.

"He's up there, Carmen. In Orion. Cendrars sees all of this. Or the spirit of Cendrars."

Carmen remained silent.

"Tell me, Carmen, in Madagascar, do they believe you can choose your ancestors?"

"Of course. They marry into families to improve their ancestry. That's what Ravalovna did."

She had learned to walk as a Betsileo. Her posture shorn of the arrogance of Western woman, she moved through space and time with apparent submission, but the submission was not to man, but to other, supernatural forces. To the ancestors, I supposed.

"That's what Celestine Cendrars has done. Blaise Cendrars re-created himself. And then she created her ancestry."

"What do you mean by that?"

"What I mean is that I'm the only person who wants to fulfil Blaise Cendrars' last wish."

"Have you considered they might try to stop you?"

"I've given it some thought," I said, but I didn't want to discuss it.

"Do you think it's your business?"

"What I believe or don't believe is not relevant."

"I understand what you mean. But don't forget what I said about *fady*."

While seated alone out on the cliff, I felt the presence of the menhir stones a couple of hundred metres away pulling at my insides. The attraction was the same force that had drawn me towards Chartres, Paris, Compostella, Staffa Island, Iona and Fingon's Cave. I operated at the lower end of the spectrum of life, obscure, unknown, governed by the magnetic fields of attraction and intuition. I de-hallowed and sullied everything I came into contact with.

X

We moved back to Noordwijk aan Zee after our four-month hiatus in Bretagne, returning home to the polder empty-handed and not even wiser for the experience. Freed of the yoke of Cendrars, I began to enjoy my life in Noordwijk aan Zee. During our walks at oceanside, I carried on monologues about Cendrars and Cendrars' points of reference, particularly his investigations into the levitating saints—St. Teresa of Avila and St. Joseph of Cupertino—and his reportages, but the theme I most often returned to was that of separation.

The only thing of note during this period of utter serenity was the curious invasion of eels into my dreams. Eels swimming up estuaries and fjords. Elvers wriggling into my ears, seeping through the pores, penetrating the bloodstream, the airways, the conductors, viaducts and ventilators of the body. Eels corrupting the organs, creating new mutant gonads, and triggering reproduction and death in stagnant waters. Eels into the deep fat, wading into the

Venus fly trap folds of the ischio-rectal zones and obliterating their indigo-coloured integument. Eels, making no distinctions, provided the cavity is deep and hidden, until they swim higher, through Meckel's Diverticulum, racing up the ascending colon, lodging in the Eustachian valve, and spawning life, while destroying the host body. I awakened from these dreams often under the mistaken belief that I had transformed into an unguent eel, stripped of its pectoral fins, and wallowing in pre-gonadal stasis.

PART IV
Mare Sargassum

From the EXTRAITS des Bulletins de l'ASMAC (Association du Souvenir aux Morts des Armées de Champagne)

In July 1915, General Joffre decided to launch two broad offensives on the same day, in Artois and in Champagne, in order to split the German front by spearheading an attack straight through its centre. The Champagne action would take place between Auberive sur Suippe in Marne department and the Aisne River. The intended target was the Vouziers-Sedan region. The Régiments Etrangers (Foreign Legions) would attack just East of the Souain-Sommepy route, onto a glacis of stunted low-growth forest, rising gradually up to a crest bounded on one side by Navarin farm and on the other by the Souain Butte. This zone was defended by a labyrinthine network of trenches and barbed wire and fortified by a massive build-up of automatic arms, in turn reinforced by heavy artillery.

The French artillery launched a pre-attack to soften up enemy positions on September 22 and continued right through September 25. In order to allow aviation to pinpoint and target enemy positions without causing friendly fire incidents, the initial waves of infantry were instructed to sew square patches of white material onto the back of their caps. This innovation proved futile on the day, as on the morning of the attack on the 25th, a wall of rain and a dense fog hung over the battle zone. As described in military reports on events (JMO du 2ième RM: 2ième RE), the colonial regiments would pour out of the trenches at 0915, and advance towards enemy defence positions in a "superbe élan". The legionnaires would assume the positions just abandoned by the French marines known as "marsouins". The initial mission called for them to stand ready to intervene and if necessary push forward as far as Sommepy.

In one hour, the colonials seized the entire forward German position, but in doing so they had already exhausted their forces prior to reaching the second objective which remained intact, just on the outskirts of Navarin farm. Towards 1030, a series of explosions just north of the buildings forced them to ground. French support artillery had failed to reach its intended targets. Poor weather and smoke prevented gunners from spotting targets which forced them to resort to a longer firing trajectory. Liaison officers who hadn't been killed or injured found themselves cut off from their command base. Communication trenches throughout were a slick of mud, but now being overrun by troops, wounded and prisoners all criss-crossing each other under the fire of German artillery who were now unleashing relentless barrages of exploding shells or gas onto the position they had just lost.

On September 28, 1915, the brigade received the mission to take Woods P-16, P-17 and P-18, marked out by the Kultur trench on the ridge joining Navarin farm with the Souain butte. At 1300, elements of the 2ième RM/1er RE moved from Wood C7 to Woods U22 and U25. To the left, the 3rd and 4th companies infiltrated into UZ Wood, notwithstanding repeated and heavy machine-gun fire. Several groups cut their way through a section of barb wire and leapt into Kultur trench heading towards P16. They were immediately peppered with machine-gun fire at point blank range. A barrage of hand grenades followed, and the task of widening the breach quickly proved impossible. A fierce firefight had broken out, both companies attempting to force the passage. A number of legionnaires infiltrated under the barbed wire, only to be wiped out by machine-gun fire. Fougasse mines exploded just short of the trench, carving out deep craters and tearing bodies to shreds. From the initial momentum, the day was now a full debacle. German guns wiped out any survivors left in the trenches, as well as those who had vainly attempted to rejoin them in support.

At the end of the afternoon, all hope was lost and the survivors of the 3rd and 4th companies fell back onto Wood U2 where they camped down until night, alongside the survivors of second company, covered by the company of machine-gunners positioned at

Wood U22 who were having some success in repelling counter attacks being conducted against the remainder of battalion B. In the right column formed by battalion A, the two head companies emerged by successive waves from Wood U25 under a rain of machine-gun fire. Virtually all officers and most of the non-commissioned officers were killed or wounded.

The remainder of the battalion fell back onto the north edge of Wood U25 where they held their ground as best as they could under the incessant bombardment of enemy artillery. At 2200, the decimated regiment received the order to return to their forward base in Wood C7. Of the 43 officers, 1960 non-commissioned officers and legionnaires, the regiment lost 20 officers and 809 non-commissioned officers and legionnaires during the morning of September 28, 1915. Among the wounded was a certain caporal Sauser Frédéric, volunteer with the 1er Régiment Etranger of the Foreign Legion, soon to become known to the world under his reincarnation as the poet Blaise Cendrars.

1

An oceanic obsidian mass of *Anguilla anguilla*, drifting out of the entropic currents of Mare Sargassum into the great North Equatorial Current eastward, floating in a stream thicker than ink, drifting, drifting, and then splitting where the North Atlantic Gyre forks northward to Iceland. Finally invading every fjord, river, estuary, belt, gut, sound and armlet of ancient Europe. Floating past the refugees at Calais, the gamblers of Deauville, the dead fishing villages of Honfleur, the jumping-off point of William the Conqueror at Barfleur, Jacques Cartier's port of St. Malo, the racing vessels in port at the fort city of Concarneau, the topless bathers at la Baule, the potters of Quimper, and covering the continent like a shroud, unnoticed by the politicians, the defence committees, the militiamen, the Institut Pasteur, the anti-pornographers.

We are seated on her terrace in Kerliou on the Brittany coast, gazing over a misty field covered with menhir stones, the outposts of Stonehenge randomly scattered over the hills and coves of

Brittany. She is holding a forged artisanal instrument in the air with a firm, sure grip, looking at me through sunglasses. Can she see me? I am thinking back to the day her father saved my life. And to another time, a grainy Kodak 1937 photo, the first day she met her father at 12 avenue de Montaigne.

"This is a *fouêsne*—used to capture eels by local fishermen."

The glare of the sun flattens out the pastel tones of the terrace. We are in Liguria somewhere. A young daughter of a woman named Féla is sitting on a wall overlooking a path in the village of Baiardo, dreaming of the day her father will finally come and see her.

Her eyes are Oriental, mulatto, untraceable. Her cheek bones high Mongolian. She is standing in the Big Sur desert with Henry Miller in front of his shack. The eels are flooding through my pores into the estuaries, arteries, veins and into the brain, infecting the cerebral passages and airways. Mare Sargassum within. The abyssal plain. The centre not holding. Across the limitless, turquoise expanse of the North Sea, a one-armed man is dropping a fathom into the sea. He's saying something! What are you saying, old man, speak!

"Take me to my place of repose."

The daughter's voice interrupting, pulling me back inside Villa Cendrars. "When I found this, I still hadn't met you, It was only later ... I purchased it from an antiquarian."

I am back in Villa Cendrars, trapped inside an aquarium in Celestine Cendrars' sunken mezzanine living room. I can make out a small sign on the aquarium wall: *Anguilla canadiensis. Loire River estuary.* June Miller wanders through with her dyke girlfriend Stasia. They disappear out the glass sliding doors for the beach, arm-in-arm. Tommy Bayou is casually discussing what to do with me.

"There's a real market for eel purses, money pouches and the like, mother. Let's just skin him alive."

The old woman smiles, caressing the rusted metal prongs of the *fouêsne* as if conjuring up a succubus. Someone is feeding thousands of eels into apertures near the top of the aquarium. I try to bang against the resonating glass walls but look down to see my hands and arms have shrunk into miniature dorsal and pectoral fins, and now more *Anguilla anguilla* are rapidly filling up my cage to join me. Nothing is audible, the rush of eels increasing in thundering cadence.

The old woman has been swept out onto the North Sea, still strapped to her chair.

I am an indistinguishable part of this mass of pitted, black sentient beings. Some have expired, others push relentlessly forward, their own lives an offering to save the species. The aquarium overflows, and the eels fill Villa Cendrars, then teem out onto the beach until the entire coast is darkened under the afternoon sky. A low, faintly discernible voice is speaking in an ancient dialect— Breton? Russian? Maria Alvares' nipples pulsating through her strapped, transparent tulle blouse. She finally speaks, but the voice is that of the old woman. "It doesn't matter whether it's an eel skin purse or wallet or suitcase. What counts is craft, not the material!"

I spot a reflection of myself: thick lips, inset eyes, scaly skin, sharp teeth. A young, feral-looking brat is pushing his nose up against the glass, making faces at me, sticking his tongue out in disgust. A thought crosses my catadromous mind. "So this is what I am."

Carmen is carrying a tray of Darjeeling tea, now assuming the role of deferential waitress. All the women are now dressed in peach-coloured maternity nightgowns, semi-transparent, floating through the room, while the voice of de Villiers sings:

In the room the women come and go
Talking of Michelangelo

My fins have receded. A fatty coat covers my elongating, slithering form, my spinal column now 700 vertebrae being played like a piano by Salvador Dali, and on each of the bony protrusions the head of Vladimir Ilyich Lenin, father of the Russian revolution, is singing in a brassy ragtime voice:

Hello, my baby
Hello, my honey
Hello, my ragtime gal

Send me a kiss by wire
Baby, my heart's on fire

If you refuse me
Honey, you'll lose me
Then you'll be left alone

Oh baby, telephone
And tell me I'm your own

Through the aquarium glass, I spot Celestine Cendrars surfing outside Villa Cendrars on a tsunami sweeping in from the Atlantic. She is wearing a white polka dot on blue bikini, circa 1952. Celestine Cendrars spots me, smiles and waves.

"So long, sucker," she shouts joyfully, spraying algae-infested Sargasso Sea entropic surf into the villa.

Maria Alvares is seated on the beach, spreading her legs from beneath her peasant dress. Beneath, a vast cavernous retreat stretches from Nevez to Port Manech: two bulbous vulva standing as sentries to the cave, and the inner passage a 6000-km vagina leading down to the Nares Abyssal Plain. The eels are swimming into her cunt, gonads sprouting out of the males as they advance towards the nexus of reproduction and oblivion.

I stare into a thick fog, which gradually breaks, and through the mist I can make out the silhouette of Carmen. She is holding a vaporiser. I finally emerge from my dream, where I have transformed into an unguent snakelike fish, stripped of its pectoral fins, wallowing in pregonadal stasis.

"I'm going to burn down Villa Cendrars. They're sucking out my vitality, Carmen. We are mutually exclusive species. I am going to burn down Villa Cendrars and toss every last one of them into sea."

"Let's go back to the house and forget about these people."

11

Three years passed and little in them that was worth saving. Money dried up, not overnight, but because this plan had moved into the attrition phase, and without being active, had depleted my reserves of enthusiasm for other endeavours—the ordinary things that provide normal human beings with the solace necessary to continue their mundane lives. My pact, unexpressed, was now unspoken, driven only by the idea that the mission of delivering Cendrars' ashes had somehow to be accomplished.

During my long walks along the windy shoreline of Nordwijk aan Zee, I'd gained some measure of calm, tempered by dissatisfaction, and a sense of incompletion unrelated to the ashes. I began a personal inquiry into the life of St. Joseph of Cupertino, the levitating saint, hero of aviators and focus of a book by Cendrars titled *Le Lotissement du Ciel* or *The Subdivision of the Heavens*. Cendrars weaves an extraordinary tapestry in this biographical set of templates around the themes of aviation and the levitation of Christian saints. A mystical subsect of Christians known as Bollandists referred to levitation as ecstatic flight, or corporeal ravishment brought on by a soul consumed by piety and love of God.

Using his techniques of matter-of-fact reportage, he makes the fantastical notion of levitation inspired by "the fire of divine love" almost believable. Cendrars' examination of Cupertino was presented in vignettes referring back to his own traumas and the premature death of his aviator son, Rémy. I began once again to think of the ashes, of completing this mission of vesting it with something, a tribute. Anything. Money was no longer possible. I had lost credibility, my name was shit in all quarters. EDL, Francesco, had something to propose, but they were also wary. I'd gone rogue, and hadn't made it back in from the cold.

Prague beckoned. Lisbon beckoned. Venice, Florence, the Parthenon, St. Petersburg—opportunities to rewrite Cendrars, to outdo him, to write a dozen novels, and I was going to a soggy corner of incestuous Brittany, where an old lady held court over a worshipping array of about the last five people still involved in promoting the cause of Freddie Sauser, aka Blaise Cendrars, the one-armed poet, to stuff his remains inside the belly of an eel and ship them off to the Sargasso Sea. We left on a rainy, cold Friday morning and drove south under a cloud of our own.

III

Once, on Christmas eve, when Joseph Cupertino heard the sound of bagpipes and flutes played by shepherds whom he had invited to celebrate with him the birth of the Heavenly Child, he began to dance because of excessive joy, and with a sob and a loud cry, flew as a bird through the air from the middle of the church to the high altar, a distance of almost forty feet [Più di cinquè canne].
—Acta Sanctorum

*I*n *Sky*, Cendrars refers to a "voluminous and anonymous old tome" recounting an unknown version of the life of St. Joseph of Cupertino. Cendrars had first discovered the tome in the basement of a fort on the Maginot Line during the First World War. He describes it as "an old, tattered book (now reduced to ashes), a voluminous work of documentation, written in Italian, printed in Padua (probably around 1860), in large Epinal script, such a blessing for the weak eyes of old women, and for the illiterate." Inside the old tome were seven crudely-coloured wood engravings illustrating the story of the levitating saint.

Twenty-five years after his discovery, Cendrars was an accredited war reporter assigned to the British Expeditionary Force in Amiens, and still lugging his life of the saint with him wherever he went. During the evening of May 13, 1940, however, and with the German juggernaut fast advancing, orders were given for any baggage cluttering the British Expeditionary Forces' trucks to be burned, and for GHQ to immediately abandon Amiens. As fate had it, Cendrars' tome was part of that baggage. Cendrars was sent to rejoin the staff of the AASF (the Advanced Fighting Forces of the RAF), and while "driving like a bat out of hell down a little road along the banks of the Aisne," he miraculously encountered his aviator son Rémy and his flight crew, only one day prior to Rémy being shot down behind German lines.

Cendrars' chronicle of the helter-skelter month when France was brought to its knees "once and for all!"—a memory which he characterises as "vivid and bleeding"—is in fact sketched out in a few staccato lines. But the memory of seven old woodcuts inserted in his lost tome, "for the distraction of idiots and to convert unbelievers" brings him to a halt, and his narrative pauses to trace out the visual details of the life of St. Joseph of Cupertino in miniaturist detail:

> **FIRST IMAGE**—It must have been a portrait of the saint. Bearded.
> **SECOND IMAGE**—Brother Joseph setting out on the high road to Bologna. He is walking in such a weird manner that people are pointing at him. Peasants in the fields are laughing at him. Some are throwing stones.
> **THIRD IMAGE**—The further he goes, the more conspicuous his unusual gait becomes. Women stare after him, follow him in his footsteps. Brother Joseph appears to be gliding, and when they see that *his feet are not touching the ground*, but move on without effort, his sandals leaving no trace, no footprint in the dust on the road and that he walks miraculously, like Christ on the waters of Galilee, the women begin crying out that it is a miracle.
> **FOURTH IMAGE**—a whole series of little scenes in which the saint is rising higher and higher, soaring above the ever increasing crowd gathering in his wake.

FIFTH IMAGE—In the university lecture hall. Brother Joseph, perched like a bird on the extreme edge of the examiner's desk, where he is balancing precariously on his knees.
SIXTH IMAGE—Rome. Brother Joseph floating just beneath the vaulted ceiling of St. Peter's, to the utter stupefaction of the prelates who are standing around a personage labeled: URBAN VIII.
SEVENTH IMAGE—Partly torn off. Portrait of another bearded man.

Here, a brief digression on Raymone, which nevertheless also provides a key. When one first discovers Raymone through Cendrars' poem—the greatest poem of vagabond love ever written by a man—"*Tu es plus belle que le ciel et la mer*"—the mind's eye sees Boticelli or Puvis de Chavannes or Degas:

Quand tu aimes il faut partir
Quitte ta femme quitte ton enfant
Quitte ton ami quitte ton amie
Quitte ton amante quitte ton amant
Quand tu aimes il faut partir

It came as a surprise and a disappointment when I first saw a photo of the real life Raymone, the actress in Louis Jouvet's troupe who was the love of his life and inspired the poem. An aquiline nose, plaintive eyes, a grimly set mouth over a square chin. All in all, a face more fitting for a convent than to inspire a man to renounce everything he owns. When I learned from Francesco that their relationship was platonic, it made even less sense.

But then there was the voice, and Cendrars himself had referred to it, and a woman's voice—particularly some of those French sopranos—have a way of blindsiding you and tethering the soul. Not to mention other parts of the body. But, visually, something evanescent, ephemeral and flight-like about the woman herself.

There is a line running through the work and life of Cendrars, one linked to his vagabond soul—that of *ekstasis,* or when he talks of the levitators, ravishment. Whether this is the body through wine or vagabonding, the soul through ravishment, or the senses through Raymone's twittering theatrical soprano, Cendrars is yielding to the desire to be transported to a higher realm. Here is a quote he cites from St. Teresa of Avila in *Sky*:

> In these ravishments, the soul no longer seems to cleave to the body ... Giving you no time to think, or to prepare yourself, this often falls upon you with such swift and forceful impetuosity that you actually see and feel this cloud that seizes hold of you and this powerful eagle that carries you off on his wings.

This fascination with the nature of levitation can be compared with his own flight from the prison of his family home in Neuchatel, described in *Bourlinguer*:

> I was never governed by a fixed plan, and still less by any act of will. When I climbed out the window of my bedroom, I was like a somnambulist, and that's probably half the reason I didn't break my neck...that was the first time that I *obeyed* this need for evasion which has so often taken control of my senses and pushed me into the wildest eccentricities, which hit me like sudden, reflexive attacks. I was always ready to risk everything, even death, and I generally came out of it absolutely gutted, but in a state of *ravishment,* wallowing in the absurdity of it all, whether I was cornered with my back against the wall, or in full flight, but regretting nothing, missing nobody, and always extraordinarily satisfied that I had once again *sacrificed* everything, while having a private laugh at my own expense. Although at times, I had the intoxicating sensation of being utterly lost, at others, I felt that I was on the verge of discovering

a new world, or that I was reborn out of my ashes, but always, always I experienced pleasure and amazement at my naive and inextinguishable belief in life.

This passage, which represents the quintessence of Cendrars' contemplative, vagabond spirit, is written out in hand and taped to my desk. I have used it throughout my life as an adult—to leave everything and everyone who fettered my happiness, obeying my own impulses for evasion. When I up and left everyone—my wife, my job, my friends—to move to China, once again there you were, Blaise Cendrars, my only breaker against a tide of second-guessers who portrayed me as an idiot. And when I was in an impasse with no solution, you gave me the strength to sacrifice everything and to see myself as nothing in the big picture.

IV

I have a passion for secrecy. For me, one of the great charms of the legion is that you can sign on under a false name and the incognito is respected.
—Blaise Cendrars

*M*aria Alvares emerged from her Renault wearing a schoolgirlish rose-coloured drop-waist crêpe dress over black panty hose and heels. She brushed a few tousled strands of rippled, ebony hair out of her eyes as she approached, revealing a set of faux-pearl drop earrings. Her face was slightly flushed as if she were short of breath. She spoke in a quick, confidential clip.

"Would you object to us discussing something *entre nous*?"

"Let's walk around to the cliffs, cove side. We can talk there."

She picked up the conversation again as we arrived at the end of the road, briefly glancing around to look back at Villa Nem Dihan.

"I want you to leave her alone."

"Leave who alone?"

"Celestine. She's an old woman."

"Shouldn't I be saying this to you?"

"I'm working for her now."

"You mean to say you're working *her* for now?"

"We are both following the same thing. The ashes."

"All right, fair enough, let's talk. You're on the inside. Do you know where she's stashed the ashes?"

"Why would I tell you?"

"Because I got something to spread around you need even more. You're a hustler, and so you're reaching the outer limits of what your brain can handle."

"Try me."

"Let's go for goal here, all right? If you can arrange for the ashes —or even some of them—to come my way, I can see a finders' fee being in order."

"I don't know. Blaise Cendrars is an institution."

"Seventy-five grand is what I'm thinking. Half up front, half on delivery."

Now it was her turn to laugh.

"Listen here, *mec*. I'm the one putting up with this *vieille salope* and her noble fucking devotion to her dead so-called father, not you. You know nothing about indignity, my friend."

"Name the price for your indignity."

She smiled. So much for weaving and papal visits.

"Two hundred grand. Plus 1 per cent royalty across the board. And, tell you what. If you decline, here's what happens, and any Alfama puta could read the future better than you, my friend. Next year, you're going to see a Netflix special called "One-armed poet" about somebody named Burnt Ashes, only he'll be American, and your story will go the way of the dodo bird, and not a cent to show for your troubles."

"Wrong question again. What are you willing to do to make sure he gets to the Sargasso Sea? I can package this thing, no worries."

"It's not that simple."

"Whatever happened to the idea of saving her father's legacy? Isn't that her mission?"

"It's not her father's legacy."

"Whose is it then?"

"Blaise Cendrars isn't her father. But that's not your concern."

There was something in that fragile, lily-white face hiding behind the curls that could turn haggard if you caught her under a different light. Right now she looked as if somebody had just cuffed her across the face, but I was pretty sure she wouldn't let that get in the way of a deal.

She moved closer to me. "It's destiny, isn't it? The way paths cross out here, the way things happen. There really is power in those menhir stones. It creates attractions that are irrational, and makes us do things we wouldn't otherwise consider. There are times when, honestly, I am afraid."

She turned to walk away, and I watched those heels clickety-clack over the chalky gravel entrance leading upwards to the road that wound back to another road and Pont-Aven, and the curly, tousled locks falling to her shoulders and that rose crêpe dress trying to grapple its way up her backside. "Oh, wait," she said, looking surprised at a recollection of something. "There's something I have to show you."

She retrieved a brown envelope from her car. It was fastened with a length of string looped around a circular patch of carton. Maria Alvares pulled out a photocopy of a drawing.

"Do you know it?"

Maria Alvares looked behind me, towards the rear of Villa Nem Dihan, trying to detect something. I noticed she had rings on both hands and a couple of bracelets on her ankles.

"No."

"It's a drawing by Marie Vassilieff. The party takes place in her atelier. Picasso and Cendrars are dancing at a party in honour of Braque. When he returned from the front in 1916."

"Everybody seemed to be doing cubism in those days."

"Do you see that thing in Cendrars' hands?"

I examined the outline of the phallic-shaped instrument.

"What do you think it is?"

"Probably a clay pipe or a corncob pipe, I'd guess. I recall seeing a photo of Cendrars in uniform holding a pipe which resembled that."

"Have you considered that it might be an eel rake?"

"Is that what it is?"

"What difference?"

She placed her hand on my sleeve. "I'm sorry I can't tell you everything now. I truly am sorry. I have to think of my future."

"What exactly is it you do for Celestine Cendrars?"

"That's the point. Everything. And beneath all the casual abuse and the lack of proper remuneration, she claims I will be named her testamentary executor and that I can do what I want. The way she put it was: 'I've become Cendrars; now you can become me.'"

"You're not all bad, are you?"

I didn't believe what I was saying, but I didn't want to believe what was staring me in the face.

"I'm not bad. I'm just so incredibly fucked up."

I pulled her towards me.

"Maybe that's what explains the attraction."

"Quit thinking so much. Just fuck me. Get it over with."

There was nothing else, but there was attraction, and it was electro-charged. That was enough for the moment.

"Someday you will kill me."

V

*D*uring four raids which took place February 13–15, 1943, 1300 heavy bombers dropped 3900 tons of high-explosive bombs and incendiary devices on the city centre of Dresden, the Baroque capital of Saxony. On February 14, Valentine's day and that year Ash Wednesday, the centre of the city, including the Altstadt, was engulfed in a firestorm, with temperatures peaking at over 1,500°C, or 2,700°F (oddly, the precise temperature of the kiln at Crane Pottery Works where I had toiled as a kiln loader when a young man), destroying almost 40 square kilometres of the city centre and killing 25,000 people.

I walked back up to the house feeling a sense of growing irritation, and something else less definable, more problematic. Sat down with a stack of books the owner had left for me—Malraux's *La Condition Humaine*, Yourcenar's *Mémoires d'Hadrien*, *La Nausée*, and a selection of books by Hervé Bazin, Balzac and Henri Troyat. I flipped open the cover of *La Condition Humaine*. On the frontispiece under the title, a handwritten note: pp. 233-4. I turned to the page. Two men, Gisors and Ferral, are engaged in a discussion. Ferral asks Gisors: "Do you not find it a form of stupidity particular to the human species that a man who has only one life would be prepared to lose it for an idea?" Gisors responds: "It is very rare that a man can bear—how can I put this?—his human condition."

I continued my stroll down the coastal path. A middle-aged man was walking from the other direction with a Jack Russell terrier and stopped for a glance out at the waters. He was watching the fishing boats in the anse.

"Those men down there, they have their work cut out for them —it's not just casting nets and having a leisurely morning of it. That sea," he added, pointing outwards, "is a graveyard."

"You're not in Brittany to mourn dead sailors, I presume."

"I'm an Air Lufthansa pilot. Allow me to introduce myself. I am Dietrich Von der Marwitz. From Dresden. Yes, that Dresden," he added smiling sadly. "My father was also a pilot. In the Luftwaffe. That's where we Prussians tended to gravitate. We weren't very thrilled about an Austrian painter taking over the country, even then."

"No goose-stepping for the Von Marwitzes."

"He wasn't in Dresden when it was bombed," he said, "as it turned out."

"So, what brings you here?"

"My grandfather, in a roundabout sort of way. Grandpa was a poet and a naïve patriot who enlisted to fight in the German infantry in World War 1 more to see the world than anything. Grandpa, however, was an inveterate francophile and adored the mavericks of the new French modern poetry, particularly Apollinaire and Cendrars, whom he venerated for his two poems *Les Pâques à New York* and *Prose du Transsibérien*."

The tale of this memory of his impractical poet grandfather came off his lips easily. It struck me as slightly rote.

"In 1915, my grandfather was posted in Champagne, the Western front, right at the position where Cendrars was posted. When I read the account of Cendrars in 'J'ai tué,' it struck me that the time and place coincided with the exact time and place where Grandpa was killed. It was very sad to read Cendrars speaking of his athletic prowess. He could not have known that his counterpart was also a poet or that he recognised him instantaneously. Upon seeing Cendrars, his childhood hero, in the flesh, Grandpa, what is the expression, refused to take arms against a sea of troubles. I like to think of his death as the ultimate poetic gesture. Of course, one never knows. Maybe it was another anonymous *poilu* who finished him off. Obviously, I prefer to hang on to my own version."

"*Auf wiedersehen*, pal."

I returned up the hill to our house in a foul mood and picked up the account of "J'ai tué" in a collection of Cendrars' writings titled *Aujourd'hui*. The short account had been written in February 1918. Unless you knew that this man would eventually be reborn as Cendrars, his account could also be read as a piece of Soviet realist propaganda or similar recruitment piece for the Kaiser, although it was in no way intended to be such:

> The hands of men and the hands of women have manufactured everything which I carry on me. All the races, all climates, all beliefs have collaborated. The oldest traditions and the most modern processes. The entrails of the globe and its mores have been overturned. Regions which are still virgin have been exploited and inoffensive beings have been taught death crafts. Entire countries have been transformed in a single day. Water, air, fire, electricity, radiography, acoustics, ballistics, mathematics, metallurgy, fashion, arts, superstitions, lamps, travels, dining, family, universal history are within this uniform that I wear. Passenger ships cross oceans. Submarines dive. Trains roll. Lines of trucks reverberate. Factories explode. The mobs

of great cities rush to the cinema and grab the newspapers. In the far reaches of the countryside, peasants sow and harvest. Pious souls pray. Surgeons operate. Financiers enrich themselves. Godmothers write letters. A thousand million individuals have devoted their waking hours, their strength, their talent, their science, their intelligence, their customs, their sentiments, their hearts. And here I am today with a cutter in hand. A Bonnot switchblade. "Vive l'humanité!" I can feel a cold truth being issued by a cutting blade. I'm in my right. My athletic past will be enough to carry the day. The nerves tense, muscles hard, ready to take a leap into reality. I survived the torpedo, cannons, mines, fire, gas, machine-guns, the entire anonymous, diabolical, systematic, blind machinery of war. Now, I'm going to survive a man. My fellow ape. Eye for an eye, tooth for a tooth. It's down to the two of us. Fists and knives. Without mercy, I jump onto my antagonist. I strike him a horrific blow, practically decapitating him. I've killed a Kraut. I was quicker and faster off the mark. More direct. I got in the first blow. I have the sense of reality; I'm a poet. I took action. I killed. Like anyone would who wants to go on living.

Whoever this Dietrich was, he'd picked his city well for emotional punch. Dresden, like Hiroshima, was a trump card for Nazi apologists and the anti-Anglo-America brigade who were itching to rewrite a few chapters on that time period under the three-sides-to-a-story doctrine. The only time the city ever came up back at ye olde family dinner table was one evening when Uncle Geoffroy was invited and he expounded at length on the crimes of the victors. My father issued his usual spare and cryptic response to a war issue, subject to the usual taboos: "We were all numbers, Geoffroy, and there's an end on it." It was pretty tough to defend fire-bombing a city, so the discussion was a non-discussion and a distasteful throwaway à la Uncle Geoffroy. Geoffroy wouldn't let up, though, and asked my mother what she thought of it. He had never forgiven my father for saving the world for democracy.

"C'mon, man, that's far too easy, not worthy of you."

He turned his attention warmly to my mother. Later, after his murder, I would discover in his private papers that he had a lifelong crush on my mother and was consumed not by the fire of eternal love like St. Joseph of Cupertino but by a fire of another order.

"What do you think, Grace?" he inquired.

My mother was Irish stock, an operating-room nurse at a military hospital, and had her ideas formed in the dust bowl years of Alberta's Great Depression. Geoffroy had never been very good at picking his friends.

"They had it coming to them," she said, meaning every word of it.

"You're not serious!" he exclaimed, taken aback.

She stood up and began gathering up the dishes of the six-course roast beef and Yorkshire pudding meal she prepared every Sunday. "Sometimes the only way to get people to the bargaining table is to fire-bomb them."

A truth straight out of County Cork and the famine years and the tough follow-up on the Canadian prairies. Geoffroy's austerity, fabricated in his Jesuit seminary, was small potatoes measured against the home truths of Mary Gallagher but, by the time he'd figured that out, he was sitting alone in a Mexico City hotel room with a rope around his neck.

VI

*I*n appearance, the whole matter is simple, cut and dried. Nothing could be easier. A man clearly expresses the wish to have his ashes scattered over the Sargasso Sea. The man dies. Because he is impoverished on the date of death, and because he is a man with the hard indifference of a vagabond, he has made no provisions for his death. Luckily, a friend has an extra plot in Division 7 of the Batignolles Cemetery. Who is the friend? No one recalls. Everyone knows Cendrars is in Division 7—very few know that he is no longer there, or that it was his own daughter who desecrated his grave, and that only part of his remains were moved to Tremblay-sur-Mauldre.

When examining photos of Cendrars at various stages of his life, it struck me that the deepening lines, creases and crags of his face strongly resembled charts of the Sargasso Sea—derelict, uncharted, dotted with flotsam, a litter of bleached white skeletons on decks, stillness, the hull trapped in dense mats of clinging seaweed

—*salgazo*—grapes, the vine again, there are Columbus' men cheering as they see the thick, brown clumps of algae—land must be near! The mind hallucinating after a month at sea, staring at the Costa Verde, we've made a U-turn; we are floating on the River Minho—home! Home! Somehow, they've made it home! No, nowhere near—they are at the sluggish centre of a gigantic whirlpool the size of Australia, rotating slowly a thousand kilometres from shore and, bizarrely, a metre above the other waters of the Atlantic Ocean. A sea mass the size of the continent, and if you're pushed out of the North Equatorial Current to the south or the Gulf Stream, running clockwise to the west and north.

In the café photo with Fernand Léger, Léger is explaining the problem of painting to the poet—the role of colour, of line, of volume, of contrast. Cendrars' left hand is wrapped around the bottle of red, both men smoking. Their gazes are locked in concentration, focussing on a midpoint on the parabola somewhere between the two red noses, and the conversation is intense, but they are both laughing, and the maritime expanse of their physiognomy is immense, without limit.

People came close to Cendrars' face but never close enough to measure it; it is roughly 700 statute miles wide and 2,000 statute miles long (1,100 km wide and 3,200 km long) or, in nautical terms, from 70° west to 40° west and from 25° north to 35° north. It is bounded on the west by the Gulf Stream; on the north, by the North Atlantic Current; on the east, by the Canary Current; and on the south, by the North Atlantic Equatorial Current. If you examine it closely, Cendrars' face perfectly mirrors the North Atlantic subtropical gyre. Cendrars wanted badly to be a man, "just a man," as he put it, but he was an ocean current. If you were to climb up his nose and look west, you'd see Bermuda. You'd see shipwrecks, and you'd see dead sailors, and five-century-old doubloons, but the one thing you wouldn't see would be the shoreline. Cendrars, like the Sargasso Sea, is a sea without shores.

He's sitting in that café with Fernand Léger, making a point. Maybe something on the history of necromancy or St. Joseph of Cupertino, or ghost-writing pornography for Apollinaire, or meeting Al Capone, or the art of trapping an armadillo—all decoys, for he was the best deflector of all time. If you looked behind the cracked skin and the marinated nose, there it was in all its terrifying depth—the Nares Abyssal Plain: the flat area of ocean floor north of the Puerto Rico Trench, 20° north to 24° north, one of the deepest in the North Atlantic, with depths of 19,029 feet (5,800 m) to 19,685 feet (6,000 m).

The painter explained to the poet the difficulties inherent in painting, the role of colour, the line, volume, contrast. Cendrars listened then set to attacking the canvas himself. Thirty of them. Those that I possess are in fact vivid experiments in colour. It is true that at times, orange dominates ...

Cendrars was already moving towards the depths of Mare Sargassum and knew that the price of the knowledge which he sought was life itself.

VII

Kermeurz'ach. The moon was full and a few fishing vessels rocked gently over the rippled backwater in Brigneau cove. An old man wearing a beret walked along the path and stopped. He pulled out a hand-rolled cigarette from the pocket of a denim shirt and lit the match with his left hand, exposing a pinned-up denim sleeve on the right. He pointed his cheroot skyward towards the Orion constellation.

"It is located on the celestial equator. Looks different from the southern hemisphere."

We sat and watched the water lap up onto the obsidian rocks of our cove, and Cendrars continued smoking.

"When I was at the front one evening, staring up at Orion, I heard a roar of propellers approaching. It was the first wave of Zeppelins coming in from Germany to bomb Paris."

"Well, I have news for you," I said to Cendrars, "the Germans made it to the sea. I see them every day down at the beach."

When a sentient being who was once a human visits you from the beyond, the contours of his features enter the mind's eye in a different manner. I could feel the man who had become Cendrars and then become something else, and something stopped me from turning to look at him.

"Go home. You're doing nothing here," he uttered flatly.

"I have a mission to complete," I responded lamely.

"A mission? What kind of a damn mission is hanging around with a bunch of women talking about literature?"

Before I could respond, I heard the crackle of a Pathé frères disk gramophone, circa 1915, playing the recording of a boys' choir singing the *Marseillaise*:

Allons enfants de la Patrie
Le jour de gloire est arrivé!
Contre nous de la tyrannie
L'étendard sanglant est levé
Entendez-vous dans nos campagnes
Mugir ces féroces soldats?
Ils viennent jusque dans vos bras.
Égorger vos fils, vos compagnes!
Aux armes citoyens
Formez vos bataillons
Marchons, marchons
Qu'un sang impur
Abreuve nos sillons!

"Some free advice, friend," Cendrars said, "you were on track with *The Imbecilic Quantum*, but you've lost the plot. Sucking up to a bunch of fairies. Where's your bloody mojo?"

"Good. Glad I have your approval to run roughshod over your daughter."

"When you wrote that book alone, you were somebody. Sales

are irrelevant. Now, you're nobody. You want the ashes, go find them. Steal them. Kill somebody in the bargain. But quit your dallying or get the hell off my turf!"

I looked up at the belt of Orion. Betelgeuse seemed brighter and the Orion Nebula visible. The hunter's sword ready to strike. Cendrars spoke.

"Be ruthless. No one else matters. Turn your pen into a sword, or hunt down a day job. But don't ever call yourself a writer again unless you're prepared to act."

I turned around and found myself alone again. There were no footprints leading either way, but I noticed the burning stub of a hand-rolled cigarette on the path, flickering then extinguishing itself. While the sound of the anthem grew fainter and fainter.

Contre nous de la tyrannie
L'étendard sanglant est levé
Entendez-vous dans nos campagnes
Mugir ces féroces soldats?
Ils viennent jusque dans vos bras.
Égorger vos fils, vos compagnes!

VIII

I was out driving alone in and around Pont-Aven when the mobile phone rang. Her voice was faint and her breath short, barely discernible.

"Jack?"

"Yes."

"Yes. I've had some kind of heart attack. Please come." Her voice faint, almost inaudible, but no fear in it.

"I'll be right there."

"Thank you."

I called the SAMU, the French emergency medical assistance service, as I accelerated out of the Nevez roundabout and pulled into her driveway five minutes later. She was prone, not moving, her eyes open and alert. I grabbed at some cushions from the divan and laid them on the ground alongside her.

"Stay still, I've called the SAMU, they're on their way."

"I have a question for you."

"Later."

"No. They've dug up the old grave, have they?"

"Yes."

She was fragile, like a little puppet doll. There had been a Norwegian figure skater in the '20s and '30s named Sonja Henje. Like her. Or Mata Hari. Or Celestine. Inimitable. Her chiselled Mongolian features hardened and resolute, evoking the hardness and readiness to kill of her father in the beige uniform of the Foreign Legion.

"And Tremblay-sur-Mauldre?"

"Yes, but I don't think they had time to do anything."

"Is that it?" She was fading, losing consciousness, but her eyes sparkled. She had guts, and I wondered why nobody seemed to have guts anymore, and why the old codes had been so easily tossed aside when life itself was nothing more than a brief exhalation before the earth reclaimed its due. Behind me, the two ambulance attendants were entering the house. She held her right hand in the shape of a claw. Like her father, putative or not, they were of the same vein of ore. Loyal to her codes, her masks and her posture and intoxicated by a belief that she was always on the verge of discovering a new world. *Deus quiser.*

"What do I do with it if I find it, Celestine?"

"*Quatre ... quatre ...*"

I watched her slide into unconsciousness. A man and a woman clad in the navy blue parkas and trousers of the SAMU had entered the room. I pointed her out and they got to work while talking to Celestine and each other.

"*Bonjour, madame, ça va?*"

"Breathing's steady. *Allez, op*, here, we'll get you up on the stretcher, all right? Get me a mask, Sophie."

I watched them fit the oxygen mask over her face, lift her carefully onto the stretcher and then exit Villa Cendrars. I listened to the crunch of gravel as the ambulance slowly backed up and drove onto the country road leading back to Pont-Aven, leaving me behind to mull over the meaning of *quatre*.

Log Book Entry
Cendrars and Marie, the Gitane

Contrary to the unchallenged myth devised by Cendrars himself, the amputation of his writing hand didn't lead him to perform extravagant dances in the military hospital, nor anything heroic of that nature. It immediately pushed him to the precipice, and the next year of his life was a ragged litany of despair, violence and suicidal conduct as he struggled to find his soul again following his return from the theatre of war. Eventually, he recovered by leaving Paris. In 1916, he rented a house from a certain Madam Samson south of Méréville in the Etampes département, near the residence of the Frenkel family where Max Jacob stayed. He sojourned there during 1916 and 1917 with his wife Féla, Odilon and Rémy. In order to write, he rented a barn in the hamlet of La Pierre nearby for 26 francs per annum, in the midst of watercress beds, a place Cendrars described as a "transverse valley on the fringes of contemporary society." It is the place where Cendrars had his "night of illumination" which exploded in a bulimic frenzy of writing and led to one of his rebirths as an *eubage gallois*, a druidic bard from the times of the Gauls.

But the period which was of interest to me was just prior, right after his amputation. Cendrars had stopped writing. In his own words, he was crippled and distraught. It was in this state that he joined a Romani caravan at Angerville, where he took a *gitane* named Marie as his mistress, and where before long, he fled the chaotic existence of the gangs of harpies and thieves who sheltered him for Courcelles, the watercress capital, in the Juine Valley.

On September 1, 1917, seated on a bale of hay under the stars, writing by the light of a candle stuck inside the neck of a wine bottle, he wrote *The End of the World, filmed by Our Lady, the Angel*, his apocalyptic poem/screenplay, in one sitting with his left hand.

IX

Our luxuries—yours and mine—have always been few, and now time itself is becoming a rare commodity, to be hoarded, but with no end in sight. So, let's deal in advance with our impending date with destiny, and with the issue of forgiveness. In fact, there is nothing to forgive, because what is to come was not your work. You are the hand that will administer the stroke, but as for *mens rea*, my friend, don't credit yourself for intent that is not your own. In the eyes of the law, I am *novus actus interveniens*, the intervening event that absolves you before man and god forever of any responsibility.

At the present time, I am swimming in a sea of intrigue—scheming heirs, bitter ex-lovers, hyenas one and all, feasting on the corpse of a poor bugger who in the end was less than a cipher on the rolls of the foreign legion, a man who attached so little importance to his identity that he threw it in the gas furnace of his ongoing self-consumption and replaced it with a term that meant "burning ember".

But, all of this is "full of sound and fury and signifying nothing". There is no point me recounting the monumental irrelevance of these backyard literary schemers feeding off a cadaver fifty years after his death, and even scavenging his DNA, and even then, even after desecrating the man, exhuming him, posthumously pulverizing him to dust, unable to generate royalties. Strange destiny that, after being ignored your whole life. But you, my son, you who will be doubly cursed—having me as a father and then being your progenitor's assassin—you are playing out a drama to rival a Greek tragedy. Just as the ideas, emotions and ideals of everyone of my race are flawed, feigned and contrived, that part of rage that governs you contains within it a raw, but true beauty.

You see what you have done to me! This is subterfuge I never suspected. Just weeks away from our date with destiny, and I am now up against the most implacable of foes—my own self. Suddenly, the mental fresco that has served as the template for my recent life—a Bosch triptych but with blank figures against a coloured backdrop—is now being filled in, and the whole enterprise bears your name and mine upon it. You unknown, inchoate entity chasing me down, while I track the evanescent corpse of a dead poet, who served as a father to the unreleased side of my eros, waiting for emancipation, only to end in this manner, with the cycle beginning anew, and me powerless to stop any of it.

So, I must now steel myself to this and kill off the rising waters of a past that preceded you and risks imperilling our entire mission. Let me bring you back to Frédérique Patella...

I'd tracked her down through some old employment records at a Quimper employment agency. Our meeting was in Pont-Aven at the Café Volpini. She had demanded money, but it turned out to be a nominal fee "for her time and trouble." A matter of principle. Her hair tied back in a bun, dressed simply, white blouse, knee-length skirt. Uniform for a head librarian or a museum conservator. About 70 years old, but good shape to her. And she was telling the story which she had said could not be discussed over the phone.

"There was a young woman there at the time of my hiring. I was introduced but have since forgotten her name. She was sulking about something. I had the distinct impression that Celestine had just accused her of doing something. Later, when I asked Celestine about this, she laughed and said: 'Oh, she was stealing the jewellery; we couldn't very well countenance that, could we?'

"One part of the house was off-limits to everyone. Once a month, an outside housekeeper, never the same, would come in and clean up the room under her supervision. One morning, a woman came by the house. There was a little girl with her. She looked like a *gitane* to me, but well-groomed, as if she came from another land. Perhaps America or England. Something not French about her. It was the only time in my life when I saw her surprised. She said nothing and allowed them in. They walked into the solarium and sat down. Celestine told me to prepare tea and something for the young woman and to take the rest of the day off.

"They were conversing in the solarium while I was in the kitchen. I am afraid that my only language is French, and I don't have a good ear for languages. But while the consonance of the language they were speaking was clearly European, I didn't have enough time to determine what it was precisely. Italian, but it wasn't Italian. *Pas tout à fait.*"

"A *gitan* dialect," I said hazarding a guess.

"Possibly. Maybe Hungarian."

Patella struck me as tense but cool, her eyes shifting sharply towards the door when anyone entered the bar. The bartender wasn't looking our way, but he also seemed aware of our presence. I decided to play out a hunch.

"You agreed to see me for reasons of your own, didn't you? Is it to do with his ashes?"

Frédérique Patella nodded.

"Do you know what killed Cendrars?" she asked.

"Sure, he got old and died. A penniless poet. With his genius friends nowhere in sight."

"No, everybody dies, and poets often finish penniless. Normally, he should have lived until he was a century and more. But he allowed himself to be consumed by a private wish for a vendetta that eventually devoured him."

"Against whom?"

"Sometime in '44, the Nazis destroyed his manuscripts. If you don't believe it, check it out in the postface to *Moravagine*, written in 1951."

"So, what was he looking for, revenge?"

"It's not what he wants. It's what I want."

Her face stony, sullen.

"I was his lover, Mr. Fingon. He posed with Raymone, but I was the object of his lust. For a time." She seemed to see she was starting to lose me with that claim, whether true or not. "It's not what you think, Mr. Fingon. I don't want a piece of Cendrars. It's more the reverse. He's gone, and I left part of myself with him."

"Look, I don't want to sound insensitive, Ms. Patella, but everybody's got a past. It's not the most interesting part of our lives."

Frédérique Patella said nothing. We were both disappointed.

"Okay, assume what you're saying is true. Why are you telling me, and what do you want from me?"

"Read the postface to *Moravagine*, Mr. Fingon. Then I'll give you the one thing you really need."

We were filling a mutual need—hers to tell her tale and mine to hear it. The principle of communicating vases reasserting its presence, or a macabre dance of the undead, science and the occult fighting for dominance of the sparse farmlands of Brittany. We continued our discussion into the afternoon. As the patrons shuffled in and out, I heard this anonymous soul telling the strange and sad tale of the tryst of a young woman with a 65-year-old poet and how, in the French way, she was allowed to do as she pleased, just so long as she didn't exist.

Back in Kermeurz'ach, I turned to the postface to *Moravagine* written in September 1951, which recounted the ignominious destruction of his manuscripts by the Nazis.

In 1925, I wrote in the Preface of *Moravagine*: "In Isle de Man, there is an old clock tower. Behind the locked door, there is a trunk with a false bottom. In the secret compartment, there is a Pravaz hypodermic syringe needle; in the trunk itself, manuscripts ... the manuscripts will remain in the trunk with the false bottom, the trunk in the garret, which is locked, inside the small house, at the foot of the old clock tower, in a small village of Isle de France as long as I, Blaise Cendrars, still drift around the world, through countries, books and men ..."

I returned there the other day after twelve years of absence. The garret was empty. The same house was still standing. The Second World War had passed through. My small country cottage had been pillaged. Of the twenty-five thousand volumes which it contained, there were scarcely two to three thousand remaining, and in what condition, my God! Filthy, torn, unrecognisable.

But all of that is nothing. The drama is that the trunk with the false bottom of *Moravagine* had disappeared, and that never, never would I be able to put any order into his papers and publish his Complete Works, including Year 2013, this premonitory anticipation of the atomic era or the Apocalypse of today.

But, even that is nothing. The shame and humiliation came with my discovery that all my files had been emptied, and even tossed out the window, and the floor of each room and even the grounds of the garden were covered with a thick layer of soiled documents.

It was under these circumstances that I was able to extract from this dung heap the few notes included herein among all the other blurred and discoloured papers and manuscripts and rendered illegible.

But, not even this represents the depths of this ignominy. The indelible blemish is that each of these recovered pages bore the print of the spiked soles of the boots of the Gestapo who had trampled over all, everything, and even my sole and unique photograph of my mother, which I found in the garden, covered in mud!

The gods had already inflicted biblical curses upon Cendrars. The loss of his writing hand, and what had been glossed over by the historians, the loss of his son, whom he truly loved, a rare thing indeed for Cendrars. It is quite conceivable that Rémy gave Cendrars a temporary reprieve, as only a child can, from the demons unleashed by the barbaric manner in which he lost his arm. Rémy replicated Cendrars' derring-do and, in that smile, the youthful insouciance of his own youth. When that happened, it surely killed off something within. And so, having concluded that barbarism would be the rule, he set out to save knowledge. Cendrars worked on an inverted pyramid of values. In the absence of the things that give a man joy—poetry, physical prowess, freedom—he set about to conceal the treasures of the mind with the private fervour of an Irish Benedictine. And being Cendrars, he set to the task with herculean ambition.

The plan was nothing less than to create his own Alexandrian library with all the arcane knowledge he had acquired through his life of vagabonding and bookworming. And now the fruits of his efforts had evaporated. A man such as Cendrars would not let such a thing lie. Something would have to be done, and something would have been done, and something remained to be done. In order to find out what that something was, I had to talk again with Frédérique Patella.

X

"I have heard of cases like Cendrars in Madagascar, where a deceased person was considered to be *very tantarana*," Carmen said.

"So, tell me what that means."

"Well, it's the worst fate you can have as a Malagasy. It literally means you have lost your history, or you no longer have a tale to tell, which means your link has been severed with the ancestors. It's actually worse than death for them."

"Go on."

"For the Malagasy, the sole goal of our life on earth is to rejoin the ancestors. In order to do that, you must have a tomb. And you cannot have a tomb without land. Land is your connection with your own ancestors, and the tomb is the portal through which you pass in order to rejoin them. From what you tell me, Cendrars had neither."

"So is this belief system totally divorced from things like morality or earning your way to the ancestors?"

"Not at all. The pure essence of good is known as *hasina* and dwells within each of us. Upon death, the role of funeral rites is to guide a person's *hasina* through the portal of the tomb, in order to rejoin the ancestors."

More than anything—her life as a slave, the malaria, the constant risk of poisoning, her time served was a procession of four-day funerals, the defining reality of a people who could hope to live until 40 but might not make it that far.

"If *hasina* escapes during the funeral rites, it can become *hery*, a form of corrupted *hasina* which causes illness, poor harvests and brings ill fortune to the families of the soul which has deviated. So, a man like Cendrars, if he voluntarily severed his link with the ancestors as you say, risked unleashing the forces of *hery*."

"Actually, it could be worse than that."

"How so?"

"Because there was no proper funeral rite when he died, and he was just left inside someone else's tomb."

"Then there is no way his spirit could go beyond a netherworld. He could be condemned to be a vagabond in the hereafter. Of course, I don't have all the facts."

"Is there any way to reverse the process?"

"Of course. But these things take time."

"How long a time?"

"Three days. Or several lifetimes. Everything passes by the tomb. And there are purification rituals and the like. I had to undergo them myself, whenever I had contact with the Andevo, considered to be untouchables."

Carmen reached for a chamois she used to polish her knives. She had told me about these three-day treks into the Ifohy mountains, then the purification ritual performed by a descendant of royalty.

"I thought all royalty was *Merina*."

"It was probably one of the 'invincible ones'."

"Uh-huh."

How do you verify the invincible one is telling the truth? I wondered. You can't, and it doesn't matter. Truth is not verifiable in the evidentiary sense. It's what people believe that gives truth its content for the Betsileo. "Sure, but this isn't Madagascar," I'd said. "That changes nothing," she had refuted, and there was an end on that.

"So in theory, the reburial of Cendrars in 1994 would have realigned him to rejoin the ancestors, and that would have been an end on it."

"Unless ..."

"There's something hanging over these people. I don't know whether curse is the right word, but it's something residual."

"There was something which occurred in Maravato, a very strange incident which arose out of a killing. Two cousins, Sava and Elie, both *tompon-tany* desired the same woman and were fiercely jealous of each other. Sava consulted an *ombiasy*—a sort of sorcerer skilled in such matters—and set about to kill his cousin, but during the preparations, he flew into a blind rage one night and allowed the hatred and jealousy to possess him, killing Elie with a machete. Later, the aggrieved family accepted the offering of a zebu, and the matter appeared to be settled. However, within a short period of time, Sava's family experienced a run of bad luck. Several members of the family died suddenly from disease, and they had a rash of poor crops. Finally, the *ombiasy* confessed that he had saved a limb of the deceased in order to use it for 'other medicinal purposes.' When it was properly buried, the curse seemed to lift. That reminds me of something I want to ask you. Are you sure the entire body was transferred from Batignolles?"

"I'm not sure of anything. But come to think of it, Celestine had said something which I discounted at the time: 'You don't think I would just hand over all the ashes of my father, do you?'"

"Is there any possibility that he wasn't completely buried in Batignolles in the first place?"

"I'll have to think about it. We need more evidence."

XI

What I have sent you is the simple account of the voyage which I undertook in the superstellar mountains, an unexplored region which is the Hinterland of the sky, where the Forces and Forms of the Spirit originate.
—BLAISE CENDRARS, IN HIS LETTER EXPLAINING "L'EUBAGE" [THE DRUIDIC BARD] TO HIS SPONSOR, THE COUTURIER JACQUES DOUCET, WRITTEN WITH HIS LEFT HAND IN 1918

Now, at Frédérique's insistence, we meet in the *Bar l'Enfer*, the bar from hell—a drab little corner Bar Tabac with a foosball table and music videos playing nonstop on a dated silver-framed Samsung large screen inside a stand-alone two-storey building at the end of a T-section on the bottom of a long, listless road. Drabness within isolation, within boredom. Frédérique Patella twisting the filter of her cigarette tensely as she lit it. There were two more in the ashtray.

"Mr. Fingon, something might happen to me. And something might happen to you. So we had best share our knowledge before this entire matter is buried in typical fashion by the Cendrarsians."

"Fair enough. What do you know?"

"Have you ever read this story, 'J'ai tué,' by Cendrars, particularly his description of Vimy Ridge and describing the German he killed?"

"Of course."

"I have brought *La Main Coupée* and want to read it to you. Wait, I have it; here is the passage:

> It was during this mopping-up operation that I stabbed to death a German who was already dead. He was in a bush behind a splinter-proof shield, watching me, his rifle at the ready. I jumped on top of him and struck a terrible blow which almost cut off his head, sending him tumbling backwards and knocking his helmet to the ground. Upon closer inspection, I discovered that he had been dead since morning. His abdomen had been torn out of him by a shell, leaving him disembowelled. Never have I been so horrified by the spectre of a fellow human being. But I am not writing this chapter to recount my own exploits. My turn will come later."

She removed a cigarette case from a beaded handbag that looked vintage, pulled out a Marlboro and lit it with an old Zippo Camel lighter, also vintage, which looked made to match the handbag.

"He told a completely different version of the same event in 'J'ai tué'."

"It's quite common for soldiers to change their stories. Every time they tell the truth, they're pilloried for it."

"At least one and maybe both stories are a complete fabrication. Have you ever heard of the book *Cendrars et la Guerre*?"

"No."

"Mr. Bastier, the author, stated that an entire volume could be devoted to the war episodes 'imagined and invented by the poet'."

She paused.

"Consider first of all the deliberate distortion by Cendrars of his war experience and the cut-and-paste by his daughter of a completely mythical passage—as if it were the actual event and which even Cendrars claims took place three months earlier. You might want to consider the possibility that his arm was not blown away by an artillery shell—although the image is striking enough—but remained attached and largely intact right up until his visit at St. Croix military hospital, where it was eventually amputated."

Patella lifted her spoon and stirred her coffee. Her veins showed through her hands. "There is a rumour circulating concerning a certain letter, signed Cendrars, which is in the Berne archives, where Cendrars allegedly denies being Celestine's father. Are you aware of this rumour?"

"Yes."

"Maria Alvares passed that on to you, I take it."

"She did."

"Celestine herself launched the rumour. Through me. There is no letter. There is no doubt that she is Cendrars' daughter."

"So why all the mystery?"

"Never mind. You know how he signed his letters. *La Main Amie*. The world always presumed he was talking about his good hand, you know."

"He wasn't?"

Her mobile phone sounded, signalling a text message, which she consulted. For the first time ever, I saw her smile.

"That was Maria Alvares."

"I didn't have the impression that you two were close friends."

"It is not possible for us to remain friends." She folded her serviette into two, and then into four sections. "Remember what Celestine told you about Batignolles, the exhumation?"

"Of course."

"Offhand, do you recall what the employee said?"

"No."

"She left out something when she told you the tale. The second employee was heard shouting: '*Putain, c'est quoi ça!*'"

"What was the *quoi ça*?"

"The *quoi ça* was an eel rake."

And then there is the story of Soeur Philomène, and she has

really caught my attention, because it's about the very thing that I want to know, that contains an answer for me—the day that Cendrars lost his arm.

"You recall the story told by Cendrars concerning Soeur Philomène?"

"The nun who took care of Cendrars after his amputation?"

"Yes. Cendrars' arm was in fact not pulverised by a mortar shell. It was machine-gun fire. Under the execrable conditions and neglect of the first hours that followed his sustaining the injury, gangrene took hold, which is the reason he had to be amputated. When he awoke from the operation, the right arm had been severed, and Cendrars went into a blind rage. Who can blame him? Almost immediately, he began threatening Soeur Philomène and other hospital staff, raging that his writing hand had been stolen and that his ability to speak had been severed. He threatened to commit suicide if she did not carry out a task for him. To return to him the severed hand."

"Coincidentally, I've been poring over these passages myself," I said. "I noticed the discrepancy between the versions. You're telling me he actually kept the hand? How did he manage that one in the middle of the spring offensive?"

"He cremated it himself and saved the ashes. In fact, Blaise Cendrars was not born out of the ashes of his past but out of the ashes of his severed writing hand. During the time prior to falling into his last coma, he confessed this to Raymone, who told Celestine about it."

"Go on."

"The rest is confabulation to cover his tracks. *La vie dangereuse* was only written in 1960. It is meant as a complement to *La main coupée* which can only be translated as *The Severed Hand* and not the pulverised hand. In fact, the entire episode had been severely edited. And Celestine Cendrars continued the duplicity in her own writing."

"Do you have any idea where he put them?"

"Cendrars became increasingly morose over the loss of his manuscripts. It plagued him not in a proprietary sense but because he had always written as a prophet and addressed his words to generations yet to be born. As the years went on, he became obsessed with the idea of transmitting knowledge in a nonliterate manner. He felt this was imperative, as he saw the Nazi phenomenon as 'annonciateur,' prescient of even worse things to come. Cendrars' experiments with media and poetry expressed in snapshot terms were techniques, but he also saw how easy it was for Nazi propagandists to use these techniques for their own ends. There was also the problem that new media techniques had created a threat that all information would be dissipated and all artistic expression cheapened through the devices of novelty. Cendrars saw first-hand the advent of the end of the world in the Champagne hills in 1915. Its playing out would take hundreds of years, and so it became the fixation of Cendrars to send out a message to the unborn using more primitive means of communication."

"A sort of drift bottle."

"Precisely. And so he instructed Celestine to deceive the public in order to assist him. And told the poor girl that, if she did, he would reincarnate within her, and in effect, she would become Cendrars. I feel sorry for her; she is actually utterly devoted to a man not really worthy of her."

"But where are the ashes now?"

"I'm still not in a position to tell you. First of all, they're not always in the same place."

"Possession is 90 percent of the law. If I can get my hands on the ashes, we can then decide on our own terms what's best to do with them, and how."

"That might prove difficult."

"Of course it's difficult; why do *you* think it's difficult?"

"Because they're not all in the same place."

Frédérique Patella was holding her cigarette in her high-strung pinch between her thumb and forefinger when the shot rang out and struck her in the chest. Frédérique Patella fell to the ground. I ran to the open door of the *Bar l'Enfer*, and I watched a scooter racing up an incline leading to the Route Nationale hit the crest and disappear.

XII

He was a wizened old goat, a squint that came at you from a long way away and a hunched over shuffle he had honed for decades on the Avenue de la Cimetière right at the entrance of Batignolles, which is where he awaited me. His name was Emil something or other, and I'd come bearing gifts, some cigars and Scottish whisky which seemed to go down pretty well.

"So you're a writer."

"Yeah, doing a human interest piece on the transfer of Cendrars' ashes. I understand you were one of the workers who exhumed Mr. Cendrars' body."

"*Oui, monsieur.* He was buried in the Lamberjack sepulchre. Come, it's close by, in Division 7."

This was the place where he'd squatted for 33 years. You had to hand it to him. Couldn't sit still, even after he died.

"His daughter, a nice woman, she arrived with a friend, and they stood at the gate for a while." He shook his head, laughed. "My boss, Joseph Czolij, he was a very short-tempered Polish man, and kept to the rules. He wouldn't let them inside until a police officer came by and lectured him about keeping Cendrars' daughter outside. Then I was called in to disinter the body."

"You were the one down there digging, shouting: 'I got the tibia!'"

He opened his mouth into a hollow grin of discoloured, damaged teeth. "It would be hard to forget that day, when you consider what was buried with him." Emil looked down at the tombstone, scratched his stubbled chin in disbelief.

"Sorry, I don't follow you."

"That thing in the place of his right hand."

"He had no right hand."

"Well, that day he had a right hand of sorts. An iron claw. That's what it was. An iron claw. What was he, anyways, a *tueur en série*? A serial killer or a rapist? It was like something out of cartoons or something, *tu comprends*?"

I showed him a sketch on a sheet of paper I'd brought.

"That's it! That's what was on the ground! *Eh bien*! There's more to this than meets the eye." Emile stopped momentarily and looked at me suspiciously. "Does this have something to do with the Masons?"

"How would I know? I'm just a writer."

"Thank you for the Scotch whisky, sir! Not often that I have the opportunity to drink it!"

I watched Emil shuffle down the Avenue de la Cimetière towards the administration office.

Log Book Entry
Documentary references to Cendrars' hand

At Châlons-sur-Marne the Sainte-Croix archdiocese was transformed into a military hospital. That's where the remainder of Blaise's right arm was amputated: strips of flesh above the pulverised elbow.
—B*LAISE* C*ENDRARS:* L*A* V*IE,* *LE* V*ERBE,* *L'*E*CRITURE,*
BY C*ELESTINE* C*ENDRARS*

We leapt, and now stared in stupefaction. Three paces from Faval, stuck in the bush like a large blossoming flower, a red lily, a human arm running with blood. A right arm sectioned above the elbow. The hand, still alive, dug its fingers into the soil as if wishing to take root there. The bloody stalk swayed gently and then regained its vertical position.
—L*A* M*AIN COUPÉE*

Oddly, in Celestine Cendrars' book, she cites the above passage in reference to the attack on Navarin farm on September 28, 1915. In fact, Cendrars recounts the event as having occurred not on September 28 but on a "beautiful morning during the month of June" at Tilleloy, well away from the principal theatre of action.

In *La Vie Dangereuse*, the section "J'ai saigné" begins as follows:

Champagne 1915.
It was the day following the failed great offensive.
Forty-eight hours after my amputation, a new attack was being prepared in the sector ... it was the 1st or 2nd day of October.

Cendrars recounts his time lying in agony amidst the ongoing horrors in this account:

Everywhere, nothing but cries, wailing, shrieking, moaning, and my injured arm hurt so badly that I bit my tongue so as not to cry out. From time to time, long shivers shook me to the core, because I was naked, freezing under the rain, stretched out on my narrow stretcher, immobile, paralysed and numb, unable to move in my restricted posture. Like a mother with her newborn, there I was with my outsized bandage, which looked like a gigantic puppet doll, hugging my flank, this grotesque appendage which I couldn't move without triggering a universe of pain. I couldn't even touch my good hand without causing this layered tampon from soaking through with crimson, while it burned atrociously. I could feel my life draining away, drop by drop. I couldn't do anything to hold it back. You can't stop the heart from beating. I could feel each beat operating the machine of the heart. At times I thought I was being sprayed by the open end of my severed arm. These spasms, which were both psychologically and physically unbearable, were my measure to mark out the tempo of passing time. Alone, at the nexus of the furious mêlée of war which raged everywhere during that horrible nocturne, I recorded all the details, as the minutes inexorably stretched out, then seconds, fractions of seconds, each of them containing an eternity of hellish pain.

XIII

*B*ut this is not just a tribute to the great man, nor even solely the delivery of his ashes to the sea, is it, my friend? This is my last will and testament to you, that you will read from the depths of whatever dungeon you are tossed into, and surely, it will be a deep and dank one, for if you have your father's traits, I think that in the end, you'll come to a bad end, the way I will, and the way my hero Cendrars did.

So, let me tell you that as much as your mother poisoned my existence with an evil ptomaine so seductive that it nearly killed me prematurely, and came damn near to preventing this final episode being played out, and as much as I enjoyed that particular road to perdition, it still paled before the true love of my life—drink, and particularly *la dive bouteille* as the French call it, the wine that I could pour down my gullet in Gargantuan dregs and with short-term impunity whenever the demi-urge took me from behind. Yes, mano-à-mano, let me tell you about drink, not what they tell you it is, what it really is. When you hear how it kills you and takes away your ability to fight like a man … and then teaches you that beyond pain and suffering, you can descend even further into abject misery. All that's true enough, but it's only the half of it, boyo. What's left out of this morality play and that is rarely told is what happens in the interval, when you are parked on a descending, but still high rung of the wheel of life. Long before your liver's bloated and your stomach lining chafed like a sheet of drywall left to bake too long in the noonday sun, long before you're forced to take one last look at the inherited jewellery prior to pawning it for a tenth of its value, long before your spirit is asphyxiated, long before you're forced to hide your trembling hands, you are granted, in the way of a false reprieve, a temporary gift enjoyed only by those who dare engage in Faustian dialogues with the Creator. It is a gift a man like me cannot resist and few ever dare suckle upon—the gift of playing at God, and then enjoying the perverse pleasure of being Adam being cast out of the garden of Eden. Maria Alvares and I had that in common, we saw it in each others' eyes, whereas Carmen and I didn't. Carmen and I had love and love alone is insufficient for a man governed by the hollow infinity of want—Maria Alvares and I had that uncommon craving that governed us like a slavemaster and bound us with the chains of a craving so hollow and debased and unconfessable, that, having survived it, or still living within it, two utterly incompatible souls paradoxically seize upon each other for no reason other than mutual recognition, then elevate their miserable condition and call it freedom, and treat the world with disdain and contempt, and laugh the laugh of recently escaped convicts, thick as thieves, as they say, just so long as the drink holds out.

Even the chains of a woman's past existence can take on meaning, and so wasted time takes on the appearance of godliness. And we confer upon this utter waste of precious minutes, hours and days with a name—sophistication. Aye, lad, listen to your vile old procreator. You'll hear harsh truths, not cheap sentiment in this quarter. Priding myself as a man of taste, a casual fuck of a sophisticated woman is a pleasure not to be denied to the self. Or at least I must have uttered such a distempered thought just prior to casually tossing the diamond of my existence—Carmen—into the sea of my own depravity. And, so it went that upon a casual entry into *Hell's Bar*, at the time of disclosure of an essential piece of information, I had just finished fucking Maria Alvares, banging my soul into perdition rhythmically against a dirty sink in a bathroom stall by a *cabine téléphonique*, while an indifferent bartender wiped his counter. This was life again in a familiar register—detrital, bacterial, filthy, on its last legs before disappearing anonymously, and the world better for my absence. Now we are enjoying cigarettes and staring with complacency out the window, two imperfect souls, each of us obsessed with a man fifty years dead, and Alvares with that brief interlude of salivating calm of having brought another life to an end. I was entirely at peace with myself and the world as well, if you call a dead man walking peace. And, I really didn't care. It was a false dawn, to be sure, but it was mine. I knew it wouldn't last because of what I had planned for myself and for you, but it was a fine moment nevertheless. Maybe those bestial predators down in places like Mosul feel moments such as this prior to decapitating or sending their own children to perfect death or after rounding up their latest catch of Yazidi sex slaves.

    Maria Alvares doused her cigarette in a pool of water in her ashtray, and the pool of water might have been a miniature cesspool, but for the two of us at the time, it was the Persian Gulf, and I was Aladdin, while she conjured up the devil out of her entrails. She is telling me that I must go to a post office box if something happens to her. That it is in Port Manech. That everything, whatever that is, will be explained there and that she might not escape having broken the omerta of the Cendrarsians.

XIV

It's a strange thing to confess to your own progeny, whom you've never even met, but I want ... no, I need you to know this. How this feeling crept upon me like a stranger in the night, and planted its grappling hooks into my mind, and then my heart and then my soul. And, it wasn't just a thought, it was the invasion of *hery*, the malignant force that Carmen had spoken to me about so often and with so many real-life anecdotes that I knew *hery* was as real and tangible as a speeding train rushing at you and that evil not only existed, it was ever-present and ready to infiltrate, for that is its nature—only awaiting the triggering event of a man deserting his freedom or redirecting this gift towards a malign purpose. The very moment it presented itself, as a What if possibility, I knew that I would do this, and that the only thing between me and this murder, for that is what I now contemplated, was the occasion when the victim, Maria Alvares, would present herself to me as the sacrificial victim.

I have always been intrigued by the manner in which at the very last moment, when an animal has been chased down by a predator, and it knows that its life is about to be plucked from it, that it surrenders and accepts the re-entry into the inevitable cycle of life and death. And, so when I thought of Maria Alvares, it was in that manner—as a Pietà-like sacrificial rag doll, that I would place upon the altar of my own warped life ambitions. Maria Alvares would surrender and I would execute the deed.

Anyone who has ever entertained these thoughts can understand this perfectly, that once entertained, you can never be the same again.

For a week, I mulled it over—my past lives, the many cronies, criminals and saints who had passed into the beyond, what those who had survived had become in order to hang out their shingle for a few more years, a few more months, a few more hours— ghoulish, macabre, hanging puppets, figurines with their cat eyes and their gym faces and their anti-aging. I would prefer something better, something more fixed—my meeting with destiny, you being one of the four horsemen of the apocalypse.

And, then, although I knew who I had marked out, and that this criminal act by my hand would occur as surely as night follows the day, I stowed the thought far into the recesses of my mind, and returned to the mundane, deceiving tempos of the day-to-day.

xv

I walked down the hill to the parking place. Bar l'Enfer had been closed up. 5:30 p.m. I walked slowly to the car, drove up the hill out of the village towards Riec sur Belon, then cut back to the N136 and drove back towards Port Manech, downshifted and accelerated. Twelve minutes later, I was in Port Manech. A stringy, empty-faced toad of a woman, all hunched up and no place to go but home, coming out of the post office. If it's for a post box, then all right, they're against the wall in the hallway. I pulled out the key to P.O. Box 38; inside there was a skeleton key on a ring. With the number four on it.

While driving back to Kermeurz'ach and, for no reason in particular, I pulled the car onto the shoulder of the D16 and parked. Ahead to the right, I spotted a gathered clump of menhir stones. To the right an abandoned, rusted-out van with a logo on the side and the sketch of a horse. *Circus Bouglione.* The weather was shit dismal, death felt close, within reach, and infinitely empty. I fingered a pack of cigarettes I'd just picked up in the town centre. Just another filthy habit.

I had come on this journey for reasons of my own, to this place, to deliver somebody's ashes, but nobody was interested. Whatever had moved Cendrars, whatever had moved these anonymous and ordinary men to lay their lives on the line, was gone. What was left was too vile for words. We were all jackals, feeding off the corpse of freedom, and there was less and less meat left. None of the heirs to the gift were worth the time of day. They wouldn't even save each other. I didn't feel any better knowing it either. Thinking about it got me nowhere.

I rolled down the car window and spat out into the mist. Looked across the road. A medical clinic. A hardware store. The Intermarché. Maybe they hid a thousand druidic graves, or the bodies of Canadians who had marched through, an unlucky last few who got caught in the crossfire of the final days of the war. It felt like Carmen's description of the extreme southern highlands. Some *hery*, the unhealthy, escaped energy of the netherworld, had been unleashed and was seeping across the plains of Finistère like a cloud of chlorine gas, asphyxiating everything in its path.

The mobile phone rang.

"Carmen?"

"No. This is Maria."

"Yeah, what?"

"Where are you?"

"On the road."

"I'm on the floor in the solarium. Do you know what I'm rubbing into my navel?"

"No."

"Ashes."

"I have to go."

"Frédérique Patella's dead."

"How?"

"I err ..." I could hear her giggling uncontrollably. "I actually uhh, disposed of her. That's right, I did, I did."

"Are the police detaining you?"

"I need someone to lick these ashes off my butt. Someone who is ready to swim back to the Sargasso Sea."

I hung up and hit the speed dial function.

"Carmen."

"Where are you?"

"I'm being set up by somebody, just don't know who."

"Get back here. Right now."

"That's not really an option for me anymore. I've got to check some things out, Carmen. I might not have any mobility once I get back. I'll be back when I'm back."

"Whatever you do, don't go to Villa Cendrars."

"See you later."

The lower fork of the D16 country road led back to Kermeurz'ach while the upper fork took me straight north again towards Kerliou and Maria Alvares. I opted for north. Instinct was back in control again. I had run out of ideas, and now I was just going wherever the wind blew me. I was surrendering, just didn't know what to. The old lady and Tommy Bayou were coming out of the hamlet as I arrived from the opposite direction. They didn't look in any hurry. There was a café at the roadside, and I decided to stop in. Bar Georges. I stepped inside and ordered a double Glenfiddich. I wasn't sure. Maybe I'd drive right through Villa Cendrars and torch the place, hopefully with these worthless sods inside; then there'd be ashes for everybody. I wondered whether I'd throw Maria Alvares into the ocean or stick her head down a well, but I knew that I also had something completely different in the back of my mind. The road would run north, and then west, where it always led out towards the sea.

XVI

From this vantage point—a long way from Vimy Ridge and the Somme and that senseless day on Navarin Farm, the Cendrars conundrum is an unidentified oracle sitting in the midst of a dense fog on the Brittany coast, and the man appears, 50 years after his death, as Joseph and his multi-coloured coat. A magician, a performer, a muse. The confusion is increased by an old lady who says she is Cendrars' daughter and is waving an eel rake and sabotaging any chance of fulfilling the request of the poet vagabond. An ex-secretary emerges out of the blue to claim the same rake was buried with Cendrars and then is shot dead before she can say why. And so forth.

But in order to see into a man's heart and to contemplate what he might or might not have done at some point in the distant past, a task which we as humans are generally incapable of performing, even on ourselves, you have to move beyond his own constructed myths, the self-interest of his putative heirs and his disciples, and the myriad believers and schools which spring up around the man who was virtually ignored during his lifetime, like the thousands of corpses of men who only days earlier had been at the peak of their vitality and now littered the Champagne plains amidst scattered clumps of meadow saffron.

And the only way to properly look into a poet's heart is to scrutinise the bare meaning of the words he uttered or wrote during his lifetime, to unearth the one thing that mattered to him. For a man may act or express himself in a thousand ways, but the *causa causans*, the *mens rea*, the moving force behind his acts is a singular, unified thing, and it is only the latter expression of that one thing which is multiple and prevents us from seeing the man.

In Cendrars' case, after three years of funereal silence during the Nazi occupation, he picked up his pen and set about to describe the indescribable—the senseless insanity of the first Great War. In a book which he titled *La Main Coupée*, he described the following in chapter XIV, which he titled "God is absent":

> God is nowhere to be seen on the battlefield. The deaths during the early part of the war—these skinny punks in madder-red kit, forgotten out in the bush, the terrain littered with stains scattered in insignificant mounds like cow dung on a prairie. It was a pathetic, sordid sight.

I had been reading tales of the Scots Canadians of the Canadian highlander regiments during World War I, the war inanely named the Great War, walking straight into machine-gun fire, a select few madmen playing pipes just in case the well-fed and warm German snipers didn't already have them in their sights from 200 yards away. The overwhelming sense you have is of their collective, bovine stupidity: tens of thousands of men being mowed down per day by massive clouds of chlorine gas, machine-gun fire and artillery, and for no apparent reason other than to comply with existing strategic doctrine. No gain on the ground, while a hundred yards might be gained at the cost of 60,000 lives only to be lost in counter attacks by equally insane strategists from the German side.

Only a century has gone by, but if there is a god out there somewhere, because he wasn't anywhere to be seen while these insignificant, ordinary men were blown to pieces on the fertile undulating plains of Champagne, may that god ensure that Field Marshal Douglas Haig of the British Expeditionary Force, *Generalquartiermeister* Ludendorff, and the esteemed Supreme Commander Maréchal Joffre all rot and fester for eternity in Dantean hells which make them pay for their sophistic addiction to spilling the blood of hundreds of thousands of innocent men. Cendrars' description of his fellow soldiers stands out in sharp contrast. Cendrars' sombre, drab, droll, mundane writing of *La Main Coupée* is his most powerful and resonates with the suffering which prevailed on these killing fields:

> ... there was not one amongst us who was made of the stuff of heroes, and it is terrible to confirm that, although we were all martyrs (in self-defence), not one of us deserves special mention ... I must confess the majority of them were indeed poor buggers who fell without knowing the why or the wherefore, and even though they still appear to me in dreams, yelling horribly and with their shattered bodies streaming blood, in many cases I myself have forgotten their names and their faces, their behaviour and the circumstances of their exemplary deaths.

There is a central paradox to Cendrars. He is a discreet man—far preferring the shadows, the hole-in-the-wall pub, the Romani camp to the limelight—but also a man with a passion for truth and a man who instinctively understood the McLuhanesque implications of media. Indeed, he was already writing of how painting and music would degenerate into becoming extensions of the family home, nothing more than *ameublement* or furnishing of a man's abode, the initial aim of art forgotten in the need for convenience. So the latter two qualities naturally meant that he made ample use of media.

In order to understand Cendrars, it is necessary to move backwards in time, because the myth and persona—through his own devices—have been distorted and inflated beyond recognition. And in order to do that it is necessary to revisit that place where anonymous men disappeared from the face of the earth in a random, horrible, equally anonymous rain of shells and bullets:

> In Frise, prior to setting up in our dugouts at water's edge, which were like the caverns of troglodytes, but at least exposed to the sun, we were stuck in miserable shallow trenches behind the sugar mill. In this corner of the sector, we occupied a muddy hole—abandoned. It was the end of the world. We couldn't even tell where our lines ended and where the German lines began. The two lines merged in a swampy prairie planted with sick, yellow, shrivelled poplars which extended up to the swamplands, where the lines were interrupted, only to resume on the other side of the flooded valley in and around the jagged meandering of the Somme. There were always a few *poilus* gazing out over this cursed prairie, and the sight of these abandoned corpses was nauseating to behold. Rotting, exposed bodies, in this green spread, steadily drenched by the suppurative Autumn rains and shrivelled progressively day after day, their sole set of clothing, their madder red trousers ballooning with vinegary water in the midst of flagons of dandelions and meadow saffron while idle, senseless discussions droned on as to whether la Sablonnière was still occupied.

These descriptions are invaluable for the tone and texture of the battlefield. But when it comes to the hand itself, Cendrars is evasive. In "J'ai saigné," a tale told in *La Vie Dangereuse*, he says:

> Forty-eight hours after my amputation, a new attack was underway in the sector. The Intendance required my bed and my bloody shirt.

And in a footnote of "J'ai saigné":

> Cendrars was injured on the fourth day, the 28th, by a German machine-gun.

Celestine Cendrars describes the event as follows:

> It was then that Blaise's right arm was amputated—a few strips of flesh remaining above his pulverised elbow.

But this affirmation is suspect considering her inclusion of the tale of the lost arm, which in fact occurred three months earlier. Cendrars lay on a stretcher, nude, as the war continued to rage around him, and he describes in an extraordinary passage the loss of this hand:

> I must have become agitated on my stretcher. Started gesticulating, gesticulating not only with this left arm, which I didn't yet know how to deploy, but at the same time, the right hand, this hand that I had just lost, that had just been ravished from me in Champagne, that I had left behind me in the Somme-Py mass grave, and whose astonishing presence revealed, manifested itself, made its presence felt in the exorbitant pains which thrust out from my stump, increased, branched out, pulled me in every direction, caused me to twist as if I had been consumed from inside by a blazing out of control inferno, but remained nevertheless very precise while multiplying, *not as if it had been severed into two by the bistoury*, but with a circular saw,

creating a Buddha-like reincarnation, a fan of arms entering the cycle of samsara to be reborn forever. This overwhelming sensation which pushed me outside of myself, and agitated my primitive reflexes, disoriented me, caused me to lose my balance until I no longer had a sense of my body and its constituent parts.

XLVII

*N*izon is a hideaway village perched on the hill just north of Pont-Aven. 47°52' north of the equator and 3°46' west of the prime meridian, more than 6,000 km from the Sargasso Sea. A long swim, even for an eel. I drove down to the Place du Calvaire and sat in the car doing something which was taking up more and more of my time—mulling over things I couldn't change which had happened a century earlier to people whose fate had long been settled. I had come a long way down in the world. From sitting in that office in Hong Kong to feeding off 50-year-old literary corpses and trying to squeeze my way past a 90-year-old woman to gain entry into a small-time world in danger of extinction known as literature when the entire world was feeding off social networking and rap music. The square was empty in front of the church. Further up the road, a sign painted on the side of a rundown building—Hôtel du ... and the remainder of the name faded out.

Celestine Cendrars was another 20 minutes away, down on

some flatlands, past Nevez. I drove through a roundabout which brought me closer to sea level, Nevez, then along a country road towards Kerliou. As I turned into another small village, Raguenez, I parked the car on the far side of the road and waited, reading the lead articles of the *Fait Divers* page of *Le Parisien*. After about ten minutes, a white Saab came by with Tommy Bayou and Celestine Cendrars, turned up, and continued in the direction of Nevez and Nizon. How could those two be together? Raguenez had a small chapel. I drove past that and into Kerliou. After 150 metres, I turned down the last lane leading down to Villa Cendrars. Maria Alvares was inside the kitchen as I entered.

"What happened to you?" she asked. I walked past her and into the solarium, looked around. She stood a few paces behind.

"What draws you towards the Sargasso Sea?"

"It's shoreless."

"A shoreless sea isn't really a sea. It's the illusion of a sea."

I moved towards Celestine Cendrars' bedroom.

"Stay out of there. It's off-limits."

"Not for me, it isn't."

I entered Celestine Cendrars' bedroom. The entire room had been renovated to resemble the inside of an 18th-century sailing schooner's pilot's cabin, designed around the panoramic view looking out over the wide expanse of the North Atlantic Ocean. A movie-size screen was attached to one of the adjacent walls. The screen saver showed the Orion constellation. The entire room was a premeditated jumble of vintage and novel. Sextants, lamps, GPS systems, star charts, gyroscopes, octants, drift indicators, and an array of globes and maps dating from antiquity to modern times with a separate map holder containing only tide and current charts for the entire Atlantic Ocean. One of the maps—displaying the trajectory of *Anguilla anguilla*, the European eel—was taped to the ground. Two pointers lay criss-cross on the centre of this last map. A set of filing cabinets, a couple of safes, drawers coming straight out of walls. The bed was a large, brass four-poster. Alongside was a side table, with log books and pens. Maria Alvares had followed me into the room.

"It's right out there," I said, pointing out to the Atlantic. "Mare Sargassum. Right on the other side. You're just not looking."

I overturned Celestine Cendrars' bed. "Nothing there."

"If you say so."

"Where are the ashes?"

"You know what I call a man who keeps talking about a place ten thousand feet beneath the surface on the ocean floor called the Nares Abyssal Plain? I call him a man with no light anywhere. A man who lives in total obscurity …"

"Where are they?"

"Where's what, *chéri*?"

"The ashes."

"*Ahh, ouais, la mer des Sargasses.* Onwards and downwards to the Nares Abyssal Plain. The place where life first burst from the ocean floor. But in the ass of an eel? Fingon's travelling three-ring circus. Come one, come all! Feast your eyes on the dead man inside the arse of an eel! So *américain*."

Maria Alvares raised her eyes to me innocently, casting for the lead as St. Bernadette at the Grotto of Massabielle.

"Leave poetry to the poets. You're far too prosaic."

"This doesn't have anything to do with poetry."

"Actually, you're not wrong about that." She was watching me, and I was looking at some other bad days a long time previous and further down the French coast. It seemed like this was just something that happened from time to time if you mixed with the species.

"Go ahead. Make my day. *Pauvre con*."

"Celestine set up this whole scene?"

"*T'es nul.* This isn't your turf; it's mine. Why have you *really* come here?"

"For the ashes."

"*Tu m'étonnes.*" She laughed. It was derisive, but it didn't look contrived. It was as close as I'd ever get to her credo of inner beliefs. "I lied to you."

"Sure you did."

"I came here to escape poverty, not to escape Paris."

The phone rang. It rang and rang again, but Maria Alvares was paying no attention. Drring. Drring.

"What do you want me to do?"

"Let it ring."

"Are you sure?"

My mobile phone rang. I shut that off. Celestine Cendrars' phone continued to ring. Ring! Ring! Ring! That passage out of Henry Miller, *Nexus*, popped into my head. Woof! Woof!

Maria Alvares perched up on the upper part of the divan, her thin muscular legs dangling from under her skirt. Credit where it's due, she was letting me weigh the options. She slid down on the divan and reached for her purse, pulled out a small packet, laid out some white powder in a line on the coffee table, and snorted it up. There was a piece of ceramic fetish art on the table in front of her carved in a phallic shape whose stem strongly suggested that of a circumcised penis.

"We all have needs. We all have desires. It's difficult to feed a woman's needs out here with these miserable Bretons."

"Even the lower forms of life can do that."

"You have misplaced loyalties. Cendrars is nowhere today. He doesn't exist. Maybe he never did. What's Cendrars worth? That's the relevant question."

"He's worth more than a few minutes with an Alfama *puta*."

She hadn't reacted yet, but her eyes were glistening. I reached over and picked up the phallic pipe, caressed it for a moment, and set it down in front of her.

"Here, suck on this for a while; it'll help bring your blood levels down."

I turned around, walked into the kitchen, ran some cold water onto my face, but it didn't do anything to stop that inner voice ordering me back into the living room. She was a poisoned chalice, but I had drunk from that chalice in the past, even when I knew the price tag probably included misery, suffering, threats and who knows, maybe even death. Death had that way of returning and inviting you to consider its earlier invitations. Death could afford to be courteous. Time was on its side. And death had that way of summoning your friends first, and leaving the scum behind, and upgrading the chamber that awaited you until finally you saw that you shouldn't overstay your welcome. Better to leave on a high note.

Maria Alvares was still sitting, those legs derisively splayed, not yet geared for attack mode. I walked through the kitchen and onto the gravel driveway, feeling the abrasive crunch of rocks and sand underneath, sweating as I fought hard to keep from looking back at her. She was watching me, but by the time I looked around to check, I was inside the car with the keys in the ignition.

Maria Alvares stood in the doorway of Villa Cendrars, fondling a long pearl necklace, her eyes coruscating right down to the iris. I pumped the gas hard, and the wheels spun a handful of gravel in the direction of the Atlantic Ocean and one Alfama hustler as I moved inland. I drove through Pont-Aven and onwards to Kermeurz'ach in a mindless intermezzo. There'd be no point in recording recent events. A Lisbon whore spreading blow over her cunt and asking an ex-solicitor to lick it off is redundant if the reader isn't developing an *emotional connection* with the characters. Even when there is none. Plus, in the brave new world of publishing, there was the semantic issue to deal with seeing as the only word I knew that fit Maria Alvares and a few others like her had been declared *fady*. A worldwide plague, but pussy had been declared a UN heritage site. *Appellation d'origine contrôlée.*

Driving past Riec-sur-Belon, mulling over the men whom I called friends and who had moved much more easily than I—like butterflies or pollinating bees briefly fluttering around the labia or, in the case of my more brutal acquaintances, stomping up to the trough like horses at a feeding post, gorging themselves before returning to the mundane, thorned savannahs of their semi-arid lives, unless they got caught *in flagrante delicte* and suddenly were consumed by a shame so penetrating that the only way out was to perform the job of the hangman themselves.

I'd heard that man *qua* man had evolved; the communiqués and the chronicles and the coded messages were displayed and implied in every Tweet, every newspaper, every chat line, every reality show—but I hadn't run across any off-screen versions of the new androids. I had nothing to do with the men who had followed, but now I wondered how much I really had to do with the men who had preceded me. I felt more the wanderer on an interstitial plane located somewhere between the warriors of the Second World War and the current larval forms who appeared partial, inchoate, mutated offspring, the products of a genetic defect or an unnamed radiation.

Whatever. The image of her standing in the doorway saying nothing had engraved itself on my mental template. The temptation to turn back had me shaking, sweating, banging the steering wheel until the pain of bruised knuckles exceeded my blind rage at having denied myself. For the time being, any knowledge that the road through Maria Alvares led directly to self-immolation, asphyxiation, extinguishment, drowning under the currents of another more powerful gyre, willing the obliteration of wonder by a baser force, offered me little solace. All things must pass, but I was snared in a place out of time which had ruined me too often in the past. Time and again the scented beauty of the outer labia had drawn me inwards and towards a system of levees and gates leading to inner lakes of tranquillity, lunar surfaces, troglodytian stalactites and stalagmites.

A woman, or more precisely the cunt, that word so reviled by women, and rightly so, for its brevity and its bluntness and for its brutal revelation of the truth within was the delivery point where a man could die to himself, where he could join his mother from which he was issued, his Sargasso Sea, his fallopian entry into the death chambers that await us all. The cunt imprisoned you, but the cunt was only the outer rim of the host body. Maria Alvares was just the prototype, but the principle was universal.

All males are eels. I believe that's how I framed my latest banal tenet of existence, and after a brief interlude in the estuaries, we move inexorably back to the spawning ground to mate and expire as is our destiny. And during this whole useless reflection, I had utterly forgotten Carmen, who put a lie to all my impulses and theories by what she was and what she pointed to, and I understood desperately and far too late that I had chosen to betray in a way which made a mere fuck in the woods superfluous, and that understanding carried with it an unexpected regret and terror that I had brought the profane into a life that was sacred.

Somehow, without recalling when the choice had been made, I'd gone beyond the pale and had become something else. This outpost of Bretagne had drawn me into its subterranean chambers and contact with this translucent, bacterial habitat had wrapped me inside a paraffinic slick. I was in a place which touched on life, but it wasn't life. It spoke of poetry, but it was the antithesis of poetry. It claimed to provide solace, security, the refuge of the altar and the confessional, but it was parasitic, a false pomade, exuding a semblance of warmth, but it was the humid warmth of death's antechamber.

It was a long way from a young man wandering the streets alone in New York at the beginning of the 20th century, conjuring up the magical lyricism that would define French poetry for the coming century. These sycophants breathed the air of desecration, and their gallows humour resonated with the hollow echo of guardians of the dungeons of the afterlife. Maria Alvares was right.

This wasn't my turf at all, and I wondered whether I wasn't subject to the curse that seemed to govern the rest of them.

When stranded alone in Alpes-Maritimes a decade previously mulling over my own fate, I had often meditated on a Géricault painting executed by the artist when he was only 27. The canvas depicted the aftermath of the French naval frigate *Méduse* which ran aground off Mauritania on July 5, 1816, when 150 people hastily constructed a raft and set out to sea. Only fifteen survived after a catastrophic hell of dehydration, cannibalism and madness had become their universe.

I looked out of the car window over a listless patch of water inland, and I started feeling like shit even from being within proximity of that Lisbon tarantula. Without even touching her, I'd become contaminated, and the betrayal was complete, pervasive, indelible. Carmen appeared on a mental shore on the nearby Ile d'Ouessant, and then the contours of her image grew fainter until she evaporated into the firmament. A fresco of grey silhouettes emerged in her place, a puppet-like macabre dance of ghosts, the same committee who summoned me inexorably to the other side. Cendrars in the sky, beckoning me to come join them on the other side and to leave behind worthless man and his vain ambitions and sultry lies, particularly my own. I had outlived my uselessness on this planet.

XVIII

Carmen sat in a low wicker chair at the edge of the open kitchen, in front of the fireplace, where a high flame was shooting up patches of black soot, some of which was flying out into the living room and forming an ugly film across the floor and on the furniture.

"What's going on?"

She threw another log onto the fire.

"I was summoned by the Pont-Aven police figure on this Frédérique Patella business."

"Impurities."

Carmen's burnt Carmine complexion triggered a memory of other places and past lives in Naples, Pompeii, Madagascar.

"*Hery.*"

"You were right. We have to leave this place"

No detectible head movement. "You were just with her, weren't you?"

"Who?" I said.

"Her," rejoined Carmen, the personal pronoun thick with *fady*.

"In a manner of speaking. Not the way you're suggesting. But we were in the same house."

No answer.

"It's not what you think, Carmen."

"You know nothing of what I think."

"Maybe it's the sea. There's some green algae out on the beaches, they say it can kill horses and drives men insane."

I had known everything about her a day before, and now she was a blank page, waiting to be filled in, but not by me. Not any more. This would just play itself out. The script had been written for casts of millions. Now it was just our turn. No more, no less.

"No. Sorry, but this time I don't believe you. I don't believe you, and I no longer believe in you."

"I'm with you on that. I stopped believing in me a long time ago. But I ran out of excuses and alibis back at the Pont-Aven police station."

I pulled the fridge door roughly open, grabbed a couple of Pilsners and cracked them both.

"Isn't a man entitled to dream?"

She shook her head.

"It's not real. It's obsession without even a reason, and explained as a dream."

"Ah; I'm delusional."

"You're unstable, unhinged."

"And the reason for that is?"

"Contamination."

"Contamination. We contaminate each other, then we create new mutant strains, and those who don't develop the immunities die."

"No. That also is a lie."

"No, I didn't mean it. Spoken in anger."

"You haven't understood anything. If your spirit isn't in order, nothing you do is of worth."

Words now dropping like ordinary men on the plains of Champagne, circa 1915.

"Have I ever given you reason to doubt?" she asked.

"Only once."

"Tell me."

"That night you were alone with Toty in the rain forest. In his words, *memorable*."

"It was memorable, all right. Toty tried to rape me, and I held him off at knifepoint. But he did his level best."

I had driven a breach into her defences with superb *élan* and then found myself alone, with no artillery in support. I stared into the face of my folly, but there was no turning back. Whatever decision had led to this catastrophe had been taken long previous. I had committed the greatest offence, breaching a trust.

"Why didn't you tell me?"

Carmen stood up and turned towards me.

"You misapprehend the true nature of freedom."

She moved past me and went upstairs and, when she returned, she was wearing a khaki shirt, beige and cut-off jeans.

"*Quitter sa femme, quitter son enfant/quand tu aimes, il faut quitter.* Goodbye."

When your *hasina* has been corrupted and you become aware of the force defiling, debasing and mutating your soul, you see the contours of *hery* attacking your moral immune system within. Its nature is mathematical, moral, spiritual, physical, botanical, cancerous, the onslaught of a wind over the savannah carrying with it a plague of locusts, malaria and something unnamed, something which requires a host body to live off. I descended to the cellar, retrieved a box of Gigondas and began feeding the fire with everything I possessed within that cursed Kermeurz'ach home that had held me captive.

For the next two days I fed the fire and drank. Who knows what thoughts, if any, crossed my mind? When Cendrars had lapsed into his three-year silence, it was the Nazi juggernaut which had forced his exile. I had brought my hell onto myself. On the third night, from my hole within the putrefied centre of a cloud of *hery*, I set to burning my manuscripts and erased the hard drive from my computer. I stepped out with the laptop, descended to the edge of the cliff and threw the carcass of 20 years' work into the ravine below.

When that didn't make me feel better, I returned to the living room. I seized both sides of the chimney and smashed my forehead against its uneven white brick exterior. Pain of another sort followed. I stared at the blood flowing out onto the floor for a long minute, listening to the high pitch of a squall raging across the ocean close by. And then in the end, even I got sick of my theatre. Because it was nothing but theatre. Carmen had left me, and the best gift I ever gave her was not following her out the door. At least I had that.

I gathered up a few basics, got in the car and drove back to Rennes and onwards north to Paris to track down someone with the answer to my question. And, then nothing, but at least I'd be done with this.

XIX

Adrift on the high seas, I often asked myself:
and if I put the sea into a bottle, will it continue to be the sea,
or is it only a bottle of dirty salt water.
And if you put life into a coffin, is that death? No.
It is no more surprising to be born several times than only once.
—BLAISE CENDRARS

The *rue de Savoie* starts at 6 *rue de Séguier* in the sixth arrondissement and ends at 55 rue des Cascades. It is 104 metres long and 10 metres wide, according to the *Dictionnaire Historique des rues de Paris*. It was inhabited by Billaud-Varennes when he arrived in Paris in late 1784. It also played a part in my personal history. Number 6 *rue de Séguier* was the site of my first night in Paris ever, a drunken all-night revelry which took me throughout the Latin Quarter and which ended 10 metres away from the place where Cendrars would leave the planet. Also, another 20 metres up on the rue de Seine was the Agence de Presse office where I first obtained the photo of Cendrars.

The name on the post-box on the ground floor was Jean Ciganer. Rez de Ch. Porte Gauche.

The man who answered the door was about 70 years old, burly, and the fact that he'd shaved that morning didn't do much to conceal the stubble covering his face. I stood in front of the door, holding the key which I had removed from the P.O. Box in Port Manech earlier that day. At first, Jean Ciganer registered nothing, and then turned around. I followed his hunched over, burly figure into the sitting room—a good-sized living room area centred on a large but unused fireplace. Jean Ciganer walked towards a long, dark brown, glass-enclosed cupboard, removed two glasses and poured out Scotch whisky for both of us.

"You know why I'm here."

"I've been expecting you. My daughter informed me you would be coming. Maria."

"Maria Alvares is your daughter."

"Monsieur, do you know what a *livret de circulation* is?" Ciganer asked.

"No."

"I am Romani. Until Mr. Cendrars gave me this shelter from the world, whatever rights I had to exist as a person were governed by a *livret de circulation*. It is a book which keeps people such as me in a netherworld where we cannot be expelled from France and yet are condemned to live on the margins of society."

"Why would he help you?"

"Our people helped the poet Cendrars in 1915. He never forgot us, and this is the favour returned."

Long curly hair to her shoulders.

"Maria Alvares is your daughter."

I looked behind him at the 19th-century fireplace. It was caramel-coloured marble with bevelled edges sloping around what should have been an opening but which had been closed off. Floral and sea shell ornamentation covered the square opening, which looked to be about four feet high, five across. It was blocked off by what appeared to be stone debris from the surrounding wall held together by sand, limestone and mortar.

"Have you ever used this fireplace?"

"No."

Nothing in his face told me he liked the question or having to lie in response.

"What I need is behind that wall. Whether it is or isn't, I'll leave you alone once this is done."

I let him ponder that for a moment. Then he spoke.

"I removed some of the bricks once, a long time ago, and they are not held fast. Wait here." He descended into the rear stairwell, returning with a small sledgehammer and a crowbar. "This will suffice."

About ten of the bricks were held together by surface mortar, and it was not long before I could pry them loose. "You've done this before."

"A long time ago. And only once."

I felt around on the floor behind the wall. "Got a flashlight?"

"Wait a minute."

Ciganer handed me an old Ray-O-Vac miner's flashlight. Using it to scope around, I was able to make out the contours of a full-sized oak chest with heavy iron accents on it. I hauled it towards the opening, propped it up on edge, and then managed to pull it through to the other side. After dragging it along the floor into the centre of the living room, I examined the wrought iron padlock holding it shut. I pulled out the key I had taken from the Port Manech post office box while Ciganer watched, expressionless. The lock opened, and the key fell to the floor. The large compartment contained one item—a grainy photo of a woman, turn of the 20th century, formal looking, dark dress, her hair tied back in a bun. The photo had been damaged, and it looked to have a footprint or scuff marks on it, still visible. I placed the photo face up on the mantle and then set to feeling my way along the bottom of the trunk. "Ah, yes, there we go."

The false bottom of the chest popped open, revealing yet another compartment. In the compartment was an old hypodermic needle with a powdery substance inside.

During this session with Jean Ciganer, he recounted what had happened to his family. Deported once after the first war from Hungary. Then, temporary refuge in France—until they were rounded up in the Vel d'hiver fiasco and sent to Auschwitz. How he had been miraculously saved as a four-year-old boy by the wife of a man who ran an antique shop before moving to the hamlet of La Pierre near Méréville, the land of the cresson beds and the place where during those very days of 1916, Cendrars had somehow moved from a suicidal frenzy to his "night of illumination," the satori experience which was to govern his writing for the next 46 years. It was Cendrars who had befriended him, asking where his family was. All gone, he had answered. But, Cendrars had insisted, he had a debt, and the debt had to be repaid.

"Cendrars understood how our culture and codes worked. He had the fibre of a true *gitan*."

He gave me that same glum look. We drank for a time and smoked and said nothing, and then he made up his mind to speak. "Maria appears to have taken to the new ways, but actually it is not money that motivates her. It's a mask to hide her true intentions."

"Revenge."

"Revenge, but not the way you understand it. It's wider, deeper, a way of remembering each other's suffering. We partake of the same spirit."

The upper part of the wall suspended over the hearth was supported by three iron bars which clamped onto the edge of the fireplace and appeared to be supporting the wall.

"What are those iron prongs holding up the granite blocks? It seems like a pretty lousy support system for eight tons of chimney breast or so."

"Decorative, I suppose," Jean Ciganer said without conviction.

"What's decorative about the inside of a chimney?"

We were well into the third bottle by this time. Jean Ciganer and I were all right with each other. I got on all fours, looked inside the hole, tapped the upper portion. A mouse ran out of the hole, landed on my shoulder and then kept on going. I stuck my hand into the hole and began feeling around the crawl space on all sides to see if anything had remained behind.

"Can you pass me that Ray-O-Vac?"

I crouched inside as best as I could and shone the lamp along the ceiling of the fireplace. I then climbed back out and stood in the living room with Ciganer, who had poured out more Gigondas, and considered it from a standing position. Two more bars were embedded into the lower portion of the wall. I climbed back inside and lay on my back. In fact, I could now see that the bars were of uneven length and were flatter and thinner than I had first presumed, forming a semi-circle, and were part of the same piece. I pushed the claw side of the crowbar into a small space between one of the bars and the stone wall, reached for a hammer, and began chipping at it steadily until it began to give.

After two hours, I had removed considerable portions of the stone from the wall and could see that the bars converged at the bottom into what appeared to be a handle. I feared that if I got out from the fireplace or slowed down my work, something might give, or someone might interrupt my work, so I kept at it. Once I could fit the crowbar between the handle and the wall above, I wrenched hard and it gave. I then started at the other end, prying out each of the five bars, which I could now already sense bore a resemblance to the instrument which Celestine Cendrars had shown me from the sanctity of Villa Cendrars long before I suspected what it might mean. I climbed outside the fireplace and examined the hard, metallic and cold instrument in my hand, covered with ash, and removed it. It was an eel rake. I removed my shirt and wiped the handle. Two initials were etched into the bottom of the handle: *B.C.*

XIX

Has he brought with him the secret message at last tracked down in the original waters of consciousness?
—Miriam Cendrars recounts her final minutes
with Blaise Cendrars prior to his death in
Blaise Cendrars, La Vie La Verbe L'Ecriture

The eel rake had been welded at the top of its handle and sounded as if it were hollow. Ciganer emerged with a hacksaw, and it was short work to sever the makeshift top, crafted no doubt by the poet. There was a note inside the hollow, rolled up as a cylinder and written on vellum paper. I removed it and opened it up:

Note liminaire: The words which follow have been reproduced in indelible ink by my own hand according to the method documented by M. Braconnet in the *Annales de Chim. et de Phys. February 1829*.

I dissolved 20 grammes of Dantzic potash in boiling water, added 10 grammes of the parings of tanned skins, 5 grammes of flower of sulphur, boiled the whole to dryness in a cast iron vessel. Afterwards, I heated, stirred until softening, then gradually added a small quantity of water, filtering it through a coarse cloth, which produced a deep coloured ink, sufficient to write out these one or two quarto pages, and possessing all the properties which are associated with indestructible ink. It flows much better than common ink and resists the most powerful chemical agents. If indeed these extraordinary and long-planned efforts on my part fail to conserve this message, then all my efforts, indeed all my life, has been to no avail.

B. Cendrars

A qui de droit:

My name is Blaise Cendrars, poet. On September 28, 1915, I was shot by a German machine-gunner on Navarin Farm in the Champagne hills of France. The day after sustaining my injury and while under sedation, my writing hand was removed without my knowledge or consent. Notwithstanding this crime, through the good efforts of Soeur Philomène, my attending nurse, my severed hand was returned to my care and custody, and I arranged for its cremation and hid its contents for safeguarding. Upon conclusion of the war, I set upon a course of dissimulation in order to safeguard for posterity the contents of my MAIN AMIE, aided and abetted by certain efforts of the only human being worthy of my trust, my daughter, Celestine Cendrars.

During the course of the next phase of my contemplative existence, I concluded that the cause of the abomination known under the laconic and poetic misnomer the Great War, its aftermath and the advent of the conflagration which followed was not monarchy, or nationalism or even conquest but modernity itself, the very essence of which divides man and turns him towards a savage destruction of himself.

My first attempt to address this problem was to compile the complete works of humanity, both known and obscure, since the beginning of time. In this manner, I accumulated, stored and catalogued 33,000 books, documents, annals, chronicles, scientific records, almanacs, containing all knowledge, equations, ratios, logarithms, theories, tenets whether from the tomes of literature, physics, physiology, botany, quantum physics, circus lore, business manuals, stock market and astronomic charts and predictors, weather maps or revolutionary manuals, and of course the voluminous secret works of wizardry, poisoning, and the dark and fetish arts. In short, everything produced by the genius of man since the beginning of recorded time.

I duly stored these documents in the base of the clock tower in Tremblay-sur-Mauldre, as I mentioned in my work *Bourlinguer*, only to discover, 30 years following the loss of my hand, in the aftermath of the Nazi debacle and the final retreat of the *boche*, that the Nazi thugs had destroyed the totality of my cache.

I therefore came to the realisation that the attempt to preserve knowledge by the storage of material media was doomed to failure. Having drawn this conclusion, I took into my confidence my daughter Celestine Cendrars, to whom I promised to subsume my spirit by a technique I learned in Africa and perfected in Brazil, and by which I proposed to access totemic powers to merge my spirit with that of my daughter. But I set a condition to this promise, to which my daughter Celestine readily acceded. That, during the 33rd year following the loss of my hand, she would deliver the urn containing the ashes of my *MAIN AMIE* to my friend Henry Miller on the cliffs of Big Sur. That on the 33rd year following my death, the remainder of my ashes would be transferred to the place of my refuge, Tremblay-sur-Mauldre.

And that finally, the recipient of this note, after review of its contents, would return to the location indicated on the map on the second quarto page, near the shack where Henry Miller sought temporary refuge from the horrors of modernity, and there, retrieve the remains of my pulverised hand and take all necessary measures to return my hand to the Sargasso Sea, and allow me to *disappear anonymously and without regret, at the originating point of our world, the Sargasso Sea, where life first burst from the depths of the ocean floor towards the sun.*

Se Deus quiser, amanhã ...

Yes, Se Deus quiser, tomorrow ... we shall arrive in the new world. Already the waves have changed in hue ...

On the second quarto page were a map and instructions on how to arrive at Henry Miller's shack and the exact location on his land where the ashes of Blaise Cendrars' hand were buried:

Find Partington Cove, 5.4 miles south of Deetjens on Highway 1. Ask for the gated fire road leading to Partington Cove, and be sure to bring a lamp, crowbar and hammer. From the gate, descend half a mile, about 200 ft altitude. Continue on the single track until you hit a junction. Follow the main path left towards the cove. Cross the creek. Turn right. You are at a 60-foot tunnel excavated out of the rock wall by John Partington in the 1880s, who transported oak from the Tanbark forests in the mountains above to ships moored in the cove.

Walk six yards into the tunnel. Touch the wall overhead left-centre. Tap the wall. In the corner of one of the two-by-fours bracing the inner wall, I have carved the letters *BC*. This brace supports the false plank I have inserted to protect the box containing the ashes. I have used the identical wood to that of John Partington—the same oak out of the Tanbark forest, and the chances are very high that my dissimulation will be successful.

B. Cendrars

I cannot tell you the feeling I had while reading this. For the first time ever, Blaise Cendrars was within reach, and for the first time, he was not uppermost in my mind. For the first time, I could see the end of my path, my perfect destination, and you my unwitting foil, about to play a role for which you need no rehearsal. Allow me to ask you a question in the form of a koan, my son, for when we meet, I shall not be so kind, so as to assist you in completing your unenviable, but necessary task. The question is:

Does free will exist?

xx

I texted Maria Alvares from the Regyn Montmartre nearby Abbesses Station. *It's me. Jack. Café Charbon. Bastille.* If you don't enter someone on the record, you don't have to strike her off. I read the one word reply. *Chouette.* Then she showed, standing in the doorway of Café Charbon like one of her ads. Black miniskirt, black nylons, an indigo pullover, and a necklace of purple glass beads. Minimalist, cool media. Both dressed for the part. Two assassins out on a date. Only one survives.

After a few drinks, we climbed inside her silver Audi and left through driving sheets of rain down boulevard Henri IV.

"What happened to the Renault?"

"Bigger things afoot, my friend."

As she hit la Concorde, the sedan went into a spin and swung into a drifting slide which brought it right up to the steps of the Orangerie, then 360'd back into the Pont de la Concorde traffic, miraculously missing three or four cars that got out of our path.

"*Putain!*" she laughed, lighting up another cigarette and pulling my hand further up her thigh.

She double parked somewhere on boulevard Raspail, and we returned inside Le Select. I recognised a bartender from the old days named Alain, a polite, soft-spoken gentleman, operating under an expression of bland indifference.

"Champagne, Alain."

"*Tchin Tchin*. That man looks like Cendrars' corpse."

She laughed.

"What ever gave you the thought you had the right to transport the poet's ashes to the Sargasso Sea?"

"He has instructed me to do it."

"Inside an eel? You're not still on that, are you?"

"That's more or less the idea."

She was studying me, unblinkingly, dissecting me and enjoying it.

"I know your wife. She never told you, did she?"

"Nobody knows my wife. Not even me."

"Do you know there is a village bearing her name in the extreme southern highlands?"

"Let's just play this out, all right?"

"You have to kill her. Otherwise, you'll never be free of her. There is no other way."

"I have an idea. Let's go back and check out the Hotel des Alliés, shall we?"

It was a quick drive down boulevard Montparnasse, boulevard Port Royal and onto *rue Berthollet*, a side street hidden in the shadow of the arcane, miniature alleyways of Mouffetard. We parked on rue de l'Arbalète and looked across at number 20, but the Hotel des Alliés had vanished. The façade of number 20 was adorned with artificial branches, with thousands of tiny lights. The entrance had two faux-neoclassical Doric columns. Over the portico was a white neon sign: *007*.

Beneath this sign, a litho of James Bond appeared in the window beside a list of bedrooms, each of which had a name, with no price displayed. "The Levitation Room," "Absolute Levitation," "Suspended Bath," "Touching the Stars," "La Sublime," or the "Marie Antoinette" or "Lovez-vous" suite. Massages, champagne, and a reception area with purple curtains which you entered by walking through a doorway shaped as a large heart. Maria Alvares whistled under her breath.

"*Putain, putain. C'est pas possible. Quand même.* This is the work of either the Mafia or the business schools. There's no difference anymore." Maria suddenly laughed. "*Enfin, bof*! Who cares? It's not the fall of Constantinople! Paris has seen worse. So your old hotel is a bordello. Whatever. It's not Kabul. C'mon. Let's go for a stroll down to Mouffetard."

The *rue de l'Arbalète* was intact. Dreary and desolate. The Marie Curie Institute, the Police precinct with a couple of officers behind the desk, riding out their shift, one of them chewing on a toothpick. We turned into the Café Egyptien just off Mouffetard for a stand-up beer and a smoke.

"Where do you stay tonight?"

"The Regyn Montmartre. Near Abbesses."

"*C'est bien*! Paris has just returned to its roots, that's all. No, wait, I have a better idea! Let's go rent the 'Lovez-Vous' suite. I love kitsch. Let's get some of this taste for authenticity out of your system."

It sounded good coming out of her mouth. We entered the 007 through the heart-shaped portico. Behind the counter was a liver-lipped man with dreamy eyes, dressed in a suit which seemed to increase his generally seedy appearance.

"I've seen you before," I said.

"The euro is worthless currency," he responded blandly. "We accept it, but we prefer dollars, or even yen. Does *monsieur* wish a room?"

XXI

The following day I decided to return to the quarter and walk along Mouffetard. While purchasing some wine, I ran into the prior owner of the hotel, Mme. Clément.

"Monsieur Fingon! What a pleasure to see you!"

"I've seen the hotel."

"Why don't you drop by for an *apéro* later in the day? We actually live right across the street at number 11!"

Later in the day, I rang up, and Monsieur and Madame Clément welcomed me into their spacious fourth-floor flat on rue Berthollet. The living room was filled with models of old sailing vessels which Clément spent his days constructing. He poured out a flute of champagne and offered me some crackers. Mme. Clément smiled.

"Do you know, you were our second-oldest client. By old, of course, I mean that you had frequented the hotel longer than anyone, except for an old Argentinean gentleman. One day, I was having a discussion with him in the breakfast room, and he suffered a heart attack right in front of me. But he survived. And he returned again to Paris to see us."

"This must be just terrible for you."

"*Il faut se résigner.* We have to accept what has happened and recall the good years we had together."

"Someone once asked me to describe what was my favourite place in the world," I recounted. "Naturally, I immediately responded: Paris. But where specifically in Paris, he pressed. I described a room with a bed, an armoire, and a desk, a simple room which looked out onto a Paris street. When I was in the room, I felt insulated from the cares of the world and that I could reconstruct my past and my future, unimpeded by fellow man and close to everything I needed for my personal happiness. Do you know where this room was?"

Madame Clément responded. "*Bien sûr, monsieur Fingon.* You were describing your room 48, at the end of the sixth floor."

Monsieur and Madame Clément sat looking at me wordlessly for several minutes. She still wore a discreet chain with a silver crucifix, and like her husband was impeccably yet modestly dressed. They had always treated me with decency, courtesy and discretion. But, all of that was over. Nothing remained of Paris. It was a shell.

"Who are these people?"

"They are a holding company known as Elegancia Hotels S.A. None of them have any hotel experience. They are out of the business schools."

Later that morning. We lay together on a platform bed designed in Osaka or Tokyo or Hiroshima at Ground Zero. I felt a gnawing in my stomach—a dis-ease I hadn't felt for a long time and something within, my moral fibre, being torn to shreds, leaving behind a cavernous wall of nothing. Inside me, shouts echoing across walls, over vast decimated savannahs and steppes as I returned to scenes of earlier madness. The cunt was either the tarmac of an airport or the beckoning follicles of a poisonous plant, siphoning your vitality as you moved closer to its dark epicentre, touching a follicle, triggering the snap shut of the electrically charged, curved labia, which goes from convex to concave, and then at a leisurely pace its digestive juices can go about dissolving your inner parts.

"Try some of this sensimilla. It'll calm you down. You look agitated."

She passed me a joint, and I sucked in a long draft, feeling it rock my cerebellum.

"Let me tell you how my mother met Frédérique Patella. She had run away from my father and relocated to Big Sur, looking for freedom, I suppose. But no money. She spots this woman wandering alone on Garrapatta Beach and decides to follow her. Then, like a good *gitane*, arranged to knock into her, so to speak. She invites her back to her cabin, and what with one thing or another, it turns out that Frédérique Patella likes women. At some point the next day Mama gets around to asking Frédérique Patella what she does for a living, and she says: 'Until I got fired last week, I was Celestine Cendrars' secretary.' Then she tells Mama about this Blaise Cendrars and his daughter, and his friendship with Henry Miller, and gives Mama this teary speech about having fucked Henry Miller the year before he died. It was pathetic. *Nul.* A hero worshipper. I detest heroes. I like to cut them down, swish, swish, to their real, puny dimensions." She gestured—a virtual machete cutting human chaff from the wheat."

"You're right about that."

She laughed. At some level, she was enjoying herself, and it was unfeigned. "Remember Dietrich from Dresden? They found Dresden Dietrich in an estuary in La Vienne last week. He had been partially eaten by catadromous fish and the fingers of both hands had been chopped off. Eels storing up for the big trip? Is that what bio-diversity means?"

"The world's not made of individuals anymore. It's corporate. It's always been corporate. Freedom is an illusion, and it never gets you anywhere. Look at the Roms."

"There was only one piece missing. The hand. And I'm thinking you know where it is, don't you?"

The sun caught her through the windows on the cheekbones like a shot. She was older again—about a decade had been added to her sandpaper features. Ten years is long enough for a life-dream to evaporate and for your vitality to go into fade mode. But she was a cameo player. The two of us were cameo players. Literature wanted to die in a final première performance. It was self-willed, and now, finally, the wish was being granted.

"You remember the *fouêsne*? The eel rake? There's a reason for that."

"Go on."

"The *fouêsne*, the original, was in your father's home."

"You're lying."

"Inside the fireplace."

"That fireplace is closed off."

"I know. I removed the *fouêsne*."

"What do you mean?"

"The real *fouêsne*. The one Celestine had failed to relocate. The reason for everything."

"Where have you put it?"

She looked hurt, and letting it show came as a surprise. She was a killer and at the same time a waif, an Alfama girl. She wasn't fighting *for* anything per se. She was fighting against everything and everyone. Maria Alvares wasn't in it for the money, and she wasn't driven by a belief or an ideology. It was just the way she was. She moved in accordance with what she was. But then again, so did woodbugs and so did pythons.

"I've put it away for safekeeping."

Maybe it was the colour of her eyes—one emerald and the other ultramarine, that gave her a fragmented, demoiselle d'Avignon look.

Her skirt hand-cut into jagged pleats. She was smoking a joint, sitting with her legs dangling along the lower-end of the bed, watching me tie her ankles to the bedposts, and then doing the same with her arms, nothing under that skirt, a bright peach of a cunt designed to fit the bucolic backdrop, and behind her hung a macabre Otto Dix. And they say expressionism is a thing of the past. "No." She smiled. Still everything in it—resignation, a mirror of pain, withering pity, *pauvre con,* come dance with me on the Styx River. She shook her head sadly. "Jack ... you look nervous. Why didn't you fuck me in Kerliou?"

"Other shores were beckoning."

"You still want to write a great book on Cendrars?"

"No."

"Given up?"

"No. Got a better idea."

"Do you recall that day in the solarium? Jack, don't tell me you've forgotten?" She stopped. Her lips parted slightly. She stood upright, a pair of pomegranate cowgirl boots pushing her ass right up to eye level from where I sat. Somebody had hijacked air traffic control and was directing me to fly straight into the Pentagon for the greater glory of God.

"Jack, nobody makes any kind of *toune* writing books," she said drawling lazily and preparing for another round. "Blackmail's your best bet in a bear market," she said, her lips moist as she watched me wrapping my belt around her neck.

"Don't you dare tell me you love me. None of this has anything to do with love."

She had never looked better, knees up and all four limbs firmly attached to the four corners of the bed, her physical imprisonment the perfect metaphor for a life of service imperfectly rendered. I leaned further down, pulled the belt tightly over her oesophagus and pressed down, then wrenched it hard, following the dilation of her surprised eyes and delivered my eulogy.

"Couldn't agree more."

XXII

I took a walk back to the *rue Lepic*, a two-hour stroll which was the reverse of my itinerary 30 years previously and which took me once again up Mouffetard and its tiny cafés, over the *Place de la Contrescarpe*, past the Sorbonne, through the Latin Quarter and past Folies Bergères in the faubourg Montmartre, and then up the *rue des Martyrs* towards Pigalle. I recalled student days, when we could only fantasize about a session with one of the petite mini-skirted whores perched on the bar stools in the lounges of late '70s Pigalle bordellos but could just scrounge up a few francs—enough to nurse a Meteor in the lounge area, tolerated by the madams of the more relaxed establishments as we watched businessmen coming in and disappearing through the rear door to sample mysteries which were not available to us.

Once up in my room, I felt heavy with the weight of the death of the Hotel des Alliés. But the Paris of *rue Lepic* was rejuvenating my spirit. I could see young Parisiennes, arm in arm, couples and locals casually strolling from café to café. Paris was still animated, mutating, organic, alive. Something in the soul of *rue Berthollet* must have died, lost its vitality, for these business school graduates to have moved in with nothing but their greed to guide them. In the meantime, free spirits roamed out and about in the great city, and I felt my peace of mind returning, and a sentiment of the incredible good luck I had enjoyed purely by following my instincts. Here I was, drinking absinthe of all things, under the shadow of the Sacré Coeur, sneaking a good cigar and mulling over the temporal nature of life itself. And it was while in this state of mind that Cendrars returned again to see me.

"I was in Aix-en-Provence during the war. I'd stopped writing for three years. Not a word. The Nazis had decided I was a Jew and placed me on the Otto list. My manuscripts were burned. But they never got close to me, to what I was as a writer, as a man. It was a good place to burn everything to ground and to start anew. Now tell me of your intentions."

"Where do you travel now?" I asked.

"One part, but only one, drifts along the Nares Abyssal Plain. I am blind and unable to detect the light, the light which moved me." For a moment, I thought I heard a groan of anguish, quickly suppressed.

"Are you a prisoner?"

He was visible through the window over the dome of the Sacré Coeur in the night sky of Montmartre. A jean shirt pinned back over the right arm.

"I cannot join the greater unity. I am a prisoner of the images which I confected during the time of my earthly passage."

His image and voice fainter now.

Deus es quiser ...

XXIII

Francesco lodged in a third-floor flat at the end of a courtyard close to Parc Monceau in the 17th. His living room was comprised largely of a collection of his own books, for the most part on Paris in the golden era of Montparnasse, the Champs Elysées and the left bank, the Pleiade and a few on his other passion, trains. His dog's name was Rabelais, and the photos were generally of Francesco receiving prizes or doling them out in the Deux Magots. Out in the hallway, there was a chin-up bar, but it was hard to see how he could use it aged 88.

"Calvados?"

"If you're offering."

Francesco removed a bottle of VSOP Busnel Calvados Vieille Réserve that had been acting as a bookend and poured out two snifters. Francesco reached for an envelope on a coffee table and opened it, removing a book. "Here's a book on Cendrars for you."

The book showed Cendrars on a ship, mid-ocean, and was called *Cendrars' Odyssey*. I flipped it open to the frontispiece, which contained a dedication. "For Francesco, who made this book possible."

"Care for a Cohibo?"

I placed the Cohibo in the emerald-green hexagonal ashtray on the coffee table and reached for more Calvados. Aged in oak casks by an able cellar master. Keeping Normans well-lubricated with oak vintage eau-de-vie since the days of Henry IV. I wondered where Pays d'Auge was. Not far. Another grey, rain-drenched corner of the Atlantic.

"Jack, after the fall season, what do you think was the fate of *The Imbecilic Quantum*?"

"Gathering dust with the instruction manual for the Editions de la Lune vacuum cleaner?"

"Within six weeks, we'd shredded the lot. The entire run."

"Should have done it sooner."

"Editions de la Lune has a tradition of rewarding those who render loyal services to the cause of literature."

"Fast-forward to present time. I'm old, and I have adjusted to the new realities. Here's the concept. Basically, we will still brand writers as in the past. But no individual writer will exist. There will only be pen names—not that I fucking care—and each profile will be backed by six to ten bunker writers who crank out the copy under the banner of the masthead writer. We're going to fuck with everything sacred. Tabula rasa. No more plot lines. Fuck plot. I'm sick of plot myself. We don't need plot. We need rap, video, sex. Senseless war. It's war. Feed the zombie troops."

"Does the masthead writer exist?" I asked.

Francesco sneered, reached for a blue folder and pulled out a sheaf of contractual documents, naming two parties to an agreement. Jack Fingon and a numbered company.

"We are buying you. You'll no longer exist—officially, that is. The masthead writer has to receive 100 percent of the glory or the public won't buy into it."

"So who's my masthead writer?"

"Who fucking cares? Jack, this is the great game. Forget about the myths. We're now a myth factory, not the myth. Assembly line. Think Mattel, think Barbie dolls, think Mars bars. Come to think of it, forget Barbie dolls. Think blow-up dolls. Assembly-line legs you get to fuck if you're a good boy. The age of the individual is over. Maybe it never existed."

Francesco choked and spluttered on his laughter, coughed, then went back to dragging off his Cohibo.

"Nobody asked you to become a writer. Quit playing the wounded ingenue. It ill becomes you. Why do you think Hemingway shot himself? No ideas left, and not because his brain was pickled. There really were no ideas left. Can't you see? Whitey's lost his nerve. No more fucking *élan*. You need history to produce literature, and history's been tossed. If it's morality or honour you're looking for, join the military, but don't hang around writers and editors.

"Jack, you've been conned. Celestine Cendrars is like Greta Garbo. She hasn't seen anyone in 30 years, unless it's strictly to do with her work. She would never dream of becoming associated with this type of crank project. When you kept on pushing to see her, Abel saw an opportunity. It actually opened up some windows of opportunity. We've been fucking laughing at you from the outset. You're nobody. You're worthless. Your writing is shit."

"You're telling me I never met Celestine Cendrars?"

"Wait here."

Francesco walked out of the room and returned a moment later with a theatre programme.

Opéra Comique/Théâtre des Variétés presents:

The Man Who Cendrars Murdered

A Tragi-Comic Play in Three Acts based on the original play by Dietrich of Dresden
    Starring:

Régine Dupuy	**as Celestine Cendrars**
Julie Pantois	as Frédérique Patella
Gabrielle Baumont	as Maria Alvares
Edmond Feydeau	as Jean-Baptiste
Arthur Mahoney	as Tommy Bayou
Jean-Louis Trintignant	**as the ghost of Blaise Cendrars**

And the members of the "Beauty Is in the Eye of the Beer Holder" Comic Troupe as the Ambulance Crew, paramedics and police officer.

"Frédérique Patella's not dead."

It was a question, uttered like a confession.

"Frédérique Patella dies every night. Then she goes home and returns the next day. Let me explain. It's like a focus group. We've deconstructed the creative process. Comes out of the workshop process. We use the theatres to gauge the audience's reactions to certain themes and shows."

"How does the public react to this scheme?"

"Bah. The public, the public. They're consumers. Mindless fucking bottom-feeders. We serve caviar; they scream for hot dogs. So, now, nothing but offal. The party's over.

"Well, we'd been looking at a takeover of five or six Paris theatres as part of a larger strategy of culling idea-feeders for the machine. Then Abel comes up with the coup de grâce. He says: Why not purchase the actors? Purchase Paris' top actors, put them on lifetime service contracts. Then we use them to test ideas on the public in real-life situations. If it flies, we write the book with the masthead writer. It's just flipping a concept. Instead of the movie based on the novel, it's the novel based on a concept played out in real time. You, are proof the concept works."

"You've vertically cornered the market of creation."

"Bah, you're a fool. Take the money and go dope yourself up. It's the end of the fucking world."

I walked down out towards the doors leading into Editions de la Lune's courtyard. There was only one person who needed killing, and he'd have to wait until my tale was told.

XXIV

*1*943.

A one-armed man walks alone in the streets of Aix-en-Provence, a beret pushed down to the eyes. He wears a ragged coat and is carrying a *cabas* containing an onion and a leek—sufficient to make a soup. He limps slowly up the road towards his desolate apartment, rue Clémenceau at Number 12, where he is taking care of *Mamaternelle,* an 80-year-old woman. He is mulling over *la débacle.* The defeat of the French army by the Nazi juggernaut and what has followed—the descent into a banal, grey darkness. France sleeps, France is comatose. France has been violated by the power of the blond, blue-eyed Aryan and the fanatics of purity.

Since April 1940, he has not written a line. He is paralysed by the shame of France's defeat. His only correspondence is with his friend Edouard: "Why did I not die of rage and shame the day when I saw two German motorcyclists laughing at the spectacle of the French in full, disorderly retreat?"

Things will get worse before they get better. Maybe things won't get better and it's the *dies a quo* of the thousand-year Reich. Everyone else has fled Aix—for Vichy, Lyon, Marseilles, and the one-armed poet has just been informed by his friend Edouard of another mortal threat. The Nazis have placed him on the Otto list. He has been classified as a Jew, and whether his new designation is due to administrative error or the hand of an enemy, he is to be shot on sight.

After a three-year absence and indescribable heart-rending pain at his adopted land losing the very thing he cherished most—liberty—in the depths of the despair of *pauvre France*, Blaise Cendrars begins to write again, and the first passages which he puts to paper will eventually become the first part of *L'Homme foudroyé*, which bears the faded title of *The Astonished Man* when in fact its clear English meaning is *The Shattered Man*, a clear reference to that Autumn day, 1915, when a German machine-gunner burst his certainties forever.

The original title of the excerpts bore the title *La Carissima*, which was not invented. As he wrote on October 4, 1943:

> I didn't invent it. It dates from the year 710! It forms part of an inscription, an old parchment found on the body of Ste Madeleine when her tomb was discovered in St Maximin in 1279. It was then buried inside the crypt, underground, so the Sarrazins couldn't find it. It's the prince of Salerno who uncovered it, overcome with grief.

The Carissima is Mary Magdalene, as Blaise Cendrars puts it, "the sole human being who during the life of Christ asked for forgiveness of her sins."

Amidst the cold of this darkest hour, in the winter of 1943, Cendrars begins to write again and recounts his misery to Raymone in his correspondence:

Monday, November 15: ... this morning, I set to work again. It went poorly. The heart wasn't in it due to events. *Pauvre France*! But I have to apply myself seriously! Peisson is in the same shape as me. He finds it impossible to work seriously. On top of that, he has occupants in the house.

November 26: I am still eking out the work in small snippets or rather I'm faking it. The other day, alert, five minutes after the passage of aircraft. It was Toulon being sacked as you read in the papers, no doubt.

Tuesday, November 30: ... As with your coal supply, my firewood is disappearing. Two alerts here last week ... I had a grey flannel suit tailored. Cost me the price of a villa! I'm now looking around for a pair of shoes ...

Friday, December 3: Alert and bombing of Marseilles as you no doubt read in the papers, and I'm still not working. I'll get back to it one day. It's a huge source of frustration. But, I have to go see my editor ...

He describes the conditions in his journal of February 11. He has burned the remainder of his wood and coal and, while searching for more, warms himself as follows:

> I have put together an unlikely outfit to survive this glacial apartment: three knit sweaters, my camel hair bathrobe, around the legs like a buggy driver, one of the red bed blankets, which is snug because it's quilted. And on top of that, the old greatcoat. And I am working. And the work is flowing. The typewriter is heating up my fingers.

May 7, 1945: Blaise to his friend Lévesque:

> The hanging of Mussolini gave me some real enjoyment. The other one, who cares. His name should never be uttered again!

May 8, 1945 to Raymone:

> It's the end of this horrible war. You aren't there. But, it's still a beautiful day.

On November 26, 1945, he learns that Rémy is killed while flying. Life is a series of traumas. But the other shock is the destruction of his work by the Nazis. And when he learns that these barbarians have destroyed the fruit of his efforts, his mind is sublimated, and his responses return again to the intuitive, somnambulist state of his initial fugue. The metaphor of *La Carissima* would re-enter his subconscious and provide him with the solution that I would discover more than 60 years later.

XXV

> *In summary, nothing is inadmissible, except life itself,*
> *unless one fully embraces it and reinvents it every single day!*
> —Remark of Carl Hess-Ruetschi,
> Freddy Sauser's music teacher at
> L'Ecole de Commerce de Neuchâtel, which allegedly
> "cast his past life into a blazing inferno"

Early evening. Top end of *rue du Cherche-Midi*. Francesco, Xavier and Abel/Dietrich of Dresden walked out of the Editions de la Lune offices heading north, no doubt towards Aux Deux Magots to plot the publication of the spring offensive.

At 7:30 p.m., Regine, the last of the Editions de la Lune staff, emerged onto the street and walked down *rue des Cannettes*, turned right onto rue du Four and disappeared. The front entrance to Editions de la Lune is a standard Parisian set of two vertical doors with the upper half divided into six panes. There is also a secretarial office which looks onto the yard. I started with that, casing two windows which swung open on hinges, but they were locked. I could make out the knob of a single cylinder deadbolt lock. I pulled out some duct tape, placed it around the corner pane, put on a glove and punched out a sufficient number of glass shards to get my hand through, then removed the duct tape and opened the door from the inside.

Up on the wall, beside the open hole where Regine held reception, there were two posters. The first showed a French foreign legion regular in World War I kit holding a knife in his hand, titled *The Man Who Cendrars Murdered: the Untold Story of how Blaise Cendrars Killed a Fellow Poet from Beyond the Rhine.* The second was an old photo of Cendrars sitting with his faithful dog Wagon-Lit in the Gare des Invalides, the PR poster for *Quiet Days at 4 rue de Savoie*, a tale of Cendrars' life just after losing his arm. Not that long ago, *The Imbecilic Quantum*, my own anti-just-about-everything rant, was being shopped up on the same wall. They'd done a hard sell to the bookshops as a cross between Donleavy and Miller, but within a week or so I'd gone the way of the other 600-odd novelists published during the fall season. Whether I was good or not was no longer relevant in the world of letters. Houellebecq, Djian, Nemirov, Russell Banks, J.B. Priestley and the rest of the immortals were brands, and if you weren't branded, you couldn't sell.

I ran up the spiral staircase to the upper conference room. Galley proofs of Dietrich's magnum opus lay spread across a series of fold-up tables assembled for the purpose. There was another mock-up of the front cover on the *Quiet Days* book, which looked ready for the dustbin. Titled only *4: Unlucky number.* That last title bore the minimalist mark of Abel, probably one of his last moves before his number was called by Editions de la Lune's chief executioner. I recalled Frédérique Patella lying there in a pool of her own blood. Another gift from the world of literature. A criminal record. "*Quatre*," she had said. "*Quatre dans le sixième.*" Four in the sixth. The sixth arrondissement. Four *rue de Savoie* was in the sixth.

I had brought two Molotov cocktails for the occasion, rolled one, down the floor and watched it explode and the first flames lapping up the far wall. Fired up a match and set the flame to a page from the first long single-column strip of *The Man Who Cendrars Murdered*, watched it curl up and blacken, then move downwards like the lava of Pompeii. If the novel were truly dead, better to purge the mind's eye by partaking in the destruction. On the floor at the edge of the desk, I spotted a slush pile of manuscripts begging to be tested for its inflammatory properties. I was feeling more like an editor with every ignition. A rack of CDs went into the bonfire next, followed by the maquettes of *The Man Who Cendrars Murdered*. I stepped out into the courtyard and stopped to check out how things were progressing. No burglar alarm, no smoke alarm, no nothing. It was true, the French were fatalistic. Still.

The fire was gathering pace, the lick of a flame blackening the walls, curtains and upholstery, and turning manuscripts to ash. I had not had such a feeling of peace in years, the calm execution of an avenging archangel carrying out missions for the legion of the damned. There would be back-up copies and ghost versions, and even if the entire building went up in flames, Editions de la Lune was being moved out to the suburbs alongside Seuil and the rest of them and maybe the files were already stored someplace else, and this was just the last façade of a front operation with all its assets gutted and sold.

It really was the end. Sooner or later, there would be only Kindle, Twitter, Facebook and Google Books. And then some underling hack from Tehran or Beijing or Waziristan would do a digital predator attack on the sum total of everything the West had ever produced, and that would be the end of it. Like a bad investment in a Ponzi scheme that fizzles out in 24 hours of virtual hell. The digital version of the Taliban attack on Buddhist art in Afghanistan. Maybe Francesco was right. Maybe it had never happened in the first place. As I reached rue du Vieux Colombier, the first police cars and the Fire Brigade trucks from the Vaugirard fire-hall were arriving at the scene.

Literature razed to the ground, nothing but refugees left. The end of literature. My greatest creative work. Outside of you. You are the sequel, the epilogue, the curtain call in this three-penny farce.

XXVI

The guillotine is the chef d'oeuvre of plastic art.
—Blaise Cendrars

After six weeks in my second-floor corner room in the San Remo Hotel on Mason Street near the wharf, the text message came through.

OK for the meeting.
B.

I waited out half the night and a rainstorm that had the sewers backing up, watched the Giants play the Dodgers into extra innings on the big screen, waking up in the Frisco darkness with a splitting headache, and finish my note to you. Nothing to do but drive out of town in my rental—a black Audi for the occasion—towards Big Sur, my final destination.

A predawn chill has siphoned the moisture out of the sky and pummelled a hole through the clouds overhead. I park the car off Highway 1 and walk up a path to a wide promontory adjacent to a cliff, which overlooks the Pacific a thousand-foot sheer drop below. I feel no vertigo whatsoever. Half a dozen California condors hang in the sky, sensing something macabre is afoot. I sit at cliff's edge for an indeterminate time, staring through my binoculars down at the shoreline with nothing much on the mind. It occurs to me that I am no longer able to gauge time properly. Nobody yet visible. Carcasses of beached sea-life, pisciform and avian, flushed onto the sand, algae and driftwood.

The gated path is easy enough to find, right on Highway 1. I follow it down, cross the bridge, veer left, and come to the tunnel. It is still early, and the cold drapes the cliffs holding up the sky. I march off the six paces. Locate the overhead supports, threaded and worn, with a mossy plant that has moved its tangled roots around them. Instead of replacing it, whoever was responsible had tacked on an extra wood brace. I pry that off with my crowbar. Underneath is a strip of wood, marked with two initials hand-carved into its rough surface. Under the woodstrip is a set of seventeen bricks which are not consistent with the remainder of the tunnel. I pull back the strip, and an aged brick, powdered with mortar, dislodges.

Behind the brick is a hole leading into the ground. I reach inside, and beneath more undergrowth, a metal casing, the dimensions of a billfold. I remove it and replace the support plank, pace out the dozen steps separating me from the other end of the tunnel, detecting movement. I emerge to the light of day and look inside. Ashes. Cendrars' Ashes.

"Hello."

That word is uttered by a faint, raspy voice delivered *sotto vocce* from a rear angle, where I can also detect his silhouette, but am unable to behold this shadow figure directly because something prohibits it. *Fady.*

It is you. You have come.

"I've been waiting for you."

He has emerged from the switchback leading up to the narrow path where I now stand. The path continues behind me, descending to a crag overlooking a waterfall and the beach a third of a mile below.

"Why have you come now?"

"I have come to stop you."

"It is too late to stop me. I am done with this."

"The road..." The tinny, decades old radio voice, echoing slightly against the antechambers of a beyond I now am about to enter, crossing the great chasm via a thousand foot drop onto hard rocks. There are worse ways to go.

The one-armed vagabond points now over the sea towards a lifeless stretch of nimbus.

"This road leads ..."

Again he stops, paralyzed by what he can see and I not.

"The place where I wander has no destination. I step out on the road and follow it in darkness, and it leads nowhere."

"But your tale, the quatrain ..."

"I cannot remember my story. It has been taken from me."

I look into his face. It is him, but a grey translucence of indescribable pain shrouds his features.

"I don't understand."

"There is nothing to understand. This is not your time."

"You were free as a man," I say, and the words now appear in all their bald naiveté. "I followed you."

He stands behind me, and I no longer dare turn to face him.

"When I left the place you still inhabit, I found myself on a suspension bridge, fashioned out of strips of damp cedar. This bridge led to another, and then to another. Each of these bridges spiralled higher, until they reached a summit, from which I fell into a pit where workmen boiled pitch and stoked a coal furnace. One of these men wore an executioner's balaclava. He guided me to a set of stocks and placed me in a yoke. There were many others like me ... *many*." That word *many* and the stare of his ghoulish eyes froze me to the spot. It seemed bereft of love, holding only the residual terror of the infinite which now held him hostage.

"And there I remained, slaving for many years and yet out of the zone of time where you still reside."

"Then, what about literature, and the flight of ideas. What of your faith in that, in the very thing that saved you here."

"Literature is dead. The master race of scribes has lost its vitality. The men who go by the name of scribes are hungry ghosts. As are we. We are now all ghosts."

I feel a numbing cold of an arm draped over my shoulder, the left arm, pointing towards the beach below and there's a sudden compulsion to end it all now, to throw myself to the earth and go the way of this grey apparition, but the voice wanes, and is interrupted by that of Cendrars.

"Take my advice. You want to do something useful. Help him," he says pointing at the young man now visible, tracing out something in the sand below. "He is alive."

"He resembles her. Better to let him kill me."

"You loved her, didn't you?"

"Didn't you love Raymone?"

"Answer me."

"Yes, I loved her. Actually, love doesn't begin to tell it. I was crazed; it was something more absolute, something more kaleidoscopic than love, that only operated under the name, but shared none of the attributes. What we had was shared, hair-line madness. We were courting death. We shared death."

"Count yourself lucky. You were temporarily unveiled. She showed you your other, your dark side. You are not worthy of such generosity.

"What is it you want? You now have the power to decide. Do you want to live, or do you want to write?"

He steps backwards, disappears onto the switchback, and is

gone. Half an hour later, I reach the bottom of the path. You don't see me. I am walking towards you, only 100 yards down the isolated strip of beach.

I stand on the wet sand of the beach. Cendrars is gone. The sky has drawn my guide back into the firmament, his message delivered, but not mine. I step on a branch. It cracks, and you turn and squint as the sunlight temporarily blinds you. Then, you notice me for the first time. We walk towards each other. The dawn is still cold, the sun has emerged, and the rhythmic tempo of waves curls like a scythe on the knife-edge of the Big Sur shoreline.

"You see?" I hear myself saying. "I am old."

You say nothing, but approach me and extend your hand, tethering me by your tactile gesture to our common past.

"What's in that box?" you ask.

"It's a long tale, but one worth telling."

"May I hear it?"

"I'll tell you all about it as we navigate towards our destination."

"And, where is that?"

"To the place where life first burst from the depths of the ocean floor towards the sun."

Fugue ...

About the Author

David MacKinnon is a Vancouver, Canada-born novelist. After reading history and philosophy at the universities of British Columbia and Louvain (Belgium), and at Université de Paris IV-Sorbonne (Paris), he worked in the Alberta oilfields and a series of jobs on the assembly line prior to being admitted to the Montreal bar, where he practiced as a trial lawyer. In '89, MacKinnon left for Hong Kong to assist Chinese nationals to escape the crackdown which followed the Tiananmen Square uprising and narrowly escaped himself after a group of Shanghai businessmen attempted to coerce him into a people-smuggling scheme. In 2004, during an extended sojourn in the Seychelles, he was declared *persona non grata* for writing on the money and gun laundering engaged in by the tinpot dictatorship which runs the Seychelles to this day. David MacKinnon has written eight novels, including *Leper Tango* (Guernica Editions).

MARQUIS

Québec, Canada

Printed on Enviro 100% post-consumer EcoLogo certified paper, processed chlorine free and manufactured using biogas energy.